Anna  All Year Round

Anna All Year Round

BY MARY DOWNING HAHN
Illustrated by Diane deGroat

CLARION BOOKS/*New York*

Clarion Books
a Houghton Mifflin Company imprint
215 Park Avenue South, New York, NY 10003
Text copyright © 1999 by Mary Downing Hahn
Illustrations copyright © 1999 by Diane deGroat

Type is 15/18.5-point Garamond 3
The illustrations for this book are executed in pencil.

Library of Congress Cataloging-in-Publication Data
Hahn, Mary Downing.
Anna all year round / by Mary Downing Hahn ; illustrated by Diane deGroat.
p.   cm.
Summary: Eight-year-old Anna experiences a series of episodes, some that are funny, others sad, involving
friends and family during a year in Baltimore just before World War I.
ISBN 0-395-86975-7
[1. Family life—Baltimore (Md.)—Fiction.   2. Baltimore (Md.)—Fiction.]   I. DeGroat, Diane, ill. II. Title.
PZ7.H1256An 1999
[Fic]—dc21 98-19985
CIP
AC

QBP 10   9   8   7   6   5   4   3   2   1

For my mother, the real Anna, with love and gratitude for sharing your stories

Contents

Fall

· 1 ·

The Language of Secrets

ANNA IS SITTING ON THE SOFA READING. IT'S A RAINY September day. Drops of water run down the front window, blurring the narrow brick row houses across the street. Leaves drift from the trees. The clock on the mantel chimes eleven. At the same moment, a horse clip-clops past, hauling a wagon.

Without looking up from her book, Anna knows it's Mr. Hausmann, the grocer, on his way to his shop at the bottom of the hill. He finishes his deliveries every Saturday morning at exactly the same time. Father says he could set all the clocks in the house by Mr. Hausmann.

Tired of sitting still, Anna slides quietly off the sofa and tiptoes down the hall to the kitchen door.

Mother's sister, Anna's aunt May, has come over from her house next door. She and Mother are sitting at the table, drinking coffee and gossiping about their other sisters. Fritzi, Aunt May's big white bulldog, is asleep at Aunt May's feet.

Anna stands in the doorway listening. Mother has five sisters and three brothers. It seems to Anna that someone in the family is always mad at someone else. This morning the two sisters are cross with Aunt Amelia. Anna isn't fond of Aunt Amelia, so she lingers, hoping to hear something interesting.

"Did you hear what Amelia had the nerve to tell Margaret?" Mother asks Aunt May. "She said her tablecloth wasn't starched properly!"

This doesn't surprise Anna. Once she saw Aunt Amelia run her finger across their dining-room table to check for dust. As if Mother would leave a speck of dirt anywhere! Why, she even sweeps the sidewalk in front of the house every morning. With Mother around, dust has no chance.

Aunt May makes a loud harrumph. "Amelia should talk. The last time I called on her, I counted three cobwebs in the corners. Poor Friedrich. I can't believe she's a good wife to him."

Mother nods in agreement and leans closer to Aunt May. "What do you think of Julianna's new beau? Have you met him yet?"

Aunt May wrinkles her nose. "I don't—"

Just then, Anna has the misfortune to sneeze.

Mother and Aunt May both turn and stare at Anna. Until now, they hadn't noticed her standing in the doorway.

Mother looks cross. "Fie, Anna. Where are your manners? It's rude to eavesdrop."

Aunt May smiles. "My little sweet potato has sprouted ears as well as eyes," she says, giving Anna a hug. Fritzi lifts his head and wags his tail. Like Aunt May, he's glad to see Anna.

Mother doesn't smile. She picks up the coffeepot and holds it over Aunt May's cup. *"Möchtest du mehr Kaffee, May?"*

Aunt May winks at Mother and pats Anna's fanny. *"Ja bitte, Lizzie."*

Anna pulls away from her aunt and scowls. Mother's family is German. When they don't want Anna to understand what they're saying, they speak in German. No one will teach Anna to speak it. It's the language of secrets.

"Was denkst du von Julianna's neuem Freund?" Mother asks.

Aunt May makes a face. *"Ich mag ihn nicht."*

Anna tugs at Mother's sleeve. "Speak English," she begs.

Mother shakes her head. "Go and play, Anna. What we say is not for you to hear."

"It's talk for grownups, very boring." Aunt May gives Anna another pat. "Do as Mother says and run along, *mein kleiner Zuckerwürfel.*"

Anna flounces to the door. When she's sure neither her mother nor her aunt is looking at her, she sticks out her tongue. She wants to be called my little sugar lump, not *mein kleiner Zuckerwürfel.*

Fritzi starts to follow Anna, but Aunt May calls him back. Mother doesn't allow Fritzi to leave the kitchen; she's afraid he'll jump on the furniture the way he does at home. Although Mother has never said it to Aunt May's face, she doesn't like Fritzi. She thinks he's ugly and smelly and spoiled rotten.

Alone in the parlor, Anna finds a book written in German. She sits in Father's big chair and opens the book. Since no one else will do it, Anna will teach herself German. She stares at the long words till her head aches. She cannot understand any of them. Some of the letters look strange. Others have funny marks over them.

Anna groans and closes the book. German children must be smarter than American children, she thinks, or they'd never learn to talk or read.

When Father comes home from his job at the newspaper, he finds Anna asleep in his chair, Mother's German book in her lap.

Anna opens her eyes and gives Father a hug and a kiss. Father picks up Mother's book and glances at the pages. "I didn't know you could read German," he says.

Anna sighs. "That's just the trouble, Father. I can't! I was trying to teach myself, but it's too hard. Why can't German be as easy as English? Why do all the words have to be so long and fancified?"

Father smiles. "I imagine that's exactly what German children say about English."

Anna loves Father too much to argue but she's certain he's wrong. Anyone can see English is much easier than German.

Father strokes Anna's long brown hair. "Won't Mother help you?"

Anna shakes her head. "All Mother has taught me is *'Gesundheit,'* which you say when someone sneezes, and *'Auf Wiedersehen,'* which means 'good-bye.' I also know *'bitte,'* which means 'please,' and *'danke,'* which means 'thank you.'"

"Those are all good words," Father says. "Why do you want to know more?"

Anna picks up her doll and smoothes its wrinkled dress. "When Aunt May visits, she and Mother talk in German to keep me from learning their secrets."

Father chuckles, and Anna lays down her doll and stares at him. "Will you teach me German?"

Father laughs. "I don't know any more German than you do. Your mother's parents were born in Germany, but my mother and father were born right here in Baltimore. So were my grandparents. As far as I know, no one in my family has ever spoken anything but English."

Anna rests her head on Father's shoulder. "I guess Mother doesn't want you to learn her secrets either."

Father smiles. "I never thought of that, Anna."

o   o   o

That night, Father reads a chapter of *The Swiss Family Robinson* to Anna. Mother sits nearby, hemming a new shirt for Father. Her needle flashes swiftly in and out of the cloth, making tiny stitches. It's a quiet, peaceful time. The fall evening has wrapped its soft arms around the houses on Warwick Avenue, hushing everything.

Father catches Anna yawning. "Time for bed," he says. Leaning close, he whispers something in her ear.

Anna walks to Mother and gives her a good-night kiss. *"Gute Nacht, Mutter,"* she says, carefully repeating what Father has just told her.

Mother stares at Anna in surprise. *"Sprichst du Deutsch, Anna?"* she asks. "Can you speak German now?"

Anna glances at Father and giggles. "Father taught me. *'Gute Nacht, Mutter'* means 'good night, Mother.'"

Mother turns to Father. "Ira, when did you learn German?"

Father laughs. "Oh, I've picked up a few words here and there, but don't worry, Lizzie. Your secrets are safe."

Mother smiles and draws Anna close to whisper in her ear. Anna goes to Father. *"Gute Nacht, Vater,"* she says, repeating what Mother has just told her.

Father winks at Mother. *"Gute Nacht, Tochter,"* he says, kissing Anna good night.

Anna leaves Mother and Father in the parlor and goes upstairs to her room. The moon shines through the skylight over her bed. Anna wonders how to say "moon" in German.

Maybe she'll ask Mother tomorrow. Like Father, she'll pick up a few words here and there. Then one day, when no one expects it, she'll join the secret conversation. Won't that surprise her mother and her aunts?

· 2 ·

Numbers, Numbers, Numbers

THE HOUSES ON ANNA'S STREET MARCH DOWNHILL IN neat rows as far as you can see. Each one has three white marble steps in front, a double window downstairs, and three windows upstairs. Inside, they are just the same. All have three rooms on each floor, plus a bathroom and a pantry. The backyards are long and narrow and separated from each other by tall white fences.

Many children live on Anna's street, but only five are Anna's age. Rosa Schuman lives two doors up, on the other side of Aunt May. Beatrice Morgan's house is at the top of the hill. Wally Heinz's house is at the bottom of the hill. Patrick Reilly lives next door to Wally, and Charlie Murphy lives across the street from Anna.

Rosa and Beatrice are best friends. They go everywhere together, holding hands and giggling. Sometimes they let Anna play with them, especially if they need her to turn the jump rope. Sometimes they tell her to go home. "Two's company," Rosa says, squeezing Beatrice's hand, "but three's a crowd."

Anna doesn't care. Rosa and Beatrice are silly, boring girls. They never do anything but play jacks and jump rope and take their dolls for walks. Anna would rather roller-skate with Charlie Murphy any day. Unlike Anna, Charlie has lots of brothers and sisters, some older than he is and some younger. Once in a while Anna wishes she had a big family like Charlie's, but usually she's happy to have Father and Mother all to herself.

This year, Charlie, Patrick, Wally, Beatrice, Rosa, and Anna are in the third grade. They go to Public School 62, a tall red-brick building just down the street from Anna's house. It's three stories high, much bigger than any house in the neighborhood. When Anna started first grade, she often got lost trying to find her classroom, but now that she's eight, she knows her way around.

Anna's teacher, Miss Levine, has divided the class into two sections: a high third for the smart children and a low third for the others. Anna is in the high third. She has more gold stars on her chart than any other child.

Anna is very proud of those stars. So are Mother and Father. Mother tells Aunt May that Anna is *"ein kluges Mädchen,"* a clever girl. Aunt May is proud, too.

Wally, Rosa, and Beatrice are also in the high third, but Patrick and Charlie are in the low. Anna feels sorry for Charlie, but he and Patrick don't care. They hate school.

One day in October Miss Levine decides the high third is ready for long division. "Suppose we have 483 oranges," she says. "And we want to divide them among 23 boys and girls. This is how we do it."

Anna watches Miss Levine's chalk fly across the blackboard as she shows the children how to divide the oranges. Ever since Anna started school, she's been a top reader but she's always had trouble with arithmetic. In her opinion, numbers are much harder than letters. And not nearly as interesting. All you can do with numbers is make problems. But you can make stories and poems with words. Stories and poems are definitely more fun than problems.

"There!" Miss Levine turns to the class with a big smile. "Each of you smart children would get twenty-one nice juicy oranges! Do you see what I did to find the solution?"

Anna nods her head like the other children. Nothing Miss Levine has said or done makes sense to her, but Anna is afraid to raise her hand and ask a question. Miss Levine might think Anna does not belong in the high third.

Rosa sits beside Anna. She cannot read as well as Anna but she is very good with numbers. Anna is afraid she will lose her place at the top of the class to Rosa.

Instead of asking Miss Levine for help, Anna secretly copies Rosa's work. If Rosa knew what Anna was doing, she'd tell the teacher or cover her problems with her hand, so Anna is careful not to be caught. She feels bad about doing this, but she cannot risk telling Miss Levine she doesn't understand long division.

No one catches Anna until the day Miss Levine sends the children to the blackboard in groups of four. She tells them they are going to have long division races. Whoever solves the problem first will receive a gold star. Anna knows she will not get one today.

Miss Levine says, "The dividend is 6281. The divisor is 47. When you find the quotient, go to your seat."

The four children write the problem on the blackboard. Anna is so nervous she drops her stick of chalk. While she's picking it up, she steals a peek at Rosa's work, but she cannot see it well enough to copy from it.

Anna stares at the numbers she's written on the blackboard. On both sides, she hears the clatter of chalk as Rosa, Wally, and Eunice zip through the problem. What Anna writes is wrong. She erases the numbers with her hand and starts again. It is still wrong. She rubs it out. The sweat on her hands makes the blackboard slippery. Her chalk won't stick to it.

Rosa finishes first and goes to her desk. She smirks as she passes Anna. Wally finishes. Eunice finishes. But Anna is still rubbing out numbers and trying to write new ones. Behind her back, children begin to giggle.

Anna's hand shakes. Her knees tremble. Tears fill her eyes. Miss Levine must know the truth now. Anna does not understand long division. She will be sent to the low third with Charlie. She will never receive a gold star again. Mother will have nothing to brag to Aunt May about. Worst of all, Father will be disappointed.

Finally Miss Levine takes the chalk from Anna. "Go to your seat," she says crossly. "You will remain inside at recess."

Before Charlie leaves, he drops a note in Anna's lap. It says, *Dere Anna, Im sory yor in trubbel. I will by you a jaw braker after skool. Yor frend Charlie.*

When the classroom is empty, Miss Levine sends Anna to the blackboard and gives her a new problem. "Perhaps you can work better when no one is watching you," she says.

Anna cannot do the problem, so Miss Levine gives her another one. And another. And then another. Anna cannot do any of the problems.

Miss Levine gives Anna one more chance. "Suppose I have 245 apples," she says. "How can I divide them among 11 children?"

Anna begins to cry. She wants to ask Miss Levine why she has so many apples. She wants to ask her why she wants to divide them up among the children. She wants to know if she, Anna, would get an apple. But she just stands there, crying.

Miss Levine scowls at Anna. "Tell me the truth," she says. "Have you been copying Rosa Schuman's answers?"

Anna twists her hands. She cannot look at Miss Levine. "Yes," she whispers.

"Anna Elisabeth Sherwood, I am ashamed of you," Miss Levine says. "Take your things and move to the back of the room. Until you learn long division, you will remain in the low third."

Still crying, Anna empties her desk. What will she tell Father and Mother?

When the children come in from recess, they are surprised to see Anna sitting in the back of the room. Rosa whispers something in Beatrice's ear that makes both girls giggle, but Charlie pats Anna's shoulder. "Don't worry," he tells Anna. "You won't stay here long. You're much too smart."

Anna hopes Charlie is right.

o o o

After dinner that night, Anna makes up the silliest problem she can think of. "If you had 517 bananas and you wanted to divide them among 28 monkeys, how would you do it?" she asks Father.

Father thinks a moment. "Why, I suppose I'd throw them all up in the air," he says at last, "and sit back and watch the fun."

Anna frowns. This is not the time for Father's jokes. "Please tell me how to divide 517 by 28," she says.

Father takes the pencil Anna hands him and begins to write. He shows Anna more than one way to divide. He lets her decide which method she understands best. Then he watches her work.

Finally Father says, "Why didn't you tell me you're having trouble with long division, Anna?"

"I was ashamed," she whispers. "I was scared you'd think I wasn't smart after all."

"Oh, Anna," Father says. "We all have trouble understanding things sometimes. You're only eight years old. I don't expect you to know everything."

Anna begins to cry. "I copied Rosa's long division and Miss Levine found out. She put me in the lower third. She says I have to stay there till I learn long division."

Father pats Anna's hand. "Promise you'll never

cheat again, Anna. If you need help, please come to me."

Every night for two weeks, Anna and Father work on long division together. Mother sits nearby, embroidering. She doesn't know any more about long division than Anna does.

When Anna is sure she understands, she asks Miss Levine to give her a long-division test at recess time.

The problems are very hard, but Anna remembers Father's lessons. When she's finished, she sits quietly and waits for Miss Levine to check her answers. She hears the children shouting on the playground. They're having much more fun than Anna.

Finally Miss Levine says, "Anna, you may gather your things and return to your desk in the front of the room." With just the hint of a smile, she adds, "And please stay there. All this moving about is distracting to the other children."

When the boys and girls come back from recess, Charlie is happy to see Anna in her old place. "I told you you were too smart to stay in the low third," he says.

Anna glances at Rosa. She doesn't look pleased to see Anna sitting beside her again. "You'd better not copy from me," Rosa whispers. "I'll tell if you do."

Anna would like to pinch Rosa's plump arm but she keeps her hands to herself. It wouldn't do to make Miss Levine cross. "If you don't stop copying my spelling tests," Anna hisses, *"I'll* tell on *you.*"

Rosa hides her red face behind her reading book, but Anna raises her hand to answer Miss Levine's first question about today's story. She can hardly wait to tell Father she's back in the top third.

· 3 ·

Anna's New Coat

ONE NOVEMBER MORNING ANNA WAKES UP AND SEES frost on her window. The bedroom floor is cold under her bare feet. She dresses quickly and runs downstairs to breakfast. At this time of year, the kitchen is the warmest room in the house.

Anna holds her cup of cocoa with both hands, feeling the heat. "Brrr," she says.

Father looks at Mother over the top of his newspaper. "I suppose it's time to order a wagonload of coal," he says. "Winter's coming. We'll need the furnace soon."

"Anna wouldn't be cold if she wore long underwear like a sensible girl," Mother says.

Anna makes a face. She hates scratchy wool underwear. When the radiator in her classroom comes on, the heat makes her legs itch.

Mother sighs. "Eat your oatmeal," she tells Anna. "Perhaps it will keep you warm."

Anna makes another face. She hates oatmeal even more than long underwear.

"Oatmeal's good for you," Mother says. "It sticks to your ribs."

"Like plaster," Father adds, with a wink. "That's why it keeps out the cold."

Before Anna leaves for school, Mother reaches into the hall closet and pulls out Anna's blue coat. "You'll need this today."

When Anna puts on her coat, it feels tight across the shoulders.

"My, my, Anna, you've grown," Mother says. "It's time for a trip to the tailor for a new coat."

Anna looks at her sleeves. They are way too short. The shoulders are too narrow. Her dress shows below the coat's hem. It looks like she's wearing someone else's coat, someone much younger than she is. "I can't wear this," Anna says. "It's too small."

Against Mother's wishes, Anna takes off her coat. But when she opens the front door, the wind roars into the house. Its icy breath makes Anna shiver. She must wear her old coat to school after all. Reluctantly she buttons it tight and runs toward school. If she's lucky, she'll get to the cloakroom and hang up her coat before anyone sees her.

Unfortunately, Rosa and Beatrice catch up with Anna at the corner. They're both wearing brand-new coats. Beatrice's is a dull gray but Rosa's is bright red. It has black satin trim and a stylish little belt. Anna would love to have one exactly like it.

"See my new coat?" Rosa asks Anna. She spins around to show off. "Isn't it beautiful?"

Anna puts her hands in her pockets, hoping to hide her coat's short sleeves. "It's very nice," she says politely.

Rosa smiles. She looks hard at Anna's coat. Even though Rosa says nothing, Anna knows what Rosa is thinking: Anna needs a new coat, too.

o o o

On Saturday, Mother, Father, and Anna ride the trolley downtown. As they walk past Hutzler's department store, Anna sees a display of girls' coats in the window. One is just like Rosa's.

Anna tugs at Mother's hand. "Look, Mother," she says. "Why can't we buy one of those coats? We could take it home today and I could wear it to church tomorrow. I wouldn't have to wait for the tailor to make it."

Mother shakes her head and frowns. "Store-bought clothes are made of cheap material. They're not well cut or well sewn. Why, one of those coats would fall apart before you outgrew it."

Anna thinks the coats are beautiful, but she knows better than to argue. Mother is an excellent seamstress. She makes dresses for Anna and herself, as well as all of Father's shirts. Sometimes she sews for other people, too. She made Aunt May's wedding dress. She makes christening gowns and caps for all her nieces and nephews.

If Mother says the coats are no good, she's probably right. Maybe Rosa's coat will fall apart soon. Anna hopes it does. It would serve snobby Rosa right.

Mr. Abraham meets Mother and Father at the door of his shop. "What can I do for you today, Mr. Sherwood?" he asks Father.

"Nothing for me, thank you," Father says. "But Anna needs a new coat."

Anna stretches out her arms to show Mr. Abraham how short her sleeves are. "I'm eight now," she says. "I've grown a lot since I was seven!"

"My goodness, Anna, you're shooting up like a stalk of corn in July," Mr. Abraham says. "If you keep growing this fast, your head will go right through the ceiling!"

Everyone laughs except Anna. She thinks Mr. Abraham is teasing her, but what if he's not? What if she grows and grows and grows like Alice in Wonderland? What if she ends up as tall as Uncle Frank? He's over six feet tall. Every time he visits, he bumps his head on the living-room chandelier.

Mr. Abraham takes a measuring tape from his pocket and leads Anna to a low stool in front of a mirror. "Stand here, please," he says. "And don't fidget."

While Mr. Abraham measures Anna, she stares at herself in the mirror. She sees a tall, thin girl with a narrow face and long brown hair. She wonders if someday she'll get prettier. Or will she just get taller?

When he's finished, Mr. Abraham smiles at Anna. "Would you like to look at the pattern books now?"

Anna and Mother go through the books together.

They look at page after page of coat patterns. Some are cut full, some narrow. Some have belts, some hang loose. Some are pleated, some are plain. Choosing the one that will look best on Anna is hard work.

At last Anna finds the perfect coat in the *Home Book of Fashions.* Its dropped waist and pleated skirt are very stylish, Anna thinks, and she loves the satin collar, the cuffs, and the matching buttons. It's even prettier than Rosa's coat.

Next Anna and Mother must pick the material from the huge bolts of fabric that Mr. Abraham lays on the table for them to admire. So many colors, so many textures. Does Anna want a solid color, a tweed, a plaid?

Anna picks up a bolt of red wool, the same red as the coat in Hutzler's window, the same red as Rosa's coat. "This is what I want," she tells Mother.

Mother shakes her head. "Red is too bright for you. It will make you pale." She shows Anna a bolt of brown tweed wool. "How about this? Brown is much more practical than red. It will be very smart with dark trim and silver buttons."

Anna shakes her head and clings to the red wool. The practical tweed is drab and boring. It won't look smart with dark trim and silver buttons. It will look ugly. No one will notice Anna in a coat like that. She'll be a plain brown sparrow instead of a gorgeous red cardinal.

Tears well up in Anna's eyes. "Please, Mother," she begs. "Please?"

Mother frowns. "Absolutely not, Anna. Red is a cheap, flashy color. I will not have a daughter of mine sashaying down the street in a common color like red."

But that's exactly what Anna wants—to sashay down the street in a flashy red coat like Rosa's.

Anna shows the bolt to Father. "Isn't this a beautiful color, Father? Don't you love red?"

Father looks at Mother. Mother is still frowning. She shakes her head again, harder this time. "Anna will look terrible in red," she insists. Father looks at Anna. She's crying now. "Red's my favorite color," she sobs, stamping one foot for good measure.

Mr. Abraham makes a little clucking sound with his tongue. "Red and brown aren't the only colors in my shop." He waves his hand at all the other bolts of fabric. "How about this nice forest green?"

He holds the bolt under Anna's chin and smiles. "Just as I thought. It brings out the color of your eyes. Not every girl has eyes as green as yours, Anna."

Mr. Abraham shows Anna her reflection in the mirror. "There. See how pretty you look?"

Anna stops crying. Mr. Abraham is right. The green is even prettier than the red. She turns to Mother hopefully. "Do you like green?"

Mother caresses the brown tweed. Father gives her a little nudge that Anna isn't supposed to see. "It's a nice shade of green," she admits. "Not as practical as the brown but much better than the red."

Mr. Abraham winks at Anna. "What would you think of dark-red velvet for the trim?" he asks. "And those silver buttons your Mother likes so much?"

Anna smiles and nods her head. She wants to hug Mr. Abraham but she's too shy. "Thank you," she whispers instead. "Thank you very much."

o   o   o

For another long week, Anna must wear her old coat to school. She keeps her hands in her pockets as much as she can. She ignores the looks Rosa gives her.

At last a parcel wrapped in brown paper and tied

tight with string arrives at Anna's door. Inside is Anna's new coat. The green wool is even softer than she remembered. The red velvet trim and silver buttons look very smart indeed.

When Anna wears it to school on Monday, Rosa touches the wool. "Your new coat is pretty," she says. "But it would be even prettier in red. Red's my favorite color."

"Mine, too," Beatrice agrees.

But Charlie says, "You look just like an Irish girl in that green coat, Anna."

Anna smiles at Charlie. She knows a compliment when she hears one.

"Red is all right," she tells Beatrice and Rosa. "But green is *my* favorite color."

Winter

· 4 ·

Rosa's Birthday Party

ONE DAY ROSA INVITES ANNA TO HER EIGHTH birthday party. It's the fourth invitation Anna has received this year. In February she went to Beatrice's party. In May she went to Patrick's party. In July she went to Wally's party. Now it's December and she's going to Rosa's party.

Anna shows Mother the invitation. Rosa's name and address, the time, and the date are printed on a pretty flowered card.

Mother wipes her hands on her apron and looks at the invitation. She is making dumplings to serve with the sauerbraten cooking in the oven. Her hands are crusted with flour.

"Oh, dear," Mother says. "Not another party, Anna."

Anna guesses Mother is tired of buying presents. "I can give Rosa a little thimble like the one I gave Beatrice," she says.

"Yes, that's a good idea. Not too expensive." Mother sighs and goes back to her work. "Parents should put an end to these parties," she says. "Such foolishness."

"I wish I could have a party," Anna says softly. She's asked Mother many times but Mother always says no. Birthday parties are too much trouble, they are expensive, they are foolish. Foolish is Mother's favorite word, Anna thinks.

Mother shakes her head. "What have I told you, Anna? It may not bother Mrs. Schuman to allow a tribe of savage children to run through her house, but I refuse to open my door to barbarians. I take pride in my home."

"But Mother—"

"No buts, Anna. My mind is made up. I will have no birthday parties here."

That is that. Anna knows better than to beg or plead or whine. When Mother says no, she means no. Father is no help. He always sides with Mother.

On the day of Rosa's party, Anna wears her best white dress, trimmed with lace and tied below the waist with a wide sash. Mother pulls Anna's hair back and fastens it with a big white ribbon tied in a bow.

"Remember to thank Mrs. Schuman for inviting you, Anna. When you leave, tell her you had a good time." Mother smoothes Anna's skirt and brushes a speck of dust from her sleeve. "And please don't spill anything on your dress," she adds.

Anna walks up the hill to Rosa's house with Charlie. For once his red hair is combed, parted in the middle, and plastered to his head with what seems to be shellac. He wears his best knee-length dark pants and a starched white shirt with a stiff collar. He looks very handsome, Anna thinks, but not very comfortable.

"I hate birthday parties," Charlie grumbles. "If it weren't for the cake and ice cream, I wouldn't go to Rosa's house today."

"The games are fun, too," Anna says.

"Pin-the-tail-on-the-donkey. Drop-the-clothespin-in-the-bottle." Charlie snorts. "Silly girl games, that's what they are."

Anna wants Charlie to like her as much as she likes him, so she says, "You're right, Charlie. Roller-skating's much more fun, and we don't have to dress up to do it."

Charlie grins at Anna. "If my mother would let me have a party, we'd play outside and wear regular clothes."

He sighs and kicks a stone. "But I'll never have a party," he adds glumly. "Our house is too crowded. There's no room for anybody except us Murphys."

"My mother doesn't approve of birthday parties, so I'll never have one either." Anna kicks a stone, too, just like Charlie did.

"If I was allowed to have a party," she tells Charlie, "we'd have the biggest cake in Baltimore, covered with the sweetest, whitest frosting you ever saw. And mountains of strawberry ice cream. Nobody would get dressed up, either."

By now Anna and Charlie are climbing Rosa's white marble steps. There isn't a speck of dirt on them. Mrs. Schuman has scrubbed and polished them in honor of the birthday party.

Charlie lifts the brass knocker and lets it fall with a nice loud thump. Rosa opens the door so quickly, Anna almost falls into the hallway.

"Happy birthday, Rosa," Anna and Charlie say together.

Rosa grins and snatches her presents. She shakes Anna's little gift and says, "I know what this is. A thimble just like the one you gave Beatrice!"

Anna is disappointed. It's no fun to give a present if the birthday person guesses what it is before she even opens it. Worse yet, Rosa doesn't look excited or pleased. Just bored.

She tosses Anna's gift onto a table piled high with bigger, fancier presents and squeezes Charlie's gift. It's small and flat and not very well wrapped. The bow is lopsided. Charlie must have tied it himself.

"I wonder what this can be," Rosa says, smiling at Charlie.

"I guess you'll find out when you open it," Charlie says and walks away to find Wally and Patrick.

Rosa giggles and pulls Anna aside. "We're going to play spin-the-bottle," she whispers. "When it's my turn, I intend to kiss Charlie Murphy. He's the cutest boy in Baltimore."

Anna frowns. She has never heard of spin-the-bottle but she doesn't admit it. Rosa is the kind of girl who makes fun of people who don't know as much as she does. "I'll kiss Charlie, too," she tells Rosa.

Rosa sticks out her tongue. "Charlie is my boyfriend," she says. "He likes me better than he likes you."

"He does not," Anna says.

"He does too!"

"Doesn't!"

"Does!"

Just as Anna is about to pull Rosa's long blond curls as hard as she can, Mrs. Schuman calls the children in to the parlor to play pin-the-tail-on-the-donkey. When it's Anna's turn, Mrs. Schuman ties a blindfold over Anna's eyes and puts a paper donkey tail in her hand. The tail has a sharp pin in one end.

Mrs. Schuman turns Anna around once, twice, three times. "Now," she says, "go and pin the tail on the donkey, dear."

Anna takes a small step toward the donkey's picture. Mrs. Schuman has tied the kerchief too loosely. Anna can see out the bottom. She knows exactly where to pin the tail.

Holding the tail before her, Anna walks toward the donkey's picture. Suddenly Rosa steps in front of her, blocking the way. Without hesitating, Anna pins the donkey's tail on Rosa in just the right place.

Rosa shrieks. Anna pretends not to know what has

happened. She staggers around the living room, her arms stretched out like a blind person's. "Where's the donkey?" she asks. "Where's the donkey?"

Mrs. Schuman comforts Rosa. She doesn't guess Anna can see through the blindfold. She doesn't blame her. "That's enough of that game," she says, untying the kerchief.

After the cake and ice cream, Rosa opens her presents. She yawns when she sees Anna's pretty silver thimble. She yawns when she sees the drawing pad Wally has given her. She yawns when she sees the colored pencils Patrick has given her. She even yawns when she sees the bottle of cologne Beatrice has given her.

But when she opens Charlie's present, Rosa smiles. "Oh, look, Mother. Isn't this handkerchief the prettiest thing you ever saw?"

Mrs. Schuman smiles and nods. Wally and Patrick make silly sounds and poke Charlie. Charlie scowls at the floor. Beatrice leans close to Rosa so she can admire the handkerchief, too.

The look on Charlie's face tells Anna he doesn't give a hoot whether Rosa likes his gift or not.

When Rosa has opened all her presents, she goes

to the kitchen and comes back with an empty milk bottle. First, she tells the children to sit in a circle. Then she says, "I'm going to spin the bottle. When it stops, I get to kiss the person the bottle points to."

"You're not kissing me," Wally says.

"Who says I want to kiss you!" Rosa says, making a face.

Beatrice giggles but Wally jumps up and says he's going home. Before anyone can stop him, he runs out the front door.

Patrick and Charlie look at each other. Anna has a feeling they want to leave, too, but they stay in their places. Maybe their mothers told them it's rude to leave before the party is officially over.

Rosa puts her chubby finger on the bottle and spins it ever so slowly. Anna isn't sure how she does it, but Rosa manages to make the bottle stop when it's pointing right at Charlie. She jumps to her feet and grabs Charlie's arm to stop him from running out of the room.

"I get to kiss you, Charlie!" Rosa says. "I'm the birthday girl and I spun the bottle right at you!"

Charlie scowls again, but he lets Rosa kiss his

cheek. Rosa aims a quick glance at Anna as if to say, "I told you he likes me best!"

Anna pretends not to notice the smug look on Rosa's face. Beatrice puts her hand over her mouth to keep herself from giggling but she giggles anyway. Patrick fidgets with his bow tie and inches closer to the door.

Rosa hands Charlie the bottle. "It's your turn to spin it," she says. "If it points at me this time, you get to kiss me!"

Charlie puts the bottle down. Anna ducks her head so she can watch him secretly. He's looking right at her, not at Rosa. Slowly he spins the bottle. When it stops, it's pointing at Anna.

Though this is exactly what Anna hoped would happen, she's suddenly afraid to raise her head. She's never kissed a boy. She sees Charlie's feet come closer. She sees him stop.

"Well, Anna," he says, "are you going to let me kiss you?"

Anna stands up slowly. Charlie leans toward her, a big grin on his face. Very carefully, he kisses Anna's cheek. He smells sweet, like birthday cake and ice cream.

"It's your turn, now." Charlie hands Anna the milk

bottle. Before she spins it, she sneaks a quick look at the birthday girl. The scowl on Rosa's face makes Anna smile.

Just as Anna is about to spin the bottle, Mrs. Schuman steps into the parlor. "Here are the clothespins, Rosa," she says. "I'm sorry it took me so long to find them. They were on a dark shelf by the coal bin. I can't imagine how they got there."

Mrs. Schuman hands Rosa a basket full of clothespins. "Now you can play drop-the-clothespin-in-the-bottle," she says.

Anna notices Rosa's red face. She has a good idea who put the clothespins on that dark shelf.

When the party is over, Anna remembers to thank Mrs. Schuman for inviting her. Charlie thanks Mrs. Schuman, too, but he doesn't look at Rosa.

As soon as he and Anna are outside, Charlie runs his hands through his hair and messes it up. Then he unbuttons his tight collar and pulls his shirt out of his trousers. "Now I feel like me," he says.

Suddenly, without any warning, Charlie grabs Anna's hair ribbon and runs down the street with it.

"Give that back!" Anna cries. "It's my best ribbon!"

"Catch me if you can," Charlie shouts.

Anna chases him but Charlie has always been able to outrun her. Before she can catch him, he dashes into his house and slams the door.

Anna sits down on her front steps and gazes at Charlie's house. Her feelings are hurt. She thought Charlie liked her, especially after he kissed her, but now he's taken her ribbon and run into his house. Doesn't he know how cross Mother will be?

Just then Mother opens the door. The very first thing she says is, "Why, Anna. What's happened to your ribbon?"

"Charlie took it," Anna says, too angry to care whether she's a tattletale or not.

"Oh, he did, did he?" Before Anna can stop her, Mother marches across the street toward Charlie's house. She doesn't even bother to put on her coat.

Anna runs behind Mother, tugging at her dress. "Stop," she says, sorry she tattled. "Charlie will get a spanking if you tell his mother he took my ribbon."

Mother keeps going. There's no stopping her when she's angry. Before she reaches Charlie's door, it opens and out comes Mrs. Murphy, dragging Charlie by the arm. In Mrs. Murphy's hand is Anna's white ribbon.

Mrs. Murphy gives the ribbon to Anna and pushes Charlie forward. "What do you have to say to Anna, young man?" Mrs. Murphy asks Charlie.

Charlie's face turns as red as Anna's face feels. "I'm sorry I took your ribbon, Anna," he mumbles.

"It's all right, Charlie." Anna smiles at Charlie and then looks at his mother. "It was just a game," she tells Mrs. Murphy. "Charlie didn't mean to be bad. Please don't spank him."

"You're too late," Charlie whispers to Anna. "She already did."

"A little spanking never hurt anyone," Mrs. Murphy says. "Don't you agree, Mrs. Sherwood?"

Mother sighs. "Just try telling Mr. Sherwood that," she says. "He doesn't believe in physical punishment, no matter what Anna does."

Charlie draws in his breath loudly. "Lucky duck," he says to Anna. "You must have the best father in all of Baltimore."

Anna smiles. It's true. Father is the best father in all of Baltimore. In fact, he's the best father in the whole world.

"Come, Anna." Mother takes Anna's hand. "It's time to go home."

"Hurry back," Charlie calls to Anna. "We'll play tag with Patrick and Wally."

Mother holds Anna's hand tighter. "Wouldn't you rather cut out paper dolls with Rosa and Beatrice?" she asks. "They're such well-behaved children. Little ladies, both of them. That Charlie is a regular hooligan."

Anna turns to wave at Charlie. She wonders what Mother would say if she told her she'd rather be a hooligan than a lady any day.

· 5 ·

Christmas Wishes

IT'S THE WEEK BEFORE CHRISTMAS. CHARLIE AND Anna are looking at a Sears Roebuck catalog, their wish book. On one page is a picture of an Erector set.

"That's what I want," Charlie says. "Nothing else. No mittens, no underwear, no warm stockings. Just an Erector set big enough to build this ferris wheel." He points to a picture of a boy playing with the ferris wheel he's made.

"Did you tell Santa about it?" Anna asks.

"Of course," Charlie says. "I wrote him a letter two weeks ago."

Anna turns the pages in the wish book. What she wants is a doll with a pretty china face, a wig of real human hair, and jointed arms and legs, the kind that closes her eyes when you lay her down to sleep. She'll name her Clarissa or Penelope. Anna can't decide which name is prettier.

Charlie looks at the dolls in the wish book and wrinkles his nose. "You should ask Santa for an Erector set, too," he says. "Then we could build things together."

Anna stares at Charlie. "Erector sets are for boys."

"There's no law that says a girl can't own one," Charlie says. "Just imagine the fun we'd have, Anna."

Anna isn't sure she wants an Erector set but she hates to disappoint Charlie. "I'll think about it," she tells him.

"Think hard," Charlie says.

o o o

After supper that night, Father asks Anna if she's written her letter to Santa.

"Not yet." She opens the wish book and shows Father the doll.

"Very pretty," he says. "Is that all you want?"

Anna turns the pages and shows Father the Erector set. "Do you suppose Santa would bring one of these to a girl?"

"I don't see why not," Father says.

Mother looks over Father's shoulder. "Surely you don't want an Erector set, Anna!"

Suddenly Anna wants the Erector set more than anything she's ever wished for. "Yes, I do!" she says fiercely.

Father chuckles but Mother frowns. "Please, Ira," Mother says. "Don't encourage this foolishness. Anna's a girl, a young lady. What use has she for boys' toys?"

"I see no harm in it," Father says. "An Erector set will teach Anna how to build things, Lizzie. It's far more educational than a doll."

Mother sighs. "We'll see," she says. "Santa may not think Anna needs an Erector set."

Anna writes her list. She uses her best penmanship and is careful not to blot the ink or misspell any words. The doll is number one. The Erector set is number two. She adds candy, hair ribbons, paper dolls, and a book. It's a lot to ask for, but, as Mother said, Santa will decide what Anna needs.

The days drag past slowly, slowly, slowly. Anna helps Mother clean the house. She polishes the silver. She buys presents and wraps them in her bedroom, keeping the door closed so no one will see what she's picked.

Finally it's Christmas Eve. Father brings home a tree taller than Anna. It's fresh and green. Soon the whole house smells like a pine forest.

Anna and Mother help Father set up the tree. They put it in front of the parlor window so people on the street will see it as they walk past the house.

They decorate the tree with big shiny glass balls and pretty ornaments from Germany. Father adds tiny candles. Anna wants to light them right away but the candles can be lighted just once—on Christmas night.

All day Mother has been cooking. The house smells of roast turkey and sauerkraut, cranberries and sweet potatoes, sugar cookies, and fondant, a special treat made of sugar and cream, colored in delicate tints of green, yellow, and pink. They are so sweet they make Anna's jaws ache.

Just as darkness falls, Mother's family begins to arrive. As they come inside from the cold, they stamp their feet and cry, *"Fröhliche Weinachten! Fröhliche Weinachten!"* Anna knows that means "Merry Christmas!"

Soon the little house is crowded with aunts and uncles and cousins, so many Anna does not know all their names. They laugh and talk, sometimes in

English, sometimes in German. They remember the old days before Anna was born.

After dinner, Grandfather Reuwer produces a bottle of homemade dandelion wine. The more he drinks, the more he talks. When Grandfather Reuwer begins telling stories that make him cry, a visiting entertainer gets out his accordion and sings. Beside him is a large chart on which the German words to the songs are written. Everyone gathers around and sings in German, even Anna. She hopes she'll remember the words, but as soon as the man turns the page, she forgets the song she just sang.

When all the songs are sung, the whole family goes to Midnight Mass at Saint Gregory's Catholic Church. This is the first year Anna has been allowed to stay up so late. She walks down the sidewalk holding Father's and Mother's hands. The street is unfamiliar in the dark. The air smells of snow and the wind is cold. All over the city, church bells are ringing. The chimes come from many directions. It's as if the bells are ringing in heaven, Anna thinks.

The church is warm. The light is soft and golden. Pine boughs garland the altar. In the crèche, Mary and Joseph kneel beside the manger, gazing at baby

Jesus. He lies on his back, wrapped in swaddling clothes, his arms spread wide. He smiles at Mary and Joseph. Like Anna, baby Jesus is an only child.

After mass, Father carries Anna home. She is too tired to walk but not too tired to look for Santa's sleigh in the sky. Even after Father puts Anna to bed, she watches for Santa. Just before she falls asleep, she thinks she hears sleigh bells.

On Christmas day, Anna wakes up before Mother and Father. She lies in bed for a while waiting for them to get up. Finally she tiptoes to the top of the steps. All is quiet downstairs. The hall is still dark.

Anna is afraid to go to the parlor by herself. Suppose Santa has forgotten her? Suppose she's been naughtier than she thought? Suppose all she'll find under the tree is a bundle of sticks or a piece of coal?

Behind her, Anna hears footsteps. She turns and sees Father coming toward her. "Merry Christmas, Anna," he says.

"Merry Christmas, Father!" Anna runs to him and gives him a big Christmas hug and kiss.

"Shall we go downstairs and see what Santa has brought?" Father asks.

"What about Mother?" Anna asks. "Shouldn't we wait for her?"

"Here I am," says Mother. *"Fröhliche Weinachten, Mädchen!"*

Holding her breath, Anna slowly opens the parlor curtain. She keeps her eyes closed for a moment, scared of being disappointed. Her heart beats so fast she thinks it might fly out of her chest.

Finally Anna dares to look. The doll she's wanted for so long sits in a brand-new wicker carriage, smiling at her. She's wearing a dress just like the one Mother has made for Anna to wear today. Under the tree, Anna finds a soft, warm beaver hat and muff for herself, and smaller ones for the doll. She also finds paper dolls and the book she hoped for, *Rebecca of Sunnybrook Farm.* In her stocking are hair ribbons, a big juicy orange, chocolate candy wrapped in shiny foil, and a pretty little gold ring for her finger.

But where is the Erector set? Anna crawls under the tree, thinking it must be hidden there, but she doesn't see it. She glances at Mother and Father. They smile at her.

"Santa has been good to you, Anna." Mother says.

"Yes, indeed he has," Father agrees.

No one says a word about the Erector set. Anna forces herself to smile. It would be ungrateful to complain, but she's very disappointed. Charlie will be disappointed, too.

Father gives Mother her present, a Victrola and records of her favorite opera singers. Mother gives Father six handmade shirts, stitched as neatly as the dresses she sews for Anna.

Anna gives Father a soft wool scarf to keep his neck warm on cold walks home from the trolley stop. She gives Mother lilac perfume.

Father likes his scarf so much he insists on wearing it to breakfast. "My neck is cold," he says.

Mother dabs a few drops of perfume behind her ears and on her wrists. The sweet smell of lilacs mingles with the waffles Mother has cooked.

All day long Father's relatives come and go. His brother, Anna's uncle Harry, comes with his wife, Aunt Grace. Father's sister, Anna's aunt Aggie, comes all the way from the farm with her husband, Uncle George. His aunt, Anna's great aunt Emma Moree, arrives in a horse and carriage. When the relatives come through the door, they say, "Merry Christmas." Like Father, they do not speak German.

Uncle Harry hands Anna a big box wrapped in splendid red and green paper. "Merry Christmas," he says. "This is from all of us. We hope you enjoy it, Anna."

The relatives gather around and watch Anna untie the shiny bow. She thinks it must be a new tea set for her dolls, but when she tears off the paper, Anna can hardly believe her eyes. Her aunts and uncles have given her the Erector set she wants so badly.

"Thank you, thank you!" Anna puts the box down and jumps to her feet. She hugs Uncle Harry and all the others and they hug her back.

Mother shakes her head. "What will Anna do with such a thing?" she says with a smile.

"I'll build a ferris wheel," Anna cries. "Me and Charlie—we'll do it together!"

"Charlie and I," says Aunt Grace. "Charlie and I will do it together."

For a moment, Anna thinks Aunt Grace wants to help her and Charlie build the ferris wheel. She's too surprised to say anything—which is lucky, because she quickly realizes that Aunt Grace is correcting her grammar, not offering to help build the ferris wheel.

"Charlie and *I*," Anna says with a smile. "Charlie and I will build the biggest and best ferris wheel in the world!"

As the day ends, the relatives gradually leave. Snow falls softly, whitening the city streets and sidewalks. Father lights the candles on the tree. He turns out the gas lights. He winds up the new Victrola and plays *"Stille Nacht"* for Mother. It's his last Christmas surprise, "Silent Night," sung in German.

Anna sits on the sofa between Mother and Father. Father sips a glass of dandelion wine. Mother eats a piece of chocolate from her favorite shop, Page & Shaw's.

Anna hugs her doll. "This is the best Christmas ever," she says.

"You say that every year," Mother says.

"And every year it's true," says Anna.

· 6 ·

Anna's Birthday Surprise

IT'S THE MIDDLE OF JANUARY. ANNA AND CHARLIE are sitting on the parlor floor, building a tower with Anna's Erector set. They cannot make a ferris wheel because they do not have enough pieces. Santa didn't bring Charlie an Erector set. He brought him mittens, socks, a scarf, and a warm hat instead. Charlie's mother says Santa knows what's best for Charlie but Charlie isn't so sure of that.

"Santa didn't bring me an Erector set, either," Anna reminds Charlie. "My uncles and aunts gave it to me."

"Maybe Santa ran out of Erector sets," Charlie says glumly.

"That must be it," Anna agrees. "Santa's elves

couldn't make enough for everyone this year. You'll get your set next Christmas."

Anna and Charlie work quietly for a while. Then Charlie says, "Your birthday is next week. Are you having a party?"

Anna shakes her head. She has pestered Mother for days but it has done no good. Mother will not say yes to a party.

Charlie looks as disappointed as Anna feels. "That's too bad," he says. "I heard Rosa tell Beatrice it's your turn to have a party. She says she won't invite you to her party next year if you don't invite her to a party at your house this year."

Anna frowns at Charlie. "That's not fair," she says. "It's not my fault Mother won't let me have a party."

"Don't get cross with me," Charlie says. "I'm just telling you what Rosa says."

"Rosa is a boring, stuck-up snob," Anna says. "I don't care if she never invites me to another party. In fact, I won't go, not even if she gets down on her knees and begs me."

Charlie agrees. "I won't go either. Rosa might kiss me again." He makes a face.

Anna giggles, but she hopes Charlie doesn't feel the same way about kissing her.

After Charlie leaves, Anna puts away her Erector set and goes to the kitchen to find Mother. "Rosa won't invite me to her birthday party if I don't invite her to my birthday party," she tells Mother.

"That's just as well," Mother says. "We won't have to buy her any more presents."

"But, Mother—"

"Anna, I've told you over and over again that you cannot have a party. If you ask once more, Father and I won't celebrate your birthday at all. There will be no gifts for you. No cake. No ice cream."

Anna knows Mother means every word. Feeling sad, she goes to the parlor and sits in Father's chair, her favorite thinking place. While Mother moves around the kitchen preparing supper, Anna stares out the window. The winter day is ending. Across the street, the housetops and chimneys are black against the sunset. They look as if they've been cut from paper and pasted onto the sky.

Slowly an idea forms in Anna's head. Mother will be very cross, but Anna doesn't care. She must have a birthday party. She absolutely must.

The next day Anna has a piano lesson at Madame Wehman's house. When it's over, she walks down North Avenue to the five-and-dime and buys a small box of pretty stationery. It costs her five cents, half of the dime Father gives her every Saturday for spending money.

That night before she goes to bed, Anna writes a note to each child on her block. At school, she hands one to Charlie, Wally, Patrick, Beatrice, and Rosa.

On the way home, Charlie reads his note out loud:

> *Dear Charlie,*
> *You are invited to a birthday party at my house on January 20. Come after school. Do not dress up. We will play outside.*
>
> > *Sincerely yours,*
> > *Anna E. Sherwood*

"A birthday party," Charlie says. "Hurrah for you, Anna!"

Anna smiles but her insides feel cold. Her birthday is only a few days away. She doesn't know what Mother will say when her friends arrive.

What will she do about cake? How will she get ice cream?

○   ○   ○

The afternoon before her birthday, Anna asks mother if she can help bake the cake. "I want a big cake this year," she says, "with lots and lots of thick, sweet icing. And gallons of strawberry ice cream."

Mother shakes her head. "The cake is always a surprise, Anna. After dinner tomorrow night, you'll see what I've baked."

"But, Mother—"

Mother frowns. "When will you learn that no means no, Anna? Not yes, not maybe, but NO."

"Will you make a big cake?" Anna persists. "And can we have strawberry ice cream with it?"

"Don't worry," Mother says. "There will be plenty of cake for the three of us."

"I'll pick up strawberry ice cream on my way home tomorrow," Father says. "A pint should do nicely."

That night Anna has trouble sleeping. What if the cake is too small for six children? What if Father doesn't bring the ice cream home in time? What if a pint isn't enough?

The party is beginning to remind Anna of one of Miss Levine's arithmetic problems. Perhaps she should tell her friends that the party has been canceled.

But when Anna arrives at school, everyone is smiling secret smiles and whispering about the packages in their coat pockets. It's too late to cancel the party.

After school, Anna runs home. Mother and Aunt May are at the kitchen table as usual. Anna hears Aunt May say, "Henry came home late again last night. We had a rip-snorting argument."

Usually Anna would lurk in the hall and listen, but not today. She goes into the parlor and peeks out the window. Rosa and Beatrice are coming down the hill toward her house. Charlie is running across the street. Patrick and Wally are with him. They are all carrying presents.

A moment later, the doorbell chimes. Anna hurries to open the door.

"Happy birthday, Anna!" says Charlie.

"Yes, happy birthday!" Rosa adds.

Anna's friends spill through the front door and fill the hall. "Happy birthday," they shout. "Happy birthday!"

Mother and Aunt May come to the kitchen door and gasp at the sight of the children.

"Anna," Mother says. *"Was ist das?"*

Mother is so startled that she has forgotten to speak English, but Anna knows what she means. "It's a surprise party," Anna says. "For me. For my birthday!"

"Anna, Anna!" Aunt May begins to laugh. *"Ach, mein kluges Liebling!* A surprise party indeed!"

Mother does not laugh. She stares at Anna. The children stare at Anna, too. No one speaks. The only sound is the hall clock ticking.

Anna's eyes fill with tears. She has made a horrible mistake. Mother will never forgive her for this clever little surprise. Nobody will invite Anna to another birthday party as long as she lives. She is disgraced.

Suddenly Aunt May steps forward. "Rosa," she says, "and Beatrice. How nice to see you." She turns to the boys. "Thank you for coming, Charlie, Wally, and Patrick."

Suddenly everything is all right. Rosa smoothes her curls and smiles at Charlie. Beatrice giggles. Wally pokes Patrick. Patrick pokes Wally. Charlie shows everyone the tower he and Anna have almost finished building on the parlor floor.

In the meantime, Aunt May pulls Mother into the kitchen. Anna hears them whispering in German. *"Das Eis,"* Mother says. *"Der Kuchen."*

Aunt May tells Mother not to worry. She comes back to the parlor and asks Anna, "Why don't you take your friends outside to play?"

Wally scowls. "If we play spin-the-bottle, I'm going home!"

"No spin-the-bottle," Anna promises, though secretly she'd love for Charlie to kiss her again. "Red-rover," she adds. "And Mother, May I. That's what we'll play.'"

Anna leads the children outside. Rosa and Beatrice are wearing their best dresses even though Anna told them not to, but the boys are wearing their play clothes.

"It's too cold to play outdoors," Rosa says, but she joins the others just the same. She doesn't want to be left out.

While the children are playing, Anna sees Aunt May scoot down the hill toward the shops on North Avenue. When she comes back, she's carrying a quart of ice cream and a big white box from Leidig's Bakery.

Anna begins to enjoy herself. It looks like she's going to have a real party after all, complete with presents, cake, and ice cream.

Soon Mother calls the children inside. A white cake sits on the dining-room table. Nine candles are stuck in the thick, sugary icing. There is plenty of strawberry ice cream.

"*Herzlichen Glückwunsch zum Geburtstag,* Anna!" Aunt May says.

"Yes," says Mother. "Happy birthday, Anna!"

"Blow out the candles and make a wish, *Liebling,*" says Aunt May.

Anna leans across the table, takes a deep breath, and blows as hard as she can. The candles flicker and go out.

As the children sing "Happy Birthday," Anna glances at Mother and smiles.

Mother meets Anna's eyes and hesitates a moment. A frown lurks in the corners of her mouth. Aunt May pats Mother's hand and whispers in her ear. To Anna's relief, Mother gives her a small smile. Anna hopes this means her wish that Mother isn't cross with her has come true.

After the children have eaten all the cake they want, they troop into the parlor to watch Anna open her presents. Rosa gives her a lacy handkerchief and Beatrice gives her a bar of scented soap. Wally gives her a drawing tablet, and Patrick gives her a bag of peppermint candy.

Last of all, Anna opens Charlie's gift. It's a tiny china dog. "He's a watchdog," Charlie explains. "He can guard our tower."

Anna smiles and puts the little dog in front of the tower. It's her favorite present, but Anna is too polite to say so. She thanks everyone, especially Charlie, and says good-bye to her guests.

Now Anna must face Mother and Aunt May. She goes to the kitchen and puts her arms around Mother. "I'm sorry," she whispers. "Please don't be angry with me."

"Anna, you embarrassed me today," Mother says. "You disobeyed me, too. I said you could not have a party and yet you went right ahead and invited those children without telling me. That was very wrong."

"Now, now, Lizzie," Aunt May says. "I admit Anna was naughty, but no harm's done."

Mother frowns at her sister. "Suppose you hadn't been here, May?" she asks. "How would I have gotten the cake and ice cream? I spent my grocery money yesterday."

Aunt May hugs Mother. "That's what sisters are for, Lizzie. To help each other. Someday you'll do the same for me."

Mother sighs and goes to the pantry. She comes back with a beautiful little cake, trimmed with pink and yellow flowers. On top Mother has written, "Happy Birthday, Anna." It's much prettier than the plain cake from the bakery but not nearly big enough for six children.

"This was to be Anna's birthday cake," Mother says. "Take it home with you, May, and surprise Henry with it. Anna has had enough cake for one day. And enough surprises, too."

Anna opens her mouth to protest but then shuts it. Now is not the time to complain.

"But what about Ira?" Aunt May asks. "He must be expecting cake for dessert."

"Ira will understand," Mother says.

Now Anna feels even worse. Because of her, poor Father won't have cake tonight.

After Aunt May leaves, Mother sends Anna to her room. Anna takes Charlie's little dog with her but she feels too bad to play with him. Instead she lies on her bed and waits for Father to come home. When she hears him at the front door, calling hello, she begins to cry. If this is how nine is going to be, she wishes she were still eight.

After a while Anna hears Father coming up the stairs. He taps on Anna's door, and she tells him to come in.

"I hear you had a party today," Father says. "A surprise party."

Anna walks the little china dog up and down her arm. She's too embarrassed to look at Father. "I'm sorry," she whispers. "Mother gave my cake to Aunt May. Uncle Henry will have it for his dessert. And you won't have any." A tear splashes down on Anna's dress.

"Who needs cake?" Father asks. "I don't want to get fat, you know."

Since Father is just as skinny as Anna, she knows he's joking to make her feel better. She puts her arms around his neck and hugs him. Because he's just come in from outside, he's still wearing the soft scarf Anna gave him for Christmas.

"Happy ninth birthday, Anna," Father says. "And many, many more to come."

Spring

· 7 ·

Stitches!

IT IS MARCH. THE DAYS ARE LONGER NOW. AND warmer.

Every day after school, Anna and Charlie put on their roller skates and head for the hill on Walbrook Avenue. Even though it's not very steep, Anna is the only girl who dares to skate all the way to the bottom. With Charlie beside her, Anna bumps over the paving stones, faster and faster. The wind blows in her face, and her skates go clickety-clack, clickety-clack like the wheels of a train.

At the bottom, Anna and Charlie roll along, slowing, slowing, slowing, until they come to a stop in front of the candy store. Sometimes Anna treats Charlie to a string of licorice. Sometimes Charlie treats Anna to a jawbreaker. They eat their candy while they climb up the hill. At the top, they skate down again, their arms spread like wings.

There is a much steeper hill a few blocks away on Bentalou Street. Sometimes Anna and Charlie sit on the curb and watch the older boys speed down the hill, but so far neither one has dared to try it.

One afternoon, Charlie and Anna are standing at the top of Bentalou Street. It's like being on a mountain peak. The houses march down the hill, row after row, one set of marble steps after another, each smaller than the one before. Anna can see the roofs of the houses at the bottom.

A big boy whizzes past, followed by two more. They shout as they go by. Soon they are at the bottom, no bigger now than the little china dolls in Anna's dollhouse.

Charlie watches the boys climb back up the hill, laughing, ready to skate down again. He takes a deep breath and squares his shoulders. "I feel brave today," he says. "How about you, Anna?"

Anna twirls the skate key she wears on a string around her neck. How can she tell Charlie she doesn't feel a bit brave? He might think she's a scaredy-cat like the other girls. He might skate away with the big boys and never play with her again. She swallows hard and says nothing—not yes, not no.

"What's wrong?" Charlie asks. "Are you scared?"

"Of course not." Anna bends down and pretends to tighten her skates. If Charlie sees her face, he'll know she's lying.

Charlie rolls this way and that, circling Anna. His skates click and clack again on the paving stones. "I dare and double dare you," he says.

Anna has never refused a dare. Slowly she straightens up and looks down the hill. While she watches, a toy-sized trolley sways past on North Avenue. Its bell chimes twice. From way up here, the sound is no louder than a bird's call.

"Are you coming or not?" Charlie asks.

Anna hears the scorn in his question, but she doesn't answer. She's so scared her mouth has dried up.

The three big boys flash past Charlie. "Hey, twerp," one shouts. "Get out of the way!"

Charlie and Anna watch them zoom down the hill again. This time, they vanish around a corner, still shouting.

Charlie frowns. "Maybe you should go home and play dolls with Rosa and Beatrice," he says.

That does it. Anna takes a deep breath and skates past Charlie. Her wheels begin to turn, slowly at first and then faster and faster. In a second, it's too late to change her mind. She's on her way down Bentalou Street with Charlie just behind her.

As she rolls over the stones, Anna feels the jolts in every bone in her body. Bumpety-bumpety-bump. She has never gone so fast in her whole life. The street rushes past in a blur. She wants to stop but she can't.

Somehow Anna keeps her balance for three long blocks. Then, right in front of Brewster's meat market, she falls flat on her face. For a moment she lies in the street, too stunned to move. Nothing hurts, everything hurts.

Then Charlie is there, kneeling on the ground beside her. "Anna," he shouts, grabbing her shoulder. "Get up! Say something!"

Now it's Charlie's turn to be scared. Anna can't think of anything to say that will make him feel better. If she opens her mouth, she'll cry. The last thing she wants to be is a crybaby.

People gather around. Anna sees men's boots, ladies' long skirts, Charlie's skates. "Stand back," someone says. "Give the poor child air."

Strong hands lift her to her feet. Anna tries to keep her skates under her but they roll this way and that. The butcher from Brewster's Market holds on to her to keep her from falling.

"Oh, no," a lady says. "Look what she's done to herself."

Anna feels something warm on her face. She touches it and sees blood. Lots of blood. She's covered with blood. The sight of it makes Anna cry in spite of herself.

"You've split your chin wide open," the butcher says. "And skinned your hands and knees raw." He pulls a handkerchief from his pocket and ties it around Anna's chin as if she has a toothache. "There, that will stop the worst of the bleeding," he says.

Turning to Charlie, the butcher adds, "Take her skates off, my boy, and help me get her home."

Charlie carries Anna's skates and the butcher carries Anna. It's a long uphill walk. People stop and stare. They ask what happened to Anna.

Since Anna's jaw is tied shut with the butcher's handkerchief, Charlie answers for her. "We were skating down Bentalou Street," he says, "and Anna fell and split her chin wide open." Charlie speaks proudly, as if he wants everyone to know how brave Anna has been.

Anna's mother is outside scrubbing the white marble steps. When the butcher comes around the corner carrying Anna, she takes one look at the blood and presses her hands to her mouth. Over goes the bucket. Soapy water sloshes across the sidewalk and into the gutter.

"Anna!" Mother cries. "Anna!"

"Don't you worry," the butcher calls. "Other than a split chin, your girl is fine. She's just had a slight mishap on her roller skates."

Charlie holds up the skates but Mother pays no attention to him. It is Anna she cares about. Only Anna. Snatching her child from the butcher, she rushes inside to call the doctor.

From over Mother's shoulder, Anna steals a peek at Charlie. He's still holding her skates. She hopes he can see she's stopped crying. If she could, she'd smile at him, but the handkerchief tied under her chin makes it impossible. She waves in what she hopes is a brave way and Charlie waves back. Anna is pleased to notice he looks worried.

Dr. Thompson comes as quickly as his brand-new car can bring him. He unties the handkerchief. The cloth sticks to the blood and Anna winces. Dr. Thompson carefully washes the cut—which also hurts—and examines it.

"Well, well," he says. "I guess I'll have to put you under the sewing machine."

Anna begins to cry again. She thinks Dr. Thompson is going to use Mother's sewing machine to stitch her up. The needle is sharp and it goes very fast when Mother sews. She doesn't know how Dr. Thompson plans to get her chin under that needle, but she's sure it will hurt.

"Oh, my heavens," Mother cries. She looks as if she's going to faint, so Dr. Thompson tells her to lie down. Then he goes to the door and tells Charlie to fetch Aunt May from next door.

Luckily Aunt May isn't a bit squeamish. She holds Anna's head still while Dr. Thompson stitches her wound by hand. Each time the needle pricks her skin, Anna flinches but it doesn't hurt as much as she'd thought it would.

When Dr. Thompson is finished, he steps back and smiles at Anna. "You're a brave girl," he says, then glances at Mother.

Mother is still lying on the couch with her eyes closed. "I cannot bear the sight of blood," she says in a small voice.

While he's bandaging the cut, Dr. Thompson says, "You didn't think I was actually going to put you under a sewing machine, did you?"

Anna is afraid to open her mouth for fear the cut will begin to bleed, so she shakes her head. She hopes Dr. Thompson believes her.

"Surely you didn't tell the poor child such a terrible thing!" Aunt May says. "You really are a rascal, Dr. Thompson!"

At that moment Charlie knocks on the door. He still has Anna's skates. Mother takes them and puts them in the closet. Anna hopes this is not the end of roller-skating.

Charlie comes closer and stares at Anna. "How many stitches did you get?"

Dr. Thompson answers for Anna who hadn't

counted. "Nine," he says, "and she didn't cry once."

Charlie whistles in admiration. "Anna's as tough as a boy," he says.

That is the greatest compliment Charlie has ever given Anna, but he tops it by adding, "And she's a whole lot prettier."

Anna decides every stitch was worth it.

· 8 ·

Fritzi and Duke

AUNT MAY'S HUSBAND, UNCLE HENRY, IS A CHAUF-
feur. He drives a limousine for a rich man who lives
in Federal Square. When Uncle Henry goes to work,
he wears a dark-green uniform with gold-braid trim,
tall polished boots, and a fancy cap with a shiny visor.
He looks very handsome.

Sometimes Uncle Henry takes Aunt May for a
ride in the limousine. She sits in the back seat and
pretends to be a great lady. Mother says Aunt May
loves to put on airs, but Anna wishes she could
ride in that big car, too. Like Aunt May, she'd
wave to people. They'd wave back. Maybe they'd
think Anna was rich. Maybe they'd think she lived
in a mansion. They might even mistake her for
a princess.

But the truth is, Anna has never ridden in a car. Not once. Every chance she gets, she begs Uncle Henry to take her out in the limousine, but he's always too busy. "Maybe some other time, sweetheart," he says, and pats her on the head.

One warm Saturday morning in April, Anna walks to the trolley stop with Father. Every day there are more cars on North Avenue. Shiny black Model T's and Oldsmobiles zip in and out of the traffic, blowing their horns and scaring horses.

"Why don't you buy a car, Father?" Anna asks. "Then you won't have to ride the trolley to work."

"I like riding the trolley," Father says. "It takes me exactly where I want to go."

"But a car would be faster," Anna says. "And we could go for drives in the country on Sundays."

Father shakes his head. "We can't afford a car, and even if we could Mother would say no. She doesn't trust cars."

Father kisses Anna good-bye. She watches him ride away on the pokey old trolley. On the way home, she counts cars. Yesterday she counted four. Today she counts six. Soon the Sherwoods will be the only family in Baltimore without a shiny, brand-new car.

Mother comes outside with a bucket of sudsy water

and a small stepladder. Today is window-washing day. Aunt May is already setting up her ladder. Mother doesn't want her sister to finish before she does.

Anna helps Mother with the ladder. "Wouldn't you like to have a motorcar, Mother? Rosa told me her father is buying one. A brand-new Model T."

Mother dips a rag into the sudsy water and begins to scrub the parlor window. "The Schumans must be even more foolish than I thought," she says.

That's that. No car for the Sherwoods.

While her mother and aunt chat, Anna sits on the front steps and plays with her paper dolls. Yesterday she cut a limousine out of a magazine advertisement, carefully making little slits in the seats for her paper dolls. Now she puts Father in his place behind the wheel. Mother sits beside him. A girl and boy sit in the back seat. They are going on a long motor trip.

"Ooga, ooga," Anna honks. "Vroom, vroom."

On their ladders, Aunt May and Mother scrub and polish. It's a contest, Anna thinks. Which sister's windows are the cleanest? Which sister's marble steps are the whitest?

When Anna grows up, she'll never wash windows or scrub steps. No, Anna will have better things to do. She'll buy a big touring car and drive all the way across America. She'll see the Rocky Mountains. She'll see the giant redwood trees. She'll see the Pacific Ocean.

Aunt May's big white bulldog Fritzi presses his nose against the window and barks. Aunt May blows him a kiss. *"Ach, mein kleiner Hund,"* she says. "You must stay inside, my naughty *Zuckerwürfel.*"

Mother mutters something under her breath. "May spoils that ugly hound," she whispers to Anna. "Next she'll be taking him to the park in a baby carriage."

As much as Anna loves Fritzi, she can't help gigling at the thought of him in a carriage, a lacy cap on his head and a dainty coverlet to keep him warm. What a sight he'd be—that huge head of his, those runny red-rimmed eyes, that pushed-in nose, that big jaw, those enormous yellow teeth. Why, Fritzi would be the ugliest baby in all of Baltimore.

While Anna is imagining Aunt May strolling in the park with her sugar lump, she sees Duke, the collie who lives up the street. Unlike Aunt May, Mrs. Anderson allows Duke to go outside by himself.

"Now there's a handsome dog," Mother says. Although she doesn't really like dogs, she can't help admiring Duke's thick fur and his pretty plume of a tail.

Anna eyes Duke with dislike. He minces toward her, his head and tail high, his long narrow nose sniffing the morning air. He reminds Anna of Rosa—too conceited for his own good.

But that's not the only reason Anna hates Duke. The collie is Fritzi's worst enemy. If Fritzi happens to be at the window when Duke passes by, the snob stops and does his business right in front of Aunt May's house. Fritzi goes crazy at the sight of the collie watering his sidewalk. He barks and growls and hurls himself at the window, but he cannot get out.

Duke knows he's safe. Sometimes he ignores Fritzi. Other times he opens his mouth and grins. It's just as if he's taunting Fritzi. "Nyah, nyah, nyah," Duke says. "You can't get me, you ugly beast!"

This morning, Aunt May is too busy with her chores to notice Duke. Just as the collie saunters past, she makes the mistake of opening the big parlor window. Like a shot, Fritzi jumps out and runs after Duke.

Aunt May screams, "Fritzi, come back!"

When Fritzi pays no attention, Aunt May tries German. *"Böser Hund, komm her!"*

But nothing can stop Fritzi. Not English, not German. He catches Duke right in front of Anna's house. The two dogs hurl themselves at each other. They jump and pounce, they snarl and growl and bite, they roll on the sidewalk. First Fritzi is on top, then Duke, then Fritzi.

Mother stands on her little ladder and screams for help in German. *"Hilfe, hilfe!"*

Aunt May shouts, "Fritzi, Fritzi, come to Mama! Stop that, Fritzi!" She tries to grab Fritzi's collar. Duke snaps at her. She tries again. This time, Fritzi snaps at her.

Anna has never seen such a terrible dog fight. She wants to run inside and hide under the bed but she cannot move. If only Father or Uncle Henry were here. They'd know what to do. They'd make the dogs stop. But there are no men in sight, not even a boy.

The dogs thrash around, snarling and biting. Mother stands on her ladder and cries. Aunt May begins to cry, too. Anna must do something. But what? If she tries to pull the dogs apart, one of them will bite her.

Then Anna remembers the bucket of water Mother was using to wash the window. She runs down the steps. Her arms feel weak and her legs shake with fear, but she picks up the bucket and rushes toward the dogs.

"*Nein,* Anna," Mother screams, covering her face with her apron. "*Nein!* You will be killed!"

Charlie runs out his front door. "Anna," he shouts. "Wait for me. I'll help you!"

At the same moment, Aunt May hurries toward Anna, but Anna is too fast. Before anyone can stop her, she hurls the water on Fritzi and Duke.

The dogs are so surprised they jump apart. Anna grabs Fritzi's collar. It takes all her strength to hold him. Just in time, Charlie grabs Duke's collar. He has to hold tight, too.

The dogs stand on their hind legs. They bark and growl. They show their big, sharp teeth. Anna knows they are calling each other names too terrible to think about.

Aunt May gets a firm grip on Fritzi. "Are you all right, Fritzi?" she asks. "Did the nasty bad dog hurt *mein kleiner Zuckerwürfel?*"

Mother climbs down from the ladder and presses her hand to her heart. Her face is as pale as her white apron. "Anna," she whispers. "*Ach, mein Liebling,* don't ever do something like that again! I thought you'd be killed for certain."

In the midst of the confusion, Mrs. Anderson runs out of her house. She pushes Charlie aside and takes charge of Duke. "You'd better do something about that ugly brute of yours!" she yells at Aunt May. "If he's hurt my collie, I'll sue you for every cent you have!"

Aunt May's face turns bright red. "How dare you blame Fritzi? It's all Duke's fault," she shouts. "He struts past our window every single day, putting on airs and teasing poor Fritzi! Why don't you keep him home where he belongs?"

Mrs. Anderson sticks her long narrow nose up in the air. She looks exactly like Duke. "My dog has just as much right to walk past your house as I have," she says in a persnickety voice.

"Tell that to the dogcatcher!" Aunt May says.

Before Mrs. Anderson can think of a reply, Aunt May drags Fritzi into the house. From behind the closed window, he barks a few more insults at Duke.

Mrs. Anderson scowls at Anna and Charlie. She doesn't thank them for stopping the fight. Holding Duke's collar, she leads her precious dog home. Anna notices Duke doesn't hold his head high nor does he mince along as if his paws are too good to touch the pavement. He walks slowly, limping a little, his tail between his legs.

Serves you right, Anna thinks.

"I'm on my way to the corner market to buy a quart of milk," Charlie says. "Would you like to go with me, Anna? I'll treat you to a big jawbreaker."

Just as Anna is about to run off with Charlie, Mother grabs her arm and says, "*Nein, nein,* Anna. You've had enough excitement for one day. Go inside and lie down for a while."

"But, Mother—"

Mother interrupts her. "You heard me, Anna. A rest is what you need, not jawbreakers."

"I'll see you later," Charlie says. He backs away from Mother, waves to Anna, and runs down the hill toward North Avenue.

Dragging her feet, Anna goes inside with Mother. She hopes Charlie won't treat Rosa to what should be Anna's jawbreaker.

o   o   o

That afternoon, Anna looks out the window just as Uncle Henry drives up in Mr. Sinclair's limousine. Anna watches Uncle Henry go into his house. In a few minutes, he comes outside with Fritzi.

Uncle Henry sees Anna at the window and grins. To her surprise, he knocks on Anna's door. Anna runs to open it. Mother is right behind her.

"Halloo, Lizzie," Uncle Henry says. "Halloo, Anna."

"*Guten tag,*" Mother says. She sounds as puzzled as Anna feels. Neither Anna nor Mother knows why Uncle Henry and Fritzi have come calling in the middle of the afternoon.

"I understand Anna was a heroine this morning," Uncle Henry says.

"Anna was very foolish," Mother says. "She could have been torn limb from limb by those vicious dogs."

Fritzi wags his tail as if he wants to show Mother how sweet he is, but Mother doesn't look at him. She dislikes poor Fritzi more than ever.

"I'd like to reward Anna by giving her something she's wanted for a long time," Uncle Henry says. "May I have your permission to take your brave daughter for a spin in my chariot?"

Anna's eyes open wide and her heart beats fast, but Mother frowns. "I don't approve of automobiles," she says. "They aren't safe."

"I'll drive just as slowly as a horse walks," Uncle Henry promises.

Anna holds her breath and waits for Mother to answer.

"You can come with us, Lizzie," Uncle Henry offers.

"Me ride in a car?" Mother's face turns pink at the very thought. "Only if May comes, too."

Aunt May pops outside just as if she knew what Mother would say. "Come, Lizzie," she says. "You must not be so old-fashioned, so *altmodisch*. Automobiles are here to stay, *meine Schwester!*"

Uncle Henry opens the limousine door with a flourish and signals to Anna. "You may ride in the front seat," he says.

Anna climbs into the car and sinks into the soft, leather seat. She feels like a princess already.

Mother stays on the sidewalk, watching, her eyes full of worry.

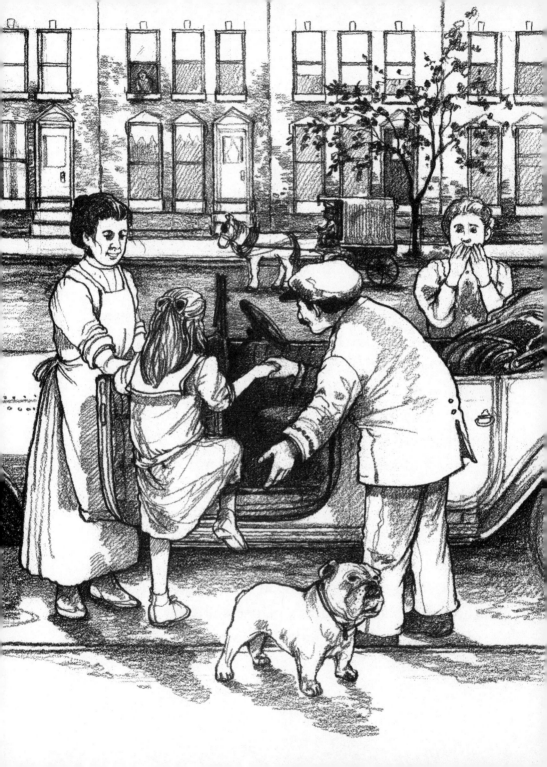

"Get in, Mother," Anna urges.

"Yes," Aunt May says. "You're holding up the fun, Lizzie."

Mother doesn't look happy, but she climbs cautiously into the back seat with Aunt May. When Fritzi jumps in between the sisters, Mother says, "I will not sit beside that ugly *Hund,* May."

Anna calls to Fritzi and he joins her in the front seat next to Uncle Henry. "Don't pay attention to Mother," Anna whispers in Fritzi's ear. "You're beautiful and I love you."

Fritzi licks Anna's nose and wags his stubby little tail. He pants doggy breath in her face and slobbers on her knee. Anna hugs Fritzi tight. If he had not gotten into a fight with Duke, Anna would not be sitting in the limousine's front seat.

"Are you ladies ready?" Uncle Henry asks.

"Yes, yes," Anna cries and bounces on the seat.

Uncle Henry starts the engine. What a noise it makes. Anna puts her hands over her ears and laughs out loud. In the back seat, Mother murmurs a prayer in German. Aunt May tells her not to worry.

As he pulls away from the curb, Uncle Henry toots the horn. Ooga, ooga! Anna glimpses her neighbors' faces peeking out from behind their lace curtains. She sits up straight and smiles at Mr. O'Neil. She smiles at Mrs. Spratt. She even smiles at Mrs. Anderson.

Mr. O'Neil and Mrs. Spratt smile and wave at Anna, but Mrs. Anderson frowns and closes her curtains with a snap, right on Duke's nose.

Fritzi sees Duke and begins to bark. Anna holds his collar tightly to keep him from jumping out. In the back seat Mother mutters something about that noisy *Hund.*

Uncle Henry passes Rosa and Beatrice. They look up from their hopscotch game and see Anna in the front seat of the limousine. Anna sticks her nose up in the air and waves in what she hopes is a royal way. Rosa and Beatrice wave back, but they don't smile. Today Anna is a princess and Rosa and Beatrice are her subjects.

Uncle Henry drives slowly downhill toward North Avenue. It's a little like riding the roller coaster at Gwynne Oak amusement park, but not as fast. And not as scary. Like Fritzi, Anna leans out of the limousine and gulps the air blowing in her face.

At the bottom of the hill, Uncle Henry waits for

a trolley to pass. Charlie comes around the corner, his hands in his pockets. Like Rosa and Beatrice, he's amazed to see Anna riding in the front seat of a limousine.

Anna touches Uncle Henry's sleeve. "Charlie helped stop the fight, too," she whispers. "Can he come with us?"

"Of course," says Uncle Henry. He beckons to Charlie. "Would you like to go for a ride?"

Charlie runs to the car, a big grin on his face, and climbs into the front seat with Anna and Fritzi. Like Anna, Charlie has never ridden in a car. He's just as excited as she is.

"What's this for?" Charlie points at a knob on the dashboard. Before Uncle Henry can tell him, Charlie points at something else. "What's that do?"

Uncle Henry answers all of Charlie's questions. While he talks, he follows the trolley downtown. Steering carefully, he weaves around horses and carts, blowing the horn now and then at other cars.

Sometimes the car's horn startles a horse, and the cart driver shouts at Uncle Henry. When this happens, Mother reaches forward and covers Anna's ears with her hands. "Such language," she says. "For shame to speak so in public where ladies and innocent children can hear."

"It's the way of world," Uncle Henry says with a shrug.

Charlie laughs but Anna isn't listening. She's just spotted Father waiting for the outbound trolley. "Stop, Uncle Henry, stop!" she cries. "There's Father! Let's give him a ride, too!"

Uncle Henry pulls up beside Father. "Hop in, Ira."

"Sit in front with me," Anna says, but there isn't enough room for Father to squeeze in between Charlie and Fritzi.

"Please, Ira," Mother pleads, "Sit back here with me."

"Yes," Aunt May says. "Poor Lizzie needs you to protect her, Ira. She's convinced Henry will kill us all."

Father laughs and gets into the back seat. "Hold my hand, Lizzie," he says. "And enjoy yourself."

Uncle Henry steps on the gas and toots the horn. Fritzi barks. Charlie asks more questions. Mother says another prayer.

Anna smiles at Father. Riding in the limousine is even more fun than she thought it would be.

∘ 9 ∘

Great Aunt Emma Moree and the Burglar

ANNA'S GREAT AUNT EMMA MOREE IS A WIDOW who lives all by herself in a tiny house on McCullough Street. She's small and thin, hardly bigger than Anna herself. Her black dresses have stiff lace collars that come up to her chin. Her long skirts sweep the floor. Her hats are decorated with plumes plucked from birds that lived long ago. Her hairstyle is many years out of fashion, but Anna loves the perfect little spit curls on her aunt's forehead.

Father says Great Aunt Emma is an anachronism. When Anna asks what that means, he says she is out of step with the times. He doesn't mean it as a criticism. He loves his tiny little aunt as much as Anna does.

Today, Aunt Emma is visiting Anna. Father is at work and Mother has gone shopping with Aunt May. Anna is playing with her doll in the front parlor and Aunt Emma is sitting nearby, reading her Bible. Suddenly they hear a loud bang on the second floor.

"What was that?" Anna moves closer to her aunt. They both stare at the ceiling.

"I don't know," Aunt Emma says. She puts her arm around Anna. "Maybe it's the wind."

Anna and Aunt Emma stare at each other. Anna knows it's not the wind. "It sounds like someone is upstairs," she whispers. "Could it be a burglar?"

"How would a burglar get in?" Aunt Emma asks.

"He could stand on top of the fence and pull himself up to the bedroom window," Anna says. She's heard Mother worry about this very thing. In fact, it happened to Mrs. Stein not too long ago. The burglar climbed through the back window and stole poor Mrs. Stein's jewelry, every bit of it, even the fake jewels.

Aunt Emma's face tightens into a scowl. "No burglar will get the best of me," she says fiercely. "No-sirree-bob!"

To Anna's surprise, her tiny aunt gets to her feet and picks up the poker Father keeps on the hearth. Gripping it tightly, she goes to the foot of the stairs. As loudly as she can, she calls, "Whoever is up there had better come down before I give you what for, you rascal!"

Anna clings to her aunt's arm. They wait for someone to come down the steps. No one does. Nor do they hear any more bangs.

"I think you scared him away," Anna says. She's very proud of her aunt.

"I believe you're right," says Aunt Emma. Looking pleased with herself, she returns to the living room and sits down in her chair. Anna notices she keeps the poker beside her—just in case.

When Mother comes home, Anna tells her what happened. "Great Aunt Emma chased a burglar away. He came in through the back bedroom window, but he was too scared to come down and face us."

Anna's mother sits down in a chair, her face pale. "Did you go up there to make sure he's really gone?"

Anna shakes her head and Aunt Emma flourishes the poker again. "I tell you I scared him away!" she says.

"Suppose he's still here?" Mother asks. "He might be hiding under a bed, waiting to kill us in our sleep!"

"Just let him try," cries Aunt Emma, waving the poker again. "I'll give him a whack he won't soon forget"

If Anna hadn't been so scared she would have laughed. Her aunt is so frail and tiny—how could she give a big fierce burglar a whack?

Just then Father comes home. "Anna, Lizzie," he says. "What's the trouble? Why are you so upset?"

"There's a burglar upstairs," Mother sobs. "He's hiding under the bed."

"There's a burglar under the bed?" Father looks puzzled.

"He came through the back bedroom window," Anna says. "Great Aunt Emma thought she'd chased him away, but Mother says he's hiding under the bed so he can kill us while we're sleeping."

Aunt Emma raises the poker over her head. "I suggest we go up there, Ira, and teach the scoundrel a lesson or two!"

Father follows Aunt Emma to the foot of the steps and takes the poker.

Mother clings to Father. "Don't go up there, Ira. Call the police!"

Father is even braver than Great Aunt Emma. Telling Mother not to worry, he goes upstairs. Anna, Mother, and Aunt Emma cower in the hall. They hear him walk into the back bedroom. Suddenly he begins to laugh. From the top of the steps, he looks down at them.

"Come up here," he says. "I want to show you something."

"I don't care to see a burglar," Mother says, pressing her hands to her chest.

"There's no burglar, Lizzie," Father says.

"I told you I chased him away," Aunt Emma says proudly.

Anna is the only one who runs upstairs to Father's side. He takes her into the back bedroom. "Do you see what I see?" he asks.

Anna stares at the window. She expects to see broken glass or a rag from the burglar's clothing caught on a splinter of wood. She sees nothing out of the ordinary.

Father points at the window shade. Unlike the shade in the other window, it's rolled up tight.

"Listen closely and tell me if this is what you

heard." Father pulls down the shade and lets it go. It flies to the top of the window with a loud bang and wraps itself tightly around the roller.

Downstairs Mother screams and Aunt Emma calls, "Give the scalawag what for, Ira!"

Anna giggles. Father is not only brave, he's smart, too. Holding his hand, she leaves the back bedroom. Together she and Father tell Mother and Aunt Emma about the window shade. In a way, Anna is disappointed it wasn't a real burglar. She would have liked to help Father give him what for.

Summer

· 10 ·

The Trolley Ride

ONE WARM EVENING IN MAY, FATHER ASKS ANNA IF she'd like to meet him in the city for lunch on Saturday. "You can ride the trolley right to the doorstep of the *Baltimore Sun* Building," he tells her.

"All by myself?" Anna asks. She's afraid to look at Mother. Surely she'll say no. Anna is only nine, much too young to ride the trolley to Charles Street.

But Mother surprises her. "You can ride on Uncle Nick's trolley," she says. "Number 573. It stops at the corner at 10:43 on the dot. Nick will look after you."

Uncle Nick is a conductor on the trolley. Anna knows he'll make sure she gets off at the right stop.

On Saturday morning, Mother walks Anna to the

trolley stop. Charlie tags along. He wishes he could go with Anna, but he's not invited.

"Maybe Father will ask you to lunch with us someday," Anna tells Charlie, but, as much as she likes Charlie, she's glad she's going alone. She doesn't want to share Father with anybody today, not even Charlie. She wants Father all to herself.

Anna, Mother, and Charlie wait on the platform with many other people. Anna wonders where they are all going. The women might be planning to shop in the big stores on Charles Street. The men might be heading for work. Anna is sure she's the luckiest one there. No one else is going to have lunch with Father. Just Anna.

At last Trolley Number 573 comes into sight. It's a summer car. The sides are open and the passengers sit on wooden benches. The motorman stands in front, his hands on the controls. Uncle Nick stands on the running board. He looks handsome in his navy blue uniform and cap.

Anna waits for the passengers to get off. The men and children jump down from the running board, but the ladies back out cautiously. They have to be careful; their long, narrow skirts get in the way.

Uncle Nick touches the visor of his cap and winks at Mother. "Welcome aboard, Anna," he says.

"Take good care of my little girl," Mother says, finally letting go of Anna's hand.

"Indeed I will." Turning to Anna, Uncle Nick says, "Sit right here on the end of the bench where I can keep an eye on you."

When all the passengers are seated, Uncle Nick pulls the bell cord twice to signal the motorman. The motorman rings his bell twice to tell Uncle Nick he's heard. Off the trolley goes.

Anna watches Uncle Nick move up and down the running board, collecting money. She thinks Uncle Nick must be very rich but, when she asks him about the coins filling the change purse on his belt, he tells her it isn't his money. It belongs to the trolley company. "They pay me a salary," he explains. "Believe me, Anna, I earn every cent of it."

The trolley bounces and sways past row after row of red-brick houses with marble steps as white as Mother's. Anna stares at the houses. It's strange to think so many mothers and fathers, grandmothers and grandfathers, children and babies, live their lives just as Anna lives hers. They are all

right here in Baltimore, yet she doesn't know any of them.

She sees a lady older than Great Aunt Emma Moree making her way slowly along the sidewalk. She sees a boy with hair as red as Charlie's. She sees a girl with curls as long and blond as Rosa's. If Anna lived here, would they be her friends instead of Charlie and Rosa?

The trolley heads down Charles Street, deep into the heart of the city. People get off and on at every stop. Now and then a man or a boy jumps off the moving trolley between stops. Others jump on, catching the grab poles with their hands and swinging onboard.

The street is crowded with all sorts of vehicles. Horses pull delivery carts, hauling meat, vegetables, milk, and ice. Motorcars weave in and out, blowing their horns—ooga, ooga! Anna catches a glimpse of a big touring car like the one Uncle Henry drives for his boss. A motorbus squeezes past a large wagon. The horse pulling the wagon rolls its eyes and neighs.

The trolley wheels shriek as they round a corner. The bell rings twice and twice again. Summer air rushes against Anna's face, cool and fresh, bringing smells from the market stalls lining Lexington Street. The sun warms her. If she weren't so eager to see Father, she could ride the trolley all day.

Suddenly Uncle Nick taps Anna's shoulder. "The next stop is Sun Square," he says. "Your father will be waiting there for you."

Sure enough, as the trolley slows down, Anna sees Father on the platform, waving to her.

Uncle Nick holds her hand while Anna jumps off the running board. She waves good-bye and runs to meet Father.

"Well, well," Father says, giving Anna a kiss. "Here's my grown-up daughter, looking very pretty. Did you enjoy your journey?"

"Oh, yes, yes!" Anna hugs Father tight. "But getting here is the best of all!"

Father holds Anna's hand while they cross the street. He shows her the *Sun* building, where he works, and introduces her to the other reporters. The newspaper office is bigger than Anna imagined. And much noisier. It smells like cigar smoke. She's glad they don't stay there long.

Father and Anna eat at Miller Brothers, the best restaurant in the city, Father says, and one of the oldest. "Even the Baltimore fire couldn't burn it down," he tells Anna.

Just inside the door, Anna stands still and stares around her. Caged canaries sing. Brightly colored fish swim in big aquariums. The tables are covered with white cloths, ironed and starched as stiff as Mother's linen. Each table has its own little lamp with a pink shade. The waiters wear white jackets with two rows of gold buttons. They carry their trays high above their heads, balanced on their fingertips. They never drop anything—not a plate, not a glass, not even a spoon.

After they're seated, the waiter gives Anna her own menu. She studies it carefully, reading each item—appetizers, soups and salads, entrées, desserts, beverages. She feels very grown-up.

"What would you like?" Father asks. "You may have anything your heart desires."

Anna frowns at the menu. It's hard to make up her mind. Should she try something she's never had? Or should she stick with familiar food?

"What are you having?" she asks Father.

Father glances at the menu. "Perhaps I'll try the escargot," he says.

Anna stares at the word escargot. She would have pronounced it the way it's spelled, but Father has left off the "t."

"Is that a German word, Father?"

"No. It's French."

"What does it mean?"

Father smiles. "Snail."

"Snail?" Anna cannot believe she's heard him properly. "You want to eat a snail?"

Father says, "Yes, I like snails. The chef cooks them in white wine and butter with a pinch of herbs. They're served in their shells."

Anna makes a face. She can't believe Father is serious. She's seen snails on the sidewalk. Nothing could make her eat one.

"Would you like to try a snail?" Father asks.

Anna shakes her head so hard the ribbon almost slides out of her hair. "If you eat one, I'll throw up," she says.

Father laughs again. "Maybe I'll have a nice hot bowl of terrapin soup instead."

Anna knows what terrapins are. She stares at Father. "Turtle soup is almost as bad as snails!"

"How about a crab cake?" Father asks. "Will Princess Anna please allow me to eat that?"

Anna nods. "Yes, Father. You may eat a crab cake."

"Thank you," Father says. "But how about you? What will you eat?"

"A ham sandwich," Anna says, deciding to choose something safe. "And vanilla ice cream for dessert."

After lunch, Father walks back to the trolley stop with Anna. He only works half a day on Saturday, so they ride home together on Uncle Nick's car.

As the trolley bounces along the tracks, Anna rests her head on Father's shoulder and watches the crowded streets and sidewalks pass by. So many people going places and doing things. And today she, Anna, has been one of them. She hopes she can have lunch with Father every Saturday. Maybe next time she'll dare to eat a crab cake. But never a snail.

· 11 ·

Ladyfingers

IT'S JULY IN THE CITY—TOO HOT TO ROLLER-SKATE, too hot to jump rope, too hot to play hopscotch. Leaves droop. Flowers hang their heads. The street venders' ponies walk slower and slower.

All day long, the sun beats down on the rooftops, streets, and sidewalks. The city traps the heat and holds it tight all night long. No one can sleep. Children stay up late. Grownups sit out front on their marble steps and fan themselves with the evening paper.

One night Aunt May and Mother are sitting side-by-side on the steps, exchanging secrets in German, while Father and Uncle Henry talk about baseball. Anna sits still and listens quietly to her mother and aunt.

"Nein, Nein, Lizzie. Henrietta ist rundlich," Aunt May says, *"nicht fett."*

Like Father, Anna has picked up a German word here and a German word there, just enough to know Aunt May has said that Aunt Henrietta is plump, not fat. At last Anna is beginning to learn the language of secrets!

Before Mother can reply, Anna says quickly, *"Nein, Tante May. Tante Henrietta ist fett, sehr fett!"* She puffs up her cheeks and stretches out her arms to show how fat Aunt Henrietta is.

Mother is so surprised she almost falls off the steps, but Aunt May bursts into laughter. "Anna, Anna," she exclaims. "Have you learned German after all?"

Anna looks at Father and giggles. He and Uncle Henry laugh too, but Mother neither smiles nor frowns. It seems she does not know what to think of Anna.

"Ach, Lizzie," Aunt May laments, "what do you expect? *Anna ist ein kluges Mädchen.* You've told me so yourself."

Winking at Mother, Aunt May begins to talk to Anna in German. She speaks so fast the words run together, long words, hard words. To Anna's dismay, she cannot understand a thing her aunt says.

Aunt May kisses Anna and smiles at Mother. "There, you see, Lizzie? Our secrets are still safe—for now, that is. But with such a clever girl in the house, we must be careful what we say, or Anna will learn all our secrets."

Mother shakes her head and sighs, but Father chuckles. Turning to Anna, he says, "Do you smell what I smell, Anna?"

Anna breathes in the sweet aroma of fresh-baked pastry drifting up the hill from Leidig's bakery. "Ladyfingers," she says. "I can almost taste them."

Father takes Anna's hand. "Come, let's walk down to the corner and treat ourselves."

"Bring something back for Lizzie and me, Ira," Aunt May calls. *"Bitte?"*

"Don't forget me," Uncle Henry shouts from the doorway.

Anna skips ahead of Father and arrives at the bakery long before he does.

"Well, well, Anna, *mein Liebling,*" Mr. Leidig says. "What will you have this evening?"

Anna closes her eyes for a moment and breathes in the sugar-sweet smell of the bakery. Then she opens her eyes and studies the pretty pink and yellow icing on the cookies, the brown sugar melting on the strudel, the cinnamon swirling on the apple dumplings, the chocolate oozing out of the éclairs, the custard bursting out of the ladyfingers. How can Anna choose? She wishes she could have two or three of everything.

But if she ate that much, she'd soon be as fat as Mr. Leidig. Father says it's a baker's duty to taste all his cakes and cookies to make sure they taste good. It must be true because Mr. Leidig looks like a gigantic gingerbread man, his round face frosted pink, his eyes little dots no bigger than raisins, his hair as white as spun sugar.

When Father arrives, Anna picks a ladyfinger. Father orders half a dozen. Anna watches Mr. Leidig put the ladyfingers in a white box and tie it shut with string. In her head she's counting—one for Father, one for Mother, one for Aunt May, one for Uncle Henry, and one for Anna. That's five. Who is number six for?

"You bought one too many," Anna tells Father.

"My goodness." Father stops at the bakery door. "Shall I return it to Mr. Leidig and ask for a refund?"

"No, no," Anna says hastily. "I'm sure someone will eat it."

"Who do you think that will be?" Father asks.

Anna seizes Father's hand. "Maybe it will be me?"

Father laughs. "That's just who I bought it for."

While Anna watches, Father opens the box and hands her a ladyfinger. "This will give you the energy to climb back up the hill to our house," he says.

When they are halfway home, Anna and Father meet the lamplighter coming slowly down the street. He lights one gas lamp after another, leaving behind him a trail of shining glass globes.

Father and Anna pause to watch the old man light the lamp on the corner. "Soon Baltimore will be electrified," Father says, "and the streetlights will come on all by themselves."

Anna smiles. She thinks Father is joking.

"Mark my word, Anna," Father says. "By the time you're my age, the world will be very different."

Anna realizes Father is serious. He works for the newspaper, so she guesses he knows more than most people about everything. "Will the world be better?" she asks.

"It will be different," Father repeats. "Some things will be better, others will be worse."

"Which will be better?" Anna asks, clinging to his hand. "Which will be worse?"

Father shakes his head. "I don't know, Anna."

Anna holds Father's hand tighter. She cannot imagine anything changing. It frightens her to think of streetlights coming on by themselves. What will the old man do if he has no lamps to light?

"There will be more motorcars," Father says. "And fewer horses."

Even though Anna loves riding in Uncle Henry's boss's big limousine, she isn't ready to give up horses.

"Why can't we have both motorcars and horses?" she asks Father.

He pats her hand. "The world isn't big enough for both," he says softly. "Automobiles go faster than horses. They are new and shiny. People like your uncle want them."

"If I had to choose, I'd pick a horse," Anna says. "You can't be friends with a motorcar."

Father laughs. "Have another ladyfinger, Anna. And then wipe your mouth. Mother doesn't like to see you with a dirty face."

By the time Anna comes home, she has eaten her second ladyfinger and cleaned her face with Father's handkerchief. She watches Mother and Aunt May divide up the four remaining ladyfingers.

"Why, Anna," Aunt May says. "Where is your ladyfinger?"

Anna pats her tummy. "I ate mine coming home."

"Oh, Ira," Mother says. "For shame. Only common girls eat in the street. Anna must learn her manners if she expects to get along in this world."

Luckily for Anna, Charlie chooses that moment to call her. Before Mother can say more, Anna runs across the street to play tag with her friends. It's dark now. Charlie, Rosa, Beatrice, Patrick, Wally, and Anna chase each other in and out of the shadows cast by the gas lamps. They play until their parents call them home, one by one.

When everyone is gone but Charlie, Anna tells him what Father told her. Charlie thinks it will be exciting to live in a world where streetlights come on like magic and the roads are crowded with motorcars.

"Do you know what I hope?" Anna asks him.

"What?"

"I hope manners go out of fashion," Anna says.

"No manners." Charlie laughs. "What a wonderful world that would be, Anna!"

Anna smiles. She likes to make Charlie laugh. Maybe she should have given the extra ladyfinger to him instead of eating it herself. Next time Father takes her to the bakery, that's what she'll do.

She tips her head back and gazes at the sky. The stars aren't as bright as they are on winter nights. The hot summer air hangs between the city and the sky, blurring everything, even the moon and the stars. *Der Mond und die Sterne,* as Mother might say.

Across the street, Aunt May laughs. Fritzi barks. In Charlie's house, a baby cries. Madame Wehman plays her piano. Down on North Avenue, a streetcar bell clangs.

No matter what Father says, Anna cannot imagine anything being different from the way it is right now. It's true that when school starts, Anna will be in fourth grade and her teacher will be Miss Osborne, not Miss Levine. But Charlie will still live across the street, the lamplighter will come every night, Mr. Leidig will bake his ladyfingers, and bit by bit, word by word, Anna will learn Mother's German secrets. As Aunt May says, *Anna ist ein kluges Mädchen*—a clever girl.

Afterword

WHEN MY MOTHER WAS EIGHTY YEARS OLD, SHE wrote a reminiscence of her Baltimore childhood, intending it for her grandchildren. She wanted them to know what the world was like when she was a little girl in 1913.

After reading Mom's account, I asked her if she'd mind sharing her memories with other children. Although she thought no one but her family could possibly be interested in her life, she gave her permission.

I must admit I changed some of the details and made up a few stories of my own, but that's the nice thing about writing fiction—I don't have to stick to the facts.

Mother is now over ninety. Her father was right about the world. In the years that have passed since

Anna roller-skated down the hill on Bentalou Street, many things have changed—some for the better and some for the worse. Cars, for instance, have replaced horses. The lamplighter is gone. At dusk, city lights come on automatically. Trolleys are no more (though you can still ride a summer car just like Uncle Nick's at the Baltimore Streetcar Museum). Public School 62 has been replaced by a modern building.

But some things have stayed the same, just as Anna knew they would. Children still roller-skate on city streets. They go to birthday parties. They build towers with Erector sets. And on hot summer nights, they sit on their front steps and stare at the moon and the stars, *der Mond und die Sterne.*

German Words and Phrases

CHAPTER 1
The Language of Secrets

Möchtest du mehr Kaffee, May?	Would you like more coffee, May?
Ja bitte, Lizzie.	Yes, please, Lizzie.
Was denkst du von Julianna's neuem Freund?	What do you think of Julianna's new friend?
Ich mag ihn nicht.	I don't like him.
Mein kleiner Zuckerwürfel	My little sugar lump
Gesundheit!	God Bless!
Auf Wiedersehen	Good-bye
Bitte	Please
Danke	Thank you
Gute Nacht, Mutter	Good night, Mother

Sprichst du Deutsch,	Do you speak German,
Anna?	Anna?
Gute Nacht, Vater.	Good night, Father.
Gute Nacht, Tochter.	Good night, daughter.

CHAPTER 5
Christmas Wishes

Fröhliche Weinachten!	Merry Christmas!
Fröhliche Weinachten,	Merry Christmas,
Mädchen!	daughter!
"Stille Nacht"	"Silent Night"

CHAPTER 6
Anna's Birthday Surprise

Was ist das?	What is this?
Ach, mein kluges Liebling!	Oh, my clever darling.
Das Eis	Ice cream
Der Kuchen	Cake
Herzlichen Glückwunsch	Happy birthday!
zum Geburtstag!	
Liebling	Darling

CHAPTER 8
Fritzi and Duke

Ach, mein kleiner Hund.	Oh, my little dog.
Böser Hund, komm her!	Bad dog, come here!
Hilfe, hilfe!	Help, help!
Nein, Anna!	No, Anna!
Ach, mein Liebling.	Oh, my darling.
Guten Tag	Good day
Altmodisch	Old-fashioned
Meine Schwester	My sister

CHAPTER 11
Ladyfingers

Henrietta ist rundlich, nicht fett.	Henrietta is plump, not fat.
Tante Henrietta ist fett, sehr fett!	Aunt Henrietta is fat, very fat!
Anna ist ein kluges Mädchen.	Anna is a clever girl.
Der Mond und die Sterne	The moon and the stars

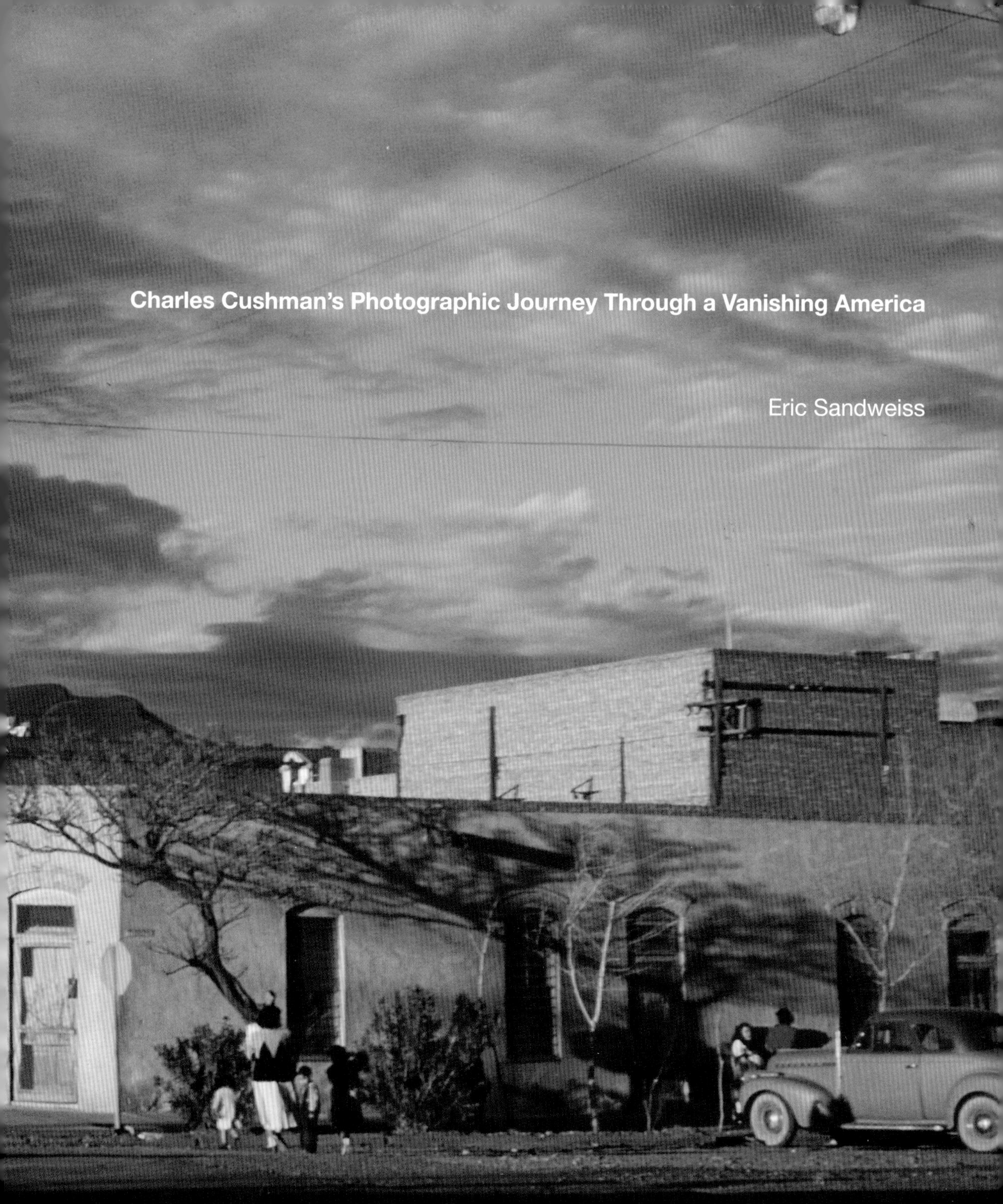

Charles Cushman's Photographic Journey Through a Vanishing America

Eric Sandweiss

OXFORD
UNIVERSITY PRESS

OXFORD
UNIVERSITY PRESS

Oxford University Press, Inc., publishes works that further
Oxford University's objective of excellence
in research, scholarship, and education.

Oxford   New York
Auckland   Cape Town   Dar es Salaam   Hong Kong   Karachi
Kuala Lumpur   Madrid   Melbourne   Mexico City   Nairobi
New Delhi   Shanghai   Taipei   Toronto

With offices in
Argentina   Austria   Brazil   Chile   Czech Republic   France   Greece
Guatemala   Hungary   Italy   Japan   Poland   Portugal   Singapore
South Korea   Switzerland   Thailand   Turkey   Ukraine   Vietnam

Copyright © 2012 by Eric Sandweiss

Published by Oxford University Press, Inc.
198 Madison Avenue, New York, New York 10016

www.oup.com

Oxford is a registered trademark of Oxford University Press

Library of Congress Cataloging-in-Publication Data
Sandweiss, Eric.
The Day in Its Color: Charles Cushman's photographic journey through a vanishing
America / Eric Sandweiss.
   p. cm.
Includes bibliographical references and index.
ISBN 978-0-19-977233-9 (hardcover : alk. paper)
1. Cushman, Charles W., 1896–1972. 2. Photographers—United States—Biography.
3. Street photography—United States. 4. Landscape photography—United States. 5.
United States—Pictorial works. 6. United States—History—20th century.   I. Title.
TR140.C87S26 2011
779.092—dc22   2011002845

1 3 5 7 9 8 6 4 2

Printed in China

"But sometimes in a man or a woman awareness takes place—not very often and always inexplainable. There are no words for it because there is no one ever to tell. This is a secret not kept a secret but locked in wordlessness . . . And sometimes if he is very fortunate and if the time is right, a very little of what he is trying to do trickles through."

John Steinbeck, *Journal of a Novel: The* East of Eden *Letters* (1969)

"America is a continent, a thing-in-process, elemental, ever changing, calling for further exploration, for constant rethinking . . . It cannot be caught or imprisoned in words of finality."

Louis Adamic, *My America, 1928–1938* (1938)

"It is never the thing but the version of the thing:
The fragrance of the woman not her self,
Her self in her manner not the solid block,
The day in its color not perpending time"

Wallace Stevens, "The Pure Good of Theory," *Transport to Summer* (1947)

CONTENTS

ACKNOWLEDGMENTS

My thanks go first to the staff of the Indiana University (IU) Archives—especially its curator of photographs, Brad Cook—for sharing their knowledge, assisting my research, and making available the images for this book. Kristine Brancolini, Kara Alexander, and many others on the staff of the IU Digital Library, who worked with the Archives to preserve the entire collection and to make it available online, introduced me to Cushman's work as they completed that project. As I did so, historian and photographer Rich Remsberg shared his knowledge of and his enthusiasm for the story, helping me to understand both the man and the significance of his photographs. The IU Institute of Advanced Study offered time for research, and the Graham Foundation for Advanced Studies in the Fine Arts underwrote some of my travels along Cushman's path. For sharing memories of one aspect or another of Cushman's life, I acknowledge Deborah Booker, Richard Dinning, Edward Laves, Elizabeth Laves Marcuson, John Moskowitz, Jr., Adolphe R. E. Roome IV, John M. Schloerb, Gerald Spore, Elsie Gergely Steg, Albert Steg, Catherine Vanderpool. Michael Corbett advised on the California research. Of the many librarians and researchers who assisted me at one stage or another in locating sources, particular mention is due to Steinbeck specialists Herbert Behrens and Carol Robles; Danielle Castronovo, California Academy of Sciences; Amy Ballmer, Art Institute of Chicago; David Pavelich, Special Collections Research Center, Regenstein Library, University of Chicago. My sister Marni discovered a key part of the story and also helped me better to understand American photographic history. Dan Carlinsky brought the book to press, and Shannon McLachlan and the staff at Oxford University Press took care of it once it arrived there. My wife Lee and my sons Noah and Ethan deserve special thanks for indulging me the spare hours needed to journey with "Cushman" when more pressing matters awaited at home. Portions of this book first appeared in the *Journal of American History*, 94:1 (June 2007).

INTRODUCTION

1. Golden Gate Bridge, San Francisco, 1938

On September 3, 1938, an out-of-work Chicago businessman named Charles Cushman pulls his new Ford Deluxe coupe into the northbound traffic lanes of the Golden Gate Bridge (fig. 1). The new bridge still sports the first coat of its distinctive orange-vermilion paint. The sky beyond it is a hazy, pale blue, suggesting the imminent arrival of the fog that pushes into the San Francisco Bay on warm fall afternoons like this one. The car is dark red; the nearby hillsides a parched brown.

We know a lot about the color of the day on which Charles Cushman and his wife, Jean, embarked on their trip up the Pacific Coast. We know it because of something they carried with them: a Contax IIA 35 mm camera, loaded with Cushman's first roll of Kodachrome color slide film. First available two years earlier, Kodak's new color film was, in 1938, still rare—for most amateur photographers it was too expensive and troublesome; for professionals, a novelty with little value for publication purposes. By the following year, the company's "Ready-Mount" developing service—offering individually mounted slides rather than unwieldy strips of positive transparencies—would hasten the coming of the age of the color snapshot. Recently launched picture magazines, with straightforward titles like *Life*, *Look*, and *Holiday*, would begin mixing color images among their photographs. And, in a rite repeated daily on movie screens across the country, Judy Garland would awaken from her gray Kansas slumber into the many-hued Land of Oz. As Charles Cushman pointed the car toward Marin County, however, few people possessed the means to record the appearance of a San Francisco afternoon—even of the newly famed Golden Gate Bridge—in anything other than shades of gray.

More than three decades would pass before Cushman turned off his ignition for the last time, unpacked the camera gear, removed the last roll of Kodachrome from his Contax, and stepped back out into a world that we now imagine, without effort or surprise, in color. In the years since he began his travels, he had driven roughly a half-million miles—from Maine to San Diego, from Vancouver to Miami, past numberless points between. He had worn out three cars, two camera bodies, three lenses, and, to judge from her expression in those occasional photographs in which she appeared, his wife's patience. He had collected, annotated, and carefully filed away his color slides—all 14,500 of them. And he had found his way out of the shadow of a personal event that nearly extinguished the light from his world altogether.

Charles Cushman was more than an obsessive collector, and his slides warrant more than the bemused indulgence that exotic collections customarily awaken in us. From 1938 to 1969, driving country roads and walking city streets, this Indiana native captured a dying America in living color. Boxed away at the time of his death in 1972, split into separate collections in the 1980s, finally reassembled and catalogued in 1999, and opened to public view only in 2003, his "fair collection of interesting pictures," as he diffidently labeled them, today startle the eye of anyone who imagines that an America untouched by the landmarks of our own time—the interstate highways, the shopping malls, the curtain-wall office buildings—must have been a quaint and distant place.[1]

Cushman's photographs, saturated in what Kodak shrewdly came to call "living" color, suggest something different. The United States that we thought we knew with photographic certainty—whether through the self-conscious artfulness of Berenice Abbott and Walker Evans or through the prosaic footage of recycled newsreels—is revealed as being but the gray shadow cast by a world no less full and tangible than our own. Ordinary subjects take on unaccustomed beauty, and beautiful colors are rendered surprisingly ordinary, as our eyes open onto an Oz filled not with magical creatures but with people who look like ourselves, living not in castles or talking forests but in apartment buildings and farmhouses— places we might even think we know as scenes from our own lives, until we see the tailfins of the car parked at the curb, notice the odd cut of a passing woman's dress, or recognize a building's location as the site we have known only as a parking lot. Looking at the photographs confounds the unspoken visual grammar that teaches us to recognize in black-and-white images something "past" and in color ones something familiar and accessible.

For its breadth of coverage and its sheer size, we know of nothing comparable to Cushman's thirty-year experiment in color photography. The recent spate of publications generated by new discoveries of other early color images—including those produced both by amateurs and by professionals such as the documentarians employed in the 1930s by the Farm Security Administration—has turned up nothing of the scale, consistency, and visual quality of the collection that this enigmatic man packed away into his slide boxes in 1969.[2]

What, besides the sheer novelty of finding such a large trove of images from color photography's earliest days, makes these pictures worth a long second glance? Perhaps it is the quality of the views themselves—sharply focused, well-exposed, intriguingly framed. Perhaps it is the voyeuristic thrill of discerning in them the habits and obsessions of a single personality over such an extended period. Whatever the source of the power that Cushman's slides hold for modern eyes, its ultimate effect is clear: in Charles Cushman's work, the past, free of the distancing scrim of black-and-white, becomes impossibly present. The foreignness of his subjects is *almost* negated by the familiarity of his medium. His camera captures a vanished America, a place lit for one moment by a brilliant flash of recall, only to fade once again into the obscurity to which we as a society have since consigned it.

Did Cushman mean to make such statements? One searches in vain for evidence that he approached his work with the self-conscious stance of professional "road" photographers in the tradition of Evans, Ben Shahn, or Robert Frank. Cushman was an amateur to the end, a traveling salesman and sometime financial analyst who happened to love taking pictures. His later correspondence confirms that he was not unaware of the quality of what he termed his "fair collection of interesting pictures," but it does not suggest that he saw himself attempting to leave behind a comprehensive historical or artistic statement. He never tried, so far as we know, to publish his photographs, nor to show them through local camera clubs. He sought neither fame nor money for what remained, to the end, a personal hobby. The very format of his chosen medium—color slides—limited its visibility to small gatherings of that limited class of personal acquaintances whom one expects to accept without protest an invitation to sit for hours in a darkened living room.

Yet something powerful—operating both from without and within the man—motivated this singular, thirty-year quest. Something, that is, in what the immigrant journalist Louis Adamic called the "elemental, ever-changing" essence of pre- and postwar America impelled this particular individual to try to express, through the language of pictures, his own particular version of the "secret locked in wordlessness" that, as John Steinbeck claimed, awaits anyone willing to look deeply enough into himself. The nation's landscape, this man, and the tool of 35 mm color film came together in a peculiar three-decade-long relationship, the results of which today lie before us like the pieces of a broken puzzle.

It is in trying to reassemble those fragmented social, personal, and mechanical destinies that we discover in Cushman's slides a value distinct from that which accompanied them into their cases in 1969. We can, to be sure, enjoy and learn from the content of the images—the cars, the bathing suits, the tractors, the neon signs. We can, alternatively, assemble them along with a smattering of letters and personal records to reconstruct the details of one man's life—a life that in many ways embodies the emergence of that larger body of middle-class Americans who made their way from the rural world of the nineteenth century to the metropolitan milieu of the twentieth. We can analyze the pictorial and aesthetic qualities afforded by the combination of a well-crafted photographic machine and the sophisticated chemistry of coated acetate film. Ultimately, though, the collection's power extends beyond the sum of its data and into the realm of its emotional effect upon latter-day viewers—us.

Even the most impersonal of Cushman's pictures, viewed today, radiates a poignancy that is likely greater than any he intended at the time. That poignancy derives not from the immediacy of a tree's fleeting blossom or a child's innocent gaze but from the very distance that now separates us from him and his subjects alike. We cannot look at these images now without knowing that the suddenly vibrant world they seem to bring to life is in fact unreachable; that even as we first make its acquaintance, that world, and the people in it, have already receded before us in a manner that not even the miracle of living color can reverse. That reminder of our own mortality—bedecked in lively reds, yellows, and blues—is surely a lesson as powerful as any conveyed in the actual content of the pictures. At some level, it is also a lesson that the photographer had, himself, to have learned.

This is a book, then, about Charles Weever Cushman (b. Poseyville, Indiana, 1896, d. San Francisco, California, 1972), a man whose life and career encompassed, at a personal level, many of the developments witnessed in American society at large during the nation's most prosperous—and most perilous—century. It is also a book about the built landscape through which Cushman and other Americans moved in the middle years of that century, and a story, finally, about the particular tool—a 35 mm camera loaded with color film—that Cushman chose to help him mark his place in that world. Like a photographic exposure calculated for maximal depth of field, Cushman's tale, if perfectly told, would depend for its coherence upon attention to all three of those points of reference. To understand the man who stands in the story's foreground—scant though we will find his (nonpictorial) legacy to be—is to understand better the motivations that impelled his particular, sustained view of the American landscape. To learn more about the roads, farmlands, towns, and cities that lie on the other side of his lens is in turn to appreciate the important role of even familiar and ordinary places in framing the choices and experiences by which people define their lives. To look more closely at the technical medium that connected him to those places is to realize the great extent to which we construct the world around us with our eyes, and not just our hands.

Finally, this is a book about ourselves, inheritors of the legacy of Charles Cushman and others like him who sought to capture the American "thing-in-process" before it proceeded to turn into something quite different. Whatever pride, nostalgia, or bitterness his pictures may call to mind, the transformations of the half century since his death assuredly color our understanding of Cushman's visual record. Like a distant cloud, our retrospective view of his images shades the work he has laid before us. To ignore the role played by our own hindsighted perceptions, to appreciate the images solely for their documentary or artistic or biographical value, is to deprive ourselves of the self-discovery—the rekindled awareness of our own choices, our own limitations, our own wordless secrets—that this powerful storyteller sought to obtain from his own life's work.

Charles Cushman was not the only mid-twentieth-century American to cloak his artistic impulses in gray-flannel and oxford cloth. In contrast to the self-conscious rebel heralded or parodied in popular images of the time—the action painter, the beat poet, the bop musician, the Method actor—Cushman and others like him willingly bridged the worlds of necessity and fantasy, of social engagement and critical detachment. Today, such part-time artists seldom engage the attention of scholars eager to explore a more fully realized expressive world, one as distinguishable from the presumed mediocrities of mass society as black is from white. Yet for Cushman and millions of others before and since, a connection to the "straight" world, an embrace of things as they happen to be, by no means necessarily lowered the level of their attentiveness or the sharpness of their critique.

A few years after Charles Cushman crossed a golden bridge into green and brown hills, another and better known businessman-artist of the day sat at his desk in the executive offices of the Hartford Accident and Indemnity Company, filing the notes for his new poem in the right-hand drawer as he went about his work day. For all of our efforts to understand the world, wrote Wallace Stevens, we see only "the version of the thing . . . [t]he day in its color not perpending time."[3] Yet it is unclear if Stevens considered that inevitable limitation on our perception, that acknowledgment of our inability really to know the world, to be a tragic thing. With an eye attuned both to corporate balance sheets and springtime flowers, and with a dedication rooted both in statistical thoroughness and obsessive wanderlust, Charles Cushman took pleasure, and found a sort of grace, in the process of gazing at his day in its color. Today, the challenge awaiting anyone confronted with his collection of pictures is to look not only at them but through them: through to the place where this enigmatic man of the American Century still stands, challenging us to understand ourselves amidst the color of our own day.

DAWN  Indiana Beginnings, 1896–1918

Writing later in his life, Charles Cushman recalled that he had been raised "pretty close to the soil," and once you have been to Posey County, Indiana, you know that he meant the phrase as more than a figure of speech.[1] Approaching Cushman's native Poseyville from the northeast, you almost feel your car sinking down into the shared floodplain of the two rivers—the Wabash, to the west, and the Ohio, to the south—that hold Posey County in their grip. This is the point at which Indiana tilts, like an off-kilter frying pan, down to its lowest elevation, at the junction of the two rivers. Despite Posey County's claim, in the words of the local chamber of commerce, to being "rich in history, industry, natural beauty, and its people," the area draws few outsiders today. The county's population peaked in 1900 and gently declined through most of the twentieth century. A few more people have arrived in recent decades (testament in part to the exurbanization of Evansville, a few miles east of the county line), but their numbers have never risen above thirty thousand countywide.[2]

Posey County's largest town, Mt. Vernon, straddles a gentle rise on the north bank of the Ohio. The center of town looks little different today from its appearance in 1876, when optimistic citizens topped off the tower of their new county courthouse. The waterfront, which was officially styled the "Southwind Maritime Center" in 1980 and which exports more than three million tons of crops and manufactured goods annually, is nevertheless still the kind of place where you might expect to find a kid with rolled-up cuffs, kicking an old bottle along the levee or throwing a line into the river.[3]

The village of New Harmony, the county's chief destination for visitors, is itself a monument to desertion. Here the German Rappites of 1814 and their successors, the followers of the Scottish socialist Robert Owen, tried to build a New World utopia—and failed. Today, little remains in the town outside of a handful of early nineteenth-century structures, a small fleet of horse-drawn buggies, and a smattering of shops and businesses primed, fittingly, to a theme of quietude and contemplation.

Residents of places like Posey County are only too aware of the differences that separate their communities from the mainstream of twenty-

2. Barnyard, Posey County, Indiana, 1941. Long after he left home, Cushman's native Posey County remained a touchstone of the photographer's ever-expanding portrait of twentieth-century America.

first-century growth and development. Some take a measure of pride in resisting the hazards of change. Their ancestors, however, had no intention of settling places that would pose picturesquely as history passed by. There was a time when the prospect of two major rivers colliding on a map excited the ambition of all those Americans convinced that greater opportunity awaited at some strategically chosen spot beyond the current frontier. This prospect of capitalizing on underdeveloped resources, a promise unleashed even before the nation itself was born, represented the first phase on this continent of the modern era—a period of widespread faith in the ultimate benefits of environmental exploitation, economic individualism, and material accumulation. "The earth is a machine," Ralph Waldo Emerson would write in his essay on farming, "which yields almost gratuitous service to every application of the intellect."[4] Charles Cushman's Posey County, seemingly the remnant of a "simpler time," as some would have it, was an integral part of the complex social machinery that Emerson and others of his generation extolled, one linking sites of extraction, storage, processing, and trade in resources into a single system that extended from remote places like southern Indiana to port cities such as New Orleans, and thence across the world. Cushman would grow up to see—and to picture—that modern landscape as it matured and then collapsed beneath the weight of a new layer of economic, technological, and cultural imperatives that shaped the United States that we know today.

The most important connective threads within the modern national landscape were its rivers, and it was for this reason that places like Posey County seemed, to many Americans in the years before the 1830s, destined for greatness. Like the canals, railroads, and highways that followed, rivers represented at the time the cheapest and fastest routes along which to move resources, and it was somewhere along the chain of handling such resources (whether extracting, processing, transporting, storing, selling, or servicing them) that most Americans made their living until the 1970s. Some of those river-junction sites (Pittsburgh, St. Louis) succeeded spectacularly, if only to settle into a slower-moving urban niche amid subsequent changes in transportation and technology. Others (Cairo, Illinois, for instance) never realized the dreams of urban glory that attended their conception. As for the place where the Wabash flows into the Ohio, Mt. Vernon's courthouse spire notwithstanding, the low-lying landscape of southwest Indiana was destined to yield farms and small market towns, nothing more.

Still, there was no shortage of Americans and European immigrants willing to set their sights on this fertile territory, even before it was legally wrested from a variety of Indian claimants in the period from 1803 to 1809, shortly after establishment of the Indiana territory. Southwest Indiana saw a steady influx of newcomers, including speculators, economic opportunists, landless farmers, and underemployed laborers, willing to gamble on such new horizons—men like the Tennessee-born George Thomas, who established a small fortune as a wharf-boat operator in Mount Vernon—the town where his granddaughter, Mabel Thomas (later Mabel Cushman) was born in 1868. There eventually came to the region, as well, a smattering of the professionals, clubwomen, ministers, and bankers who considered it their lot in life to elevate frontier American towns and cities from the status of crass commercial outposts into orderly and civil communities. Such a person was Cushman's maternal great-grandfather, Charles Weever, a Maine native who in the 1830s established his medical practice in Posey County; such too were Charles Cushman's paternal grandparents, Elizabeth Cushman and her husband Reuel, a Methodist circuit-rider. Himself a first-generation Hoosier, Reuel and his descendants still prided themselves on their direct ties to Robert Cushman, one of the original settlers of Plymouth, Massachusetts, in 1620, and the namesake of a monument dedicated in that historic town in 1858. Reuel and Elizabeth's son Wilbur, born the year following the erection of the family monument, grew up to operate the local lumber mill and grain warehouse that stood along Railroad (later Water) Street in Poseyville, and he earned enough money from his operations to build a big frame house for Mabel, whom he had married in 1895, and their son, Charles, born the following summer. The house still stands on a quiet block of Second Street, a block from the stores of Main Street, around the corner from the local Carnegie library, up the street from the Methodist Church.[5]

This was the world in which Charles Cushman grew up. Sunday drives to his grandparents took him either south to Mt. Vernon (where his mother's father, the county sheriff, lived with his wife and their younger children in the residence adjoining the county jail), or north, to the Gibson County land where Reuel farmed after he retired from the ministry. Back in town, the census taker who passed through Poseyville in 1900 needed only seven pages of his ledger to record the name of every one of Wilbur and Mabel's neighbors; surely the Cushmans knew them all. Family photos tempt a viewer to imagine young Charles the coddled only child of small-town gentry (a sister, Dorothy, died at the age of two), the cherished offspring of ambitious parents who must have considered their little community a pleasant enough place but not the mercantile or cultural center that earlier generations of Cushmans, Thomases, and Weevers

3. Charles Cushman, c. 1898

4. Indiana University, c. 1908

might have foreseen in their early flights of entrepreneurial fantasy (fig. 3). Their son played his own games of make-believe as he sat in the child-sized, wire-back chair that they bought for him and gazed out at the quiet street from the front porch. It is hard to imagine that Charles's ambitious relatives would not have encouraged him to imagine a life for himself beyond the Posey County line.

That he in fact did so is first evident in a telegram that Cushman sent to the Indiana University (IU) registrar in December, 1913. "As I contemplate entering your institution next term," wrote the teenager, "I would like you to send me a credit blank so I may get it filled out as soon as possible."[6] A month later he was in Bloomington. Like his near-contemporaries, Hoagy Carmichael and Ernie Pyle (both of them just enough younger than Cushman to have missed him in school), Cushman arrived at IU a small-town Hoosier with big-time ambitions; like them, too, he found at the college the opportunity to develop those ambitions in a setting that, while sheltered as all colleges are, brought him into contact with ideas not easily accessible to the resident of the farmlands and small towns of early twentieth-century Indiana (fig. 4). The university,

MAXWELL HALL.   OWEN HALL.   WYLIE HALL.

US· INDIANA STATE UNIVERSITY, BLOOMINGTON, INDIANA.

not yet the center of international learning that it would become under the hand of President Herman B Wells, was nevertheless well on its way to joining the ranks of the nation's more prestigious state campuses. Indiana University, like other American universities at this time, had begun to fashion itself as the training ground for a range of increasingly well-defined and exclusive professions — law, medicine, business — as well as to forge links, in the fashion of the Progressive Era, between traditional liberal arts education and a curriculum more reflective of the social, economic, and political concerns of the day. Cushman and his classmates would hear progressive education's best-known proponent, John Dewey, deliver the Phi Beta Kappa oration at their 1917 graduation ceremony.[7]

The rise of Indiana University also reflected in part the rise in the fortunes of the state that it served. Cushman had come of age (and IU had grown) amidst an efflorescence of Hoosier culture. The movement was reflected in the voices of writers like James Whitcomb Riley, who affected a vernacular Hoosier style; in the passion for "pioneer" culture

5. "Mystical Evening," Theodore C. Steele (1918)

evident in the pages of the fledgling *Indiana Magazine of History*, which first appeared in 1905; and in the images of artists such as Theodore C. Steele, many of them working from studios in rural Brown County, who made a study of Indiana's distinctive rustic scenery (fig. 5). The regional-culture fetish boomed beside the state's concurrent rise as an industrial powerhouse, ever-more closely tied to, and indistinguishable from, other urbanizing states. U.S. Steel's Elbert Gary established his new company town on the shores of Lake Michigan when Cushman was nine years old; immigration and manufacturing growth catalyzed a more-than-two-fold increase in Indianapolis's population from 1890 and 1920; and production in the capital as well as in other urban centers such as South Bend, Fort Wayne, and Evansville helped to elevate the value of the state's industrial output to nearly $2 billion—ninth in the nation—by 1920 (fig. 6).[8] Under the shadow of rising smokestacks, the image of a simpler, more peaceful time—an image formed as much from modern desire as from historical evidence—shone surprisingly bright in Indiana.

6. "Looking N.E. by N. at Gas Washer and #4 Blast Furnace," U.S. Steel Works, Gary, Indiana, 1917

Cushman, a child of the industrial age, absorbed the image like other twentieth-century Hoosiers with similarly worldly experiences. In years to come, as he traveled the country and then the world, the largely unaltered backroads of Posey County remained a touchstone of his view of American life.

More than 2,500 students, nearly all of them from Indiana, attended IU with Cushman in the mid-1910s. Their choice of courses included not only obscure university fare such as Old High German and Latin Epigraphy, but also classes with titles like "Public Finance" and "Social Pathology: Poverty and Charities." Cushman, an English major, exemplified the union of traditional liberal arts and the growing professional curriculum. Alongside his classes on the English novel and Elizabethan prose, he pursued coursework in commercial law, journalism, and advertising—all of which, as he later wrote, would prove vital to his professional choices in life.[9]

In addition to their studies, IU students participated in a predictable mix of campus athletics, club and fraternity life, and local carousing. As Pyle would several years later, Cushman found his niche on the staff of the campus newspaper, the *Indiana Daily Student* (IDS). The features he wrote in his post as "sporting editor" reflect the snappiness of the prose associated with the great sports writers of the day whom he may have admired—men such as Ring Lardner and Grantland Rice—as well as a penchant for skeptical analysis and persuasive rhetoric that would serve him well in his later work. "[T]o get down to the cold facts," Cushman warned readers at the close of the 1915 collegiate Big 9 football season, "there is no one man that can make a fair and just selection that might safely be called the REAL All-Star team."[10] Such reasoning of course framed, and in its careful use of qualifiers lent additional weight to, his own attempt to do just that.

Cushman's columns, like the clippings and programs that he collected for his college scrapbook, reveal him as a serious but ever-reserved sports enthusiast; more a watcher than a doer. Too small for football and basketball, his own sporting activities were limited to such more leisurely activities as golf and bowling. And when it came time to state, in the IDS, his opinion as to the value of collegiate sports, the sporting editor struck a surprisingly equivocal note, suggesting that varsity teams cost too much money, placed too much pressure on athletes, and generally slighted "the individual undergraduate" who ought righfully to remain at the center of all college activities.[11]

Like many of those undergraduates (and influenced in no small measure by the absence of campus dormitories), Cushman took part in local fraternity life. He pledged Delta Tau Delta, and evidently enjoyed— to guess from the jocular caption appearing beside his photograph on the pages of the campus yearbook, the *Arbutus*—the reputation of a lady's man (fig. 7). Too young yet to bear the adjective that best describes his appearance in later years—"dapper"—Cushman nevertheless cut a spry figure on campus. Small and wiry, he carried himself with an air of pride and alertness, bearing the slight, squint-eyed grin that suggested, then and later, a man enjoying a joke that he preferred not to reveal to his companions. He filled his scrapbook with mementoes of fraternity life, theatre programs, and dance invitations, and he seems, to judge from his report card, not to have sweated a great deal over his grades. Finishing his coursework in mid-1917, he applied his new business training to a temporary job in the local freight office of the Illinois Central Railroad. Within a few months he had moved north to Indianapolis to serve the company as a passenger agent.[12]

Aside from the pride with which Cushman traced his paternal ties to Plymouth Rock, we know nothing of Charles' relationship with his father. But it was a turn in that relationship that represents the first clue we have as to the end of the relative ease of his young life, and to the commencement of a life spent on the move. In November 1917, Wilbur turned ill and Charles returned to Poseyville. From there, he wrote to IU Dean of Liberal Arts Horace A. Hoffman of his father's grave condition. "As it is his earnest desire to see my diploma," Cushman added, he needed to learn whether or not recent course credits had been added properly to confirm his formal graduation as of the previous summer. The following May, his

7. Charles Cushman, 1916, Indiana University *Arbutus.*

Cushman (right) established himself at IU as a relatively indifferent scholar, a talented writer, and a socially active student.

degree ensured but his father still ailing, Cushman left home to face a second transition: service in the United States Navy. By his own account, he volunteered for duty; given his age, he likely did so in order to avoid the virtual certainty of being drafted following the implementation of the Selective Service Act, passed by Congress that same month. Cushman was sent to Great Lakes Naval Base in Chicago, and it was there that he learned, just a month later, of his father's death.[13]

A widow's only child, Charles Cushman was destined for what he later called "about as unpoetic a military career as any of the war"; serving at the rank of seaman 2d class, he recalled, he "never got further east than Buffalo, New York."[14] The service proved for him less significant in what it might have imparted about discipline or patriotic duty than it did as an introduction to the city of Chicago—the place that Cushman would call home for more than three decades. He received his release from active duty a month after the Armistice, and went back to Indiana to spend his first Christmas without his father.

MORNING An Eye for Business, 1919–1940

Having become, in the space of a little over one year, a college graduate, a veteran, and a fatherless son, Cushman must have felt suddenly far from the relatively untroubled life he had led in either Poseyville or Bloomington. In his struggle, at this point, both to establish a career for himself and to provide for Mabel, he channeled his affinities for language and for business into the world of advancing technologies and corporate salesmanship. In the twentieth-century corporate milieu that Cushman joined after the war, machines that processed information would become as important as those that processed resources. Words and images, in this world, represented a product as important as blades, gears, and boilers. Not yet leaving behind the central precepts of modern economic life—the quest for resources, the need for technical innovation, the drive for individual gain—the key features of mid-twentieth-century American economic culture nevertheless pointed toward a future in which images and impressions would acquire central importance in and for themselves, rather than solely for the sake of selling goods. Charles Cushman's professional journey into this culture belonged to its time as surely as the journeys that brought his ancestors and others to antebellum southern Indiana had belonged to theirs.

With his first sales position, working for the Addressograph Company of Chicago, Cushman encountered firsthand a corporate pioneer of the information technology on which the new economic culture depended. As one of a growing number of "commercial travelers" on the road for corporations like Addressograph, National Cash Register, and Burroughs Adding Machine in the 1920s, Cushman practiced an art similar in its outline to—but more sophisticated in its detail than—that of the nineteenth-century "drummer," the salesman who had traveled to crossroads stores with a full selection of items from wholesale houses in such cities as Boston and Chicago. Like the inventions marketed by its fellow innovators in business technology, Addressograph's product—a line of machines that enabled businesses to mass-produce mailings—served a more specialized clientele, required a higher consumer investment, and demanded greater technical know-how and financial discretion on the

Film—first black-and-white and then color—helped Cushman to express the relationships of commerce, industry, and landscape that he had analyzed through his employment in Chicago, New York, and elsewhere along the road.

8. Brooklyn Bridge, New York, c. 1929

part of its sales representatives than had the goods distributed by the early wholesale houses. It was here, presumably, that Cushman first became accustomed to life on the road. Indeed, he traveled enough that year to have turned himself into a statistical anomaly, showing up on the 1920 census rolls both in Chicago—with Mabel in their South Side apartment at 39th and Ellis Streets—and again, this time on the road, in a rooming house on Seventh Street in Terre Haute.[1]

The Addressograph job proved short-lived, a fact that appears to have been due to that very travel schedule. Owing to what he later described obliquely as a "difference with [the] district sales manager over territorial allotment," Cushman left the company in the summer of 1920— less than a year after he had begun. What the Addressograph job lacked in length of tenure, however, it made up in terms of its importance in other areas of Cushman's subsequent career. First, it took advantage of Cushman's personal skills. "In whatever work I have been engaged," he would tell a prospective employer two decades later, "I have relied mainly on my contacts with people." Salesmanship of the sort demanded by corporations like Addressograph relied on personable, upbeat men—but it also required of them a more subtle, and presumably more sincere, form of persuasion, one informed more by psychological know-how and social science data than had the hard-sell craftiness of the drummers whose lives have been fictionalized by writers from Cushman's fellow Hoosier Theodore Dreiser to Meredith Willson. The successful salesman operated at a "a higher and more rational plane of psychology," than had his predecessor, according to Archer Wall Douglas, the author of one of many salesmanship guides of the period. His life "is taken up in perpetual study of human nature," a study that, with his constant travel, makes him "essentially cosmopolitan in his attitude of manner and thought." Such a profile meshed perfectly with the aspirations, the natural talents, and the training of the young man from Poseyville.[2]

The complement of the modern salesman's sophistication, however, was his willingness to operate as part of a larger, disciplined organization. Big companies organized their sales forces, trained them, familiarized them with market research, and left specific directions as to their comportment. Cushman seems to have bridled at the discipline associated with working as part of a larger sales force. Territorial allotment or no, the fact remains that Charles Cushman never again sought his fortune within the ranks of a large corporation. In a manner that echoed his approach to college athletics, he spent most of his subsequent working life watching and writing about business, not taking part in it.

A second important aspect of the short-lived Addressograph job was the opportunity it provided for Cushman to immerse himself further in the technology of printing and reproduction, which he had first encountered in his work at the IDS. Addressing machines had been available in one form or another since at least the 1850s; Addressograph's improved Graphotype, which Cushman sold, allowed an office worker to emboss names on metal plates (fig. 9). Linked on a motorized chain, the plates quickly stamped addresses upon thousands of envelopes. Despite a range of models and prices, the technology appealed primarily to businesses large enough both to require its capabilities and to afford the

9. "Office with thirteen Graphotype machines," c. 1920s.

investment that it demanded. By 1924, Addressograph marketed machines capable of printing nearly ten thousand addresses in an hour and
costing as much as $1500. It was a small step from these innovations to
still larger machines (offered by Addressograph as well as its competitor
and eventual partner, American Multigraph) capable of mass-producing
letters with common text but distinctive addresses, dates, and saluta-
tions. The "age of mechanical reproduction," as the philosopher Walter
Benjamin would soon term the period, made itself felt first and foremost
to ordinary citizens in the everyday business transactions—once initiated
in face-to-face conversation and concluded with handshakes and signatures—that technology and corporate organization now allowed to take
place across thousands of miles between people who never met. Successful businesses in mid-twentieth-century America would be those
that bridged this physical and conceptual gap with sales, marketing, and
public relations strategies that returned the "aura" of originality, as Benjamin would have it. Such strategies placed a comprehensible, human
face—just as the Addressograph machines graced their clients' mechanized correspondence with seemingly handwritten signatures—upon
relationships and products whose origins were increasingly automated
and distant. At Addressograph, Cushman found his niche as an agent in
the process of bridging the mechanical and the personal. A better de-
scription of the talent required of a photographer might not be found.[3]

The recession years of 1920 and 1921 were likely difficult for Cushman, as they were for many Americans. Living with his mother in Chicago, he turned from one job to another: first, a stint in the adjustments
and returns department of Montgomery Ward, then an experiment as the
co-owner of a South Side rugwashing business. Both experiences proved
temporary. At some time in this period, Mabel married Adolphe Riviere
Edward Roome. Roome, a native of Louisiana, was like Wilbur Cushman
a modestly successful product of the industrial age. A railroad telegraph
operator, he rose to a supervisory position in the telegraph department
of the Southern Pacific in Los Angeles, and moved from there to a managerial job with that city's new Pacific Electric Railway. In 1916, Roome

LaSalle Extension University

ADMINISTRATION BUILDING,
MICHIGAN AVENUE AT FORTY-FIRST

CHICAGO

10. LaSalle Extension University
letterhead, c. 1924

had divorced his wife Lillian and left her and their three children to take a
job with the American Railway Association, a trade group first established in 1891. He lived at 42nd and Drexel, not far from Charles and
Mabel's apartment, and it may be that he met her in the neighborhood.
Mabel became a beloved figure who would soon to be known to Roome's
family as "Mumsie"; Charles, to judge both from his absence in Roome
family memories and from the utter lack of evidence of contact among
his own papers, chose not to connect with her new family in any mean-
ingful way. His relationship with Mabel, by later accounts an extremely
close one during his childhood and young adulthood, now seems to
have become more distant, and as he set out on his own he opened
himself to new emotional, as well as professional, connections.[4]

It was in 1922, with the economy on the rebound, that Cushman
acquired a deeper glimpse into the inner workings of the American economy and, in the process, further developed the "eye" that would distin-
guish his photography of the American landscape in the coming decades. LaSalle Extension University, headquartered at the corner of 41st
Street and Michigan Avenue in Cushman's South Side, was a quite different school from Indiana University—or virtually any other at the time
(fig. 10). A school for professional training in business and law, LaSalle

had been established by Chicago advertising man Jesse Grant Chapline in 1908 as a business in its own right; the university sold shares, offered dividends, and eventually opened branch campuses in cities such as New York and Los Angeles. In addition to the "dollars and cents training" promised by its curriculum, LaSalle speculated in other commercial ventures related to its mission of education for the modern business environment. In 1927, for instance, the school acquired the rights to manufacture the Stenotype machine (like the Graphotype another of the semiautomated office machines that helped to elevate the efficiency of white-collar work in the early 1900s) and, in 1935, it established a national Stenotype Institute—designed as a "national laboratory" for the machine's use—in leased downtown office space.[5]

LaSalle ventured, as well, into the business of forecasting conditions in the enterprises in which its students trained. From 1916 forward, the university published a monthly newsletter, the *LaSalle Business Bulletin*. The *Bulletin*, through its principal columnists Franklyn Hobbs and Archer Wall Douglas (the same Douglas whose *Traveling Salesmanship* had helped to define the character of the contemporary traveling salesman), operated on Hobbs's premise that "[f]act finding has become the order of the day." That new day for American business would, as Hobbs boasted in words sure to awaken the poetic spirit that lurks in the heart of every statistician, be "lighted by the rising sun of statistical compilations." The *Bulletin* offered its subscribers just such a compilation, enlivened by simplified maps and readable prose. Cushman joined the newsletter's staff as a research analyst in 1922. He used his position, as he later wrote, as an opportunity to develop "direct contacts with business executives" in an effort to discern national market trends in agriculture, finance, and industry.[6]

Cushman's name never appears on the pages of the *Business Bulletin* (none of the editorial staff's names do) but the essays penned by its two named columnists—Hobbs (a Chicago statistician and financial analyst) and Douglas (the St. Louis–based businessman who, in addition to writing popular business books, served as chairman of the United States

Chamber of Commerce's Committee on Statistics and Standards)—echoed the kind of fast-paced journalism that he himself had learned at the sports desk of the IDS. Whether reporting on future prospects for nonferrous metals or predicting the winter wheat crop, the *Bulletin*'s editors proved surprisingly adept at placing mundane economic details within a bigger picture of American life and culture during an increasingly (and, ultimately, precariously) prosperous decade. As both an illustration of an increasingly current mode of social analysis, and a precursor of Cushman's own visual presentation of the functional characteristics of the American landscape, the *Bulletin* bears some examination.

More than a simple market rundown, each issue of the *Bulletin* painted, in word and image, a broad portrait of American economic life during the weeks just past. Douglas's articles, in particular, enacted his own earlier call, in *Traveling Salesmanship*, for the salesman to be "the observer and student *par excellence* not only of material conditions, but of the trend of thought among his people." To the successful salesman, as Douglas had written, "[t]he story of the crops, of industrial life, of mining interests, of the probable cut of lumber, and of the enterprises of construction and development, are matters of vital moment."[7] If nothing else, Douglas's writing for the *Business Bulletin* confirmed that he sought to fashion himself from the same cloth. His research staff and editors, including Cushman, charged with the task of fleshing out the details of the last month's economic activities, could not have failed to absorb the same lesson.

Every issue of the *Business Bulletin* included several iterations of "the original Douglas Condition Map, in use over thirty years for business purposes"—a rudimentary U.S. map, shaded according to a key indicating "fair," "good," or "very good" conditions in one of a variety of areas of economic activity (fig. 11). Douglas and Hobbs's accompanying text illustrated the map, as it were, explaining regional variations in conditions within a range of economic sectors (usually including, at the least, construction, agriculture, iron and steel, and automobiles) and offering their overall thoughts on the nation's economic health. In the process,

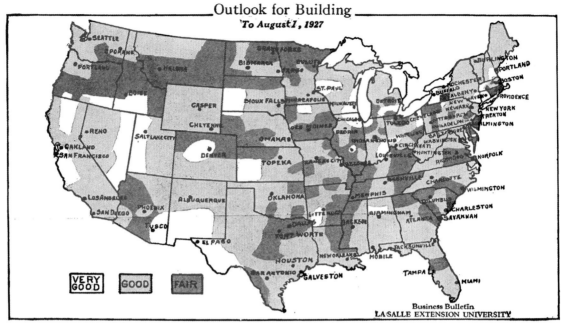

Outlook for Building
To August 1, 1927

VERY GOOD   GOOD   FAIR

Business Bulletin
LA SALLE EXTENSION UNIVERSITY

The favorable outlook for building is principally in the large centers and manufacturing districts, where many commercial and public buildings are being erected. There is also much construction in the suburbs of the large capitals because of the steady movement of population away from the congested districts of the cities to outlying towns and villages. New construction is hampered in many agricultural localities by the farmers' lack of money and credit, and in a number of Southern, Southwestern, and Central Western states by bank and commercial failures.

11. Douglas Condition Map, LaSalle Extension University *Business Bulletin*, June 1927

the columnists revealed much both about American culture and about the economist's own presuppositions about the place of business within that culture.

To read the *Business Bulletin* of the 1920s is to see the fulfillment—through economies of scale, improved communications, and mechanical innovation—of the promise of modern culture as it was pioneered by families like the Cushmans a hundred years earlier. Information replaces uncertainty, as "[p]rovincialism is fast vanishing under the educational influence and the wide mailing range of newspapers, the magazine, and the printed book . . . and the limitless scope of the radio." Farming still undergirds the economy, but now, reports Douglas, "the farmer no longer determines the nature and acreage of his products merely by local happenings, but he is being more and more influenced by the world-wide story of agricultural events." Not far from those farm fields, "in the Central West and in the South, the small towns are becoming more and more the sites of manufacturing plants" operated by big-city companies in search of cheaper labor and more efficient distribution. In these fac-

tories and elsewhere, coal-fueled power, dependent on mining operations that are excessive in their number and perennially troubled in their
labor relations, is yielding to the greater efficiency of oil-based fuel and
hydroelectric power. The revolutionary effect of the internal combustion
engine is especially pronounced among "the individuals of the countryside," giving them "opportunity to become much better acquainted with
their neighbors and their country." Meanwhile, mobility characterizes, as
well, the "increasing tendency of wage earners to invest in small and
moderate-sized homes on the fringes and in the suburbs of the great
cities." Fueled by such movement, as well as by the tremendous growth
of central business districts like Manhattan's, construction comprises
"perhaps the greatest single factor" in the nation's prosperity. In all its
salient features—communication, transportation, technology, and trade—
the economy described in the *Bulletin* represented the improvement and
refinement of trends evident for a century or more. Yet amidst those familiar features, the very task of managing and packaging that economy
emerges as a significant area of creative growth and prosperity in its own
right.[8]

Beside their value in pointing out the underlying continuity of traditional economic activities within even the most advanced-seeming in-
novations of the 1920s, these descriptions of American economic and
cultural life stand out for several additional reasons. The first is the degree to which leisure, consumption, and travel—hallmarks of what John
Kenneth Galbraith, himself educated as an economist in these same
years, would later dub "The Affluent Society"—had come to be considered both culturally desirable and economically imperative. "Thousands
upon thousands of families now take transcontinental tours," wrote
Douglas of the increasingly widespread ownership of automobiles, adding that "[t]he educational and recreational gains are of untold value."
Such gains were by no means the only benefit of consumer spending
and leisure time: "[O]ur excess of capacity is being employed by the
spread of ability to buy radios, automobiles, grand pianos, and the like."
The consumer-driven economy—an economy that rested ever more upon

the work of advertisers and image-makers to cultivate demand for a growing productive capacity—had arrived.[9]

The second striking point is the *Bulletin*'s editors' faith, shared with other analysts of the time, in the virtues of a well-regulated and coordinated economy in place of the laissez-faire marketplace of a generation earlier. The success of World War I–era government-business partnerships such as the War Industries Board, the U.S. Shipping Board, and the U.S. Housing Agency had suggested to analysts and business leaders the power of government planning to spark, and not simply constrain, economic output. The authors of the *Bulletin* were no exception. In their articles, the new Federal Reserve system earns repeated praise for its judicious management of the "conservative prosperity" of the period; the Federal Farm Loan Bank Board draws a nod for its role in reducing the uncertainty of the farmer's credit cycle; professionals, workers, and government regulators alike garner credit for fostering "co-operative competition" and making "notable progress in the psychological problem of smoothing out our human relations in business."[10] Douglas's and Hobbs's faith in the good of judicious government regulation, enlightened corporate self-governance, and conservative unionism put them squarely in line with the mainstream of economic and financial analysts of the day— as it would with the planners who would soon exercise power both in the Hoover administration and in the Roosevelt White House that replaced it.

Characteristic of its time, too, was the *Bulletin's* effort to place economics within a broader social framework that both comprehended and isolated (as the simplifying quality of the maps nicely illustrates) the nation. Like Rexford Tugwell, the Columbia economics professor who had coauthored the 1925 college text, *American Economic Development: And the Means of Its Improvement*, before heading FDR's Resettlement Administration, the editors sought a language for instructing a wide audience on the relationship of the economy to everyday life among a nation of people who presumably shared, for all their variety, a common set of values and cultural reference points (fig. 12). Such broad-brush social-economic analysis did not appeal to everyone, but it did mesh with a

12. Detail, Rexford Tugwell, *American Economic Development: And the Means of Its Improvement*, 1925

growing interest among intellectuals of the time in developing original explanations of the American "character." As Constance Rourke, Edmund Wilson, Lewis Mumford, H. L. Mencken, and other critics would do for the cultural realm, social scientists like Tugwell, Robert and Helen Lynd, and Robert Park sought to discern in the turmoil and variety of the American experience common threads from which to weave a coherent tapestry of post–World War I society. Whether focused on government, literature, or architecture, the cultural critics of the 1920s shared a commitment to making what Tugwell, describing his own work, called "a great generalizing effort to locate the germinal forces of the present"; to asserting the existence of a describable national character; to framing that character in terms of common ideals rather than (in the manner of supporters of immigration restriction or followers of the revived Ku Klux Klan) of common blood; and to highlighting "the means of its improvement" for the good of the country.[11]

Broadly framed as the social science effort of the 1920s was, it depended for its authority on the growing collection and accuracy of statistical collection and analysis. The United States Census, established in the Constitution and first taken in 1790, had since the late nineteenth century taken increasingly precise measure of the nation, its people, and its economy. Overseeing the 1890 Census, the most detailed to date, was the nation's first commissioner of labor, Carroll Wright, who as director of the Massachusetts Bureau of Statistics of Labor had compiled detailed economic data since 1873. Wright's tenure, first in Boston and then in Washington, signaled the increasing ubiquity of quantitative data as an underpinning of efforts toward social reform and economic modernization. Progressive Era housing and city planning advocates weighted their recommendations with quantitative data on disease, illiteracy, and poverty.[12] Trade groups such as the U.S. Chamber of Commerce, established in 1912, carried Wright's tradition to the private sector, hiring analysts like Archer Wall Douglas to comb government statistics (and to develop their own) for the private benefit of their constituents.

The technical means for assessing such growing quantities of data grew apace with their increasing utility to government and industry. Calculating machinery, popularized since the late 1800s by Burroughs, NCR, and other successful corporations, became increasingly sophisticated in the 1920s. This development owed its success, in part, to concurrent developments in the fields of photography and optics—developments with which Cushman may have been peripherally familiar based on his own experience with Addressograph. Yet Cushman was still relying on firsthand interviews as a means of gathering information for the LaSalle *Bulletin* when in 1927 Emanuel Goldberg, the Russian-born director of the German-based optical company Zeiss-Ikon, patented an "Apparatus for Selecting Statistical and Accounting Data"—a microfilm-based data reader whose capabilities for making precise and predictive judgments from statistical collection pointed toward the eventual development of the computer. Goldberg's adoptive countryman Walter Benjamin, writing his essay on art and mechanical reproduction in 1936, likewise noticed the congruity between advancing visual technologies and "the increasing importance of statistics," both of which rested, as Benjamin noted, on a "'sense of the universal equality of things'" that lay beneath the apparent particularities of individual objects.[13]

Government and trade groups were not the only ones to draw on the value of statistical data and computational tools. Private investors, as the editors of the *Bulletin* knew, stood to benefit from increasingly accurate information regarding business and financial activity. Among the companies offering to sell such information to a growing clientele of market speculators, the best known was Standard Statistics, a financial-research firm established in 1906. Standard's five hundred staff analysts produced more than twenty specialized publications—graced with no-nonsense titles like *Standard Monthly Bond Offerings* and *Standard Trade and Securities Services*—to help professional investors divine the direction of selected market sectors. In 1928, as opportunities for American investors continued to multiply without apparent limit, the company sought to broaden its customer base with a more popular and broadly focused newsletter, *Your Money*. To head up the new venture, they brought to their New York headquarters a new research analyst and editor with a knack for explaining economic data in terms that the general reader could understand. His name was Charles Cushman.

Cushman was not alone when he arrived in New York that August. With him came his new wife, the former Jean Hamilton (fig. 13). The two had married on June 21, 1924, in Chicago—the city where Jean grew up and (earlier that month) graduated college. Cushman's papers offer no clue as to how they met—fellow South Siders, they may have encountered one another at a social event or simply on a sunny day in Jackson Park. But given Cushman's association with LaSalle (and the school's ties to local business and advertising executives), and given his growing knack for establishing personal and professional ties with mentors whom he found useful to his research, one suspects that it was Jean's father, Joseph R. Hamilton, who provided Charles with his first link to the family that would, in the wake of his mother's recent remarriage, become his own. With the marriage, and then the move to New York, Cushman found himself drawn by the powerful gravitational pull of the Hamilton family.

13. Jean Hamilton Cushman,
Wisconsin Dells, 1924

The elder Hamilton offered Cushman not only the fatherly mentor that he had lacked since the death of his own father (and maybe longer), but also a professional role model and, perhaps most important, a source of the financial support that would alter Charles's subsequent career decisions.

The best place to begin to understand Joe Hamilton, and to appreciate his importance to Cushman's life, is in the pages of the book that most nearly approaches a biography of the man. From it, we learn that Joe had been "a kind of mooning boy, greatly beloved and protected by the family." The "family" in question is that of his father, Samuel Hamilton, a northern Irish immigrant who arrived in the Central Valley of California in the 1860s. The words are those of Samuel's grandson (and Joe's nephew), John Steinbeck. The biography is Steinbeck's sprawling family memoir, first drafted in 1952 under the working title "Salinas Valley," and finally published, the following year, as *East of Eden*.[14]

The young Joe Hamilton occupies only a walk-on role in the family drama that is *East of Eden* (albeit a larger one than that occupied by his sister, Steinbeck's own mother, Olive), but Steinbeck's quite specific portrayal of this well-loved youngest child betrays the fact that the writer remained close to his uncle throughout the latter's life, and that the adult Joe's recollections were key to the construction of the book's substantial factual backdrop. Unlike his siblings, Steinbeck writes, Joe "daydreamed out his life." A misfit in the world of toil that characterized the Hamiltons' California just as it did the Cushmans' Indiana, Joe's "inability to function at farm and forge . . . headed him for a higher education"—specifically, at the newly opened Stanford University, some seventy miles north of the family farm near Salinas (fig. 14).[15]

14. Joseph R. Hamilton (left) and roommates, Stanford University, c. 1899

Steinbeck leaves Joe—as Joe leaves California—a young man. His geographic and dispositional drift away from the family proved a poor fit for the narrative wholeness that Steinbeck required in a tale of families whose fates are intertwined with that of the austere landscape of the Salinas River valley. We learn only in passing, then, that Joe "had gone east and was helping to invent a new profession called advertising," a field in which, as the writer notes with apparent pleasure, "Joe's very faults were virtues."[16] If the fictional character thus merits only a quiet, ironic exit from Steinbeck's dramatic stage, the real Joseph Hamilton was, as of 1900, just beginning to construct a life of greater historical importance—to his family, his profession, and even, to some extent, the nation—than any one of the Hamilton clan short of Steinbeck himself. Unlike his generational contemporaries Adolphe Roome, in Louisiana, or Wilbur Cushman, in Indiana—but very much in a manner that prefigured the life of Wilbur's son Charles—Joe Hamilton left behind the world of farms, factories, and trains for a world that valued his words, ideas, and images above his sweat and his muscle.

Hamilton's faults first turned to virtues at the doorstep of the modern department store—the institution that, as much as any other, embodied the dreams of all those Americans (not only of "mooning boys" such as himself) of the modern era who aspired to a material reward in exchange for the tedium of working life. Department stores served as a fulcrum in the transition from that era to the consumption- and image-based culture whose birth was suggested in the pages of the LaSalle *Bulletin*. Such stores did not produce new goods, but they showed those goods in a new light. They did not create an economy built upon word and image, but their effort to build demand for commodities required that they foreground imagery to an extent not yet seen in the world of business and commerce. But the history of department-store retailing, as it happens, reflects more than the larger changes afoot in twentieth-century American culture. It also bears directly on the more particular fortunes of the Hamilton and Cushman families.

Since 1848, when Alexander T. Stewart opened his emporium on lower Broadway in downtown Manhattan, big-city department stores had done more than simply provide shelf space for the growing evidence of American ingenuity. Their rise had fueled the nascent advertising industry, and advertisement had in turn fueled the notion that not only wealthy Americans (the all-too-obvious targets of Thorstein Veblen's 1899 critique of "conspicuous consumption") but working men and women, too, could surround themselves in the trappings of taste and luxury. Advertisement was one crucial component of the department stores' success formula. Buying in greater quantity and relying on constant, nonnegotiable prices, men like Marshall Field or the brothers Edward and Lincoln Filene also assumed a lower profit margin on their merchandise. To compensate for this lower margin, they endeavored to turn over their goods more quickly—to sell a greater number of units each day than could specialized shopkeepers. This they accomplished, first, through location (selecting for their sites those street corners by which the greatest number of potential customers would pass on a given business day); second, through the adornment of their buildings (which typically boasted brightly decorated display windows and open, skylit interiors); and third, through relentless promotion and advertisement.

Each of these responses to the challenge of mass merchandising would affect Joe Hamilton's life and, in a less direct fashion, Charles Cushman's. Following his graduation from Stanford, Hamilton married Augusta (Gussie) Moskowitz, the child of German-Jewish immigrants who had settled, first, beside California's Morro Bay and eventually in San Francisco. Hamilton briefly pursued a journalism career and then, around the time of the 1902 birth of the couple's only child, Jean, refashioned himself as a department-store advertising manager. He first entered the profession at Prager's in San Francisco, then quickly moved to Kansas City's Jones Store—at a time when such stores were not only changing Americans' consumption habits but reshaping the American central city. In New York's Herald Square, Chicago's Loop, San Francisco's Union

Square and elsewhere, the big stores took over the "hundred-percent corners" at the heart of the central business districts and forced less high-yielding tenants—offices, hotels, smaller retailers—into place around them. Residential and manufacturing uses, once intermixed throughout the city, then scattered to the downtown fringe and beyond. Hamilton, a child of the ranch, became a man of this new downtown—a place devoted to consumption and display rather than to production; a place that in this sense modeled the kind of broader economic changes that awaited the twentieth-century United States.[17]

The technologies of reproduction and design aided the department-store owners in their success. Retailers displayed images of their new buildings in their advertisement and on their business stationery—just as factory owners had done before them.[18] With the appearance of his trade journal, *The Show Window*, Chicago retail specialist L. Frank Baum could earn a respectable living offering store managers advice as to the proper design—and, increasingly important, the proper color scheme—of the displays that they erected behind the plate-glass panes that faced crowded corners. Within those buildings, retailers sought to complement their goods with other sorts of stimuli—fashion shows, music, art exhibitions—designed to draw potential customers in from the street.[19] Spectacle—even without direct relation to the goods traded across the store counter—became integral to the merchant's technique.

The task of promoting public awareness of, and interest in, the events and commodities offered behind the display windows fell to a new sort of professional, the advertising manager. At his best, the advertising manager asserted himself as a partner in the store's success, turning sales into matters of public interest. Manly Gillam, working for Philadelphia's John Wanamaker, bought for that store its first full-page newspaper advertisement in 1888—an act that set in place a partnership between retailer and newspaper that persists today. Wanamaker had snatched Gillam from his position as managing editor for the *Philadelphia Record*, and it was under the latter's influence that the Philadelphia store organized its advertising staff as though it were a news bureau;

Wanamaker himself further equated promotion and news with his insistence to employees that "newspaper statements must tell plainly and interestingly of the goods that are to be sold."[20]

In more than simply his aggressive approach to advertising and public relations, John Wanamaker proved the most influential of the late-nineteenth- and early-twentieth-century merchant princes (fig. 15). As his store expanded, first in Philadelphia and then in New York, he burnished his reputation both through public service (serving as President Benjamin Harrison's postmaster general) and through commercial showmanship (luring customers in to hear the famous Wanamaker organ, or to see some of his many photography exhibitions, including a six-year-long series of exhibits drawn from the grandly conceived Rodman Wanamaker

15. Wanamaker's, Philadelphia, c.1902

Expeditions to the American Indian). During these years of expansion and innovation, Wanamaker relied for the promotion of his efforts on the services of his advertising department. That department was managed variously by his longtime confidant Gillam, by the famous adman John E. Powers, and finally by a newcomer who had traveled east from California by way of Kansas City: Joseph R. Hamilton.[21]

Hamilton's quick rise to what one home-town reporter called, with justifiable boastfulness, "the highest standing in his profession" is a mystery not readily explained. But the prestige and influence of managing the advertising business of a retailer who operated at the scale, and with the visibility, of Wanamaker—particularly one who so identified his success with the power of advertising—is indisputable. For several years, the career of this child of California's Salinas Valley farmland orbited closely around the brightest star in the universe of American retailing and advertising. During that time, Hamilton made his mark as the author of regular store ads that one journalist of the time described as "a newspaper in little," each opening with a peppy, illustrated editorial extolling some aspect of American society, and only then working its way into a discussion of actual sales merchandise. By the time that Hamilton, Gussie, and Jean left Philadelphia for Chicago in 1910, his experience qualified him both as one of the nation's leading advertising professionals and as a witness to one of the most remarkable careers of the Progressive Era.[22]

Hamilton's departure from Philadelphia brought him into the employ of Herbert Kaufman, a prominent Chicago adman, playwright, and aphoristic journalist who, although one year younger than his new associate, had already made a name for himself in England and America. Kaufman probably met Hamilton on a visit to Philadelphia, where John Wanamaker had called on the promoter to offer his counsel on the growing Wanamaker empire. If we can take at face value Steinbeck's characterization of young Joe's personality, then we can also imagine the attraction to Hamilton of this fast-talking visitor, who claimed to earn $1000 per week on a schedule of six-hour days and five-month vacations, and who advised aspiring professionals that "when you play, go at it harder than you work." Kaufman's writings in the *Chicago Daily Tribune* paralleled Hamilton's own brisk editorial voice in the Wanamaker advertisements; from 1908 to 1915, Kaufman's weekly column dispensed encouragement and advice under such peppy headlines as "The Snail Can't Get the Giraffe's Viewpoint," "Find an Abandoned Mine and Work It," and "Nature's Family Name is 'Persistence!'"[23]

As Hamilton set to work in Chicago, his renown in professional and political circles grew alongside his contacts and, from all appearances, his personal wealth. At some point (perhaps upon Kaufman's 1918 departure to serve as assistant secretary in Woodrow Wilson's State Department), Hamilton opened an agency under his own name—eventually operating from an office on the 10th floor of the Lake Michigan Building at 180 N. Michigan Avenue at the north edge of the Loop—which he would maintain for the remainder of his life.[24] According to later family recollections, Joe and Gussie hosted a Sunday salon in their Hyde Park apartment, the regular guests at which included the likes of Clarence Darrow and the sculptor Jo Davidson. Among their well-connected friends the family numbered the prominent Chicago attorney Angus Roy Shannon (a man who, in addition to his professional accomplishments, could also lay claim to having married the sister-in-law of the writer Hamlin Garland, who was also the sister of the sculptor Lorado Taft) and oil company executive Henry M. Dawes, a formidable man next to anyone other than his own brother Charles, who had served as Calvin Coolidge's vice president and earned a Nobel Peace Prize for his role in aiding Germany's postwar rebuilding. Daughter Jean absorbed naturally the mingling of politics, business, and the arts that livened the Hamilton family home; she also considered her mother's Jewish heritage—conspicuous in the midst of this largely Anglo-Saxon social circle—as an additional source of pride and distinctiveness. For Charles Weever Cushman of Poseyville, Indiana, the family and their friends must have seemed heady company indeed: company that proved as alluring, in its way, as Jean herself.[25]

Steinbeck, too, was impressed by the ease with which his uncle moved in influential circles. It could not have been entirely the young writer's want of a good meal that accounts for the awe with which he described entering Uncle Joe's room at New York's Commodore Hotel one night in February 1926. Steinbeck, working construction and living with his sister and her husband in Brooklyn, enjoyed an expensive dinner that evening, courtesy of his uncle; he then watched as Joe, with a few quick phone calls, arranged for him to obtain his first professional writing job, as a reporter at William Hearst's New York *American*. Hamilton also tried to engage Steinbeck to join his own agency—an offer the writer refused, though the two men would remain in touch for the remainder of Joe's life.[26]

Whether or not Joe Hamilton extended the same job offer to his new son-in-law, Cushman seems likely to have enlisted Hamilton's aid in securing his own move to New York in 1928—nearly two years after his writer cousin, tired and disgusted, had found work on a ship bound for California. As much as it depended on writing and editing skills, Cushman's position at Standard Statistics' *Your Money* demanded an ability to relate easily to corporate leaders. In contrast to his still-struggling cousin, Cushman had educated himself specifically to acquire such skills, and had developed them further through his recent professional experiences. Still, his new appointment likely depended on Hamilton's connections as much as had Steinbeck's own short-lived foray into journalism. In the subtle struggle of two young writers for the favors and approval of their successful elder, it was Cushman who seemed, at this point, better positioned to turn personal connection into professional success.

As its title suggested, *Your Money* aimed to establish a personal connection between the company's services and the client's perceived needs (fig. 16). Its features translated—much as Joseph Hamilton's advertising work did—abstract concepts into personal stories designed to appeal at an individual level. In contrast to the company's specialized, sector-specific market reports, Standard's new magazine was designed

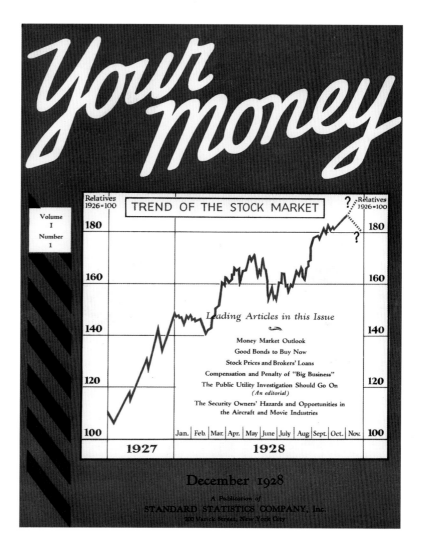

Your Money

Relatives 1926=100

TREND OF THE STOCK MARKET

? Relatives 1926=100

Volume I Number 1

180

180

160

160

Leading Articles in this Issue

Money Market Outlook
Good Bonds to Buy Now
Stock Prices and Brokers' Loans
Compensation and Penalty of "Big Business"
The Public Utility Investigation Should Go On
(An editorial)
The Security Owners' Hazards and Opportunities in
the Aircraft and Movie Industries

140

140

120

120

100

Jan. | Feb. | Mar. | Apr. | May | June | July | Aug. | Sept. | Oct. | Nov.

100

1927

1928

December 1928

A Publication of
STANDARD STATISTICS COMPANY, Inc.
200 Varick Street, New York City

16. *Your Money*, December 1928

to attract everyday investors to the increasingly lucrative world of stock market investment. As editor, Cushman adopted a solicitous, but not deferential, tone toward his prospective readers. "Probably it weakens one's strategic position to offer an apology before one makes a bow," he wrote in his first editor's note, before going on to establish his own intent of putting a more personal stamp (including, if the whim suited him, "a description of the floral life of the Amazon valley") than readers customarily expected from a market newsletter.[27] In a manner at once professionally contrived and innately suited to his own disposition, Cushman spoke familiarly to the everyday investor—the physician, the attorney, the store owner, the insurance executive—a man with the intelligence, but not the time, to navigate corporate financial reports; a man more concerned, ultimately, with his own and his family's well-being than with the minutiae of the market. To this ideal reader, Cushman translated the unsentimental facts of the statistician or the banker into the reassuring language of a trusted brother or a college roommate. *Your Money* continued the premise of the *Business Bulletin*—that the American economy could be explained in simple, comprehensive terms—but the newer publication reflected its editor's affinity for those personal, quirky, and particular stories that lay within the bigger abstractions of the statistician. Cushman's opening apology, so similar in tone to his earlier IDS disclaimer about predicting "all-league" team picks, carved out a space for himself as an idiosyncratic but trustworthy observer of the American scene.

Cushman arrived at *Your Money* during the best of times; like most others riding the crest of the market wave, he hesitated to anticipate the worst. As of late 1928, Standard Statistics still refused to offer more than a gentle cautionary nudge to its clients concerned about ever-higher stock prices: "how long they will continue to [rise]," wrote Cushman, "and whether in the early future the rise will be succeeded by a precipitous decline are questions that we shall make no attempt to answer here."[28] For Cushman, that early future proved noteworthy primarily for a change of a more personal sort: in April 1929, just eight months after arriving in New York, he returned with Jean to Chicago.

Why the abrupt end to the New York adventure? Cushman, in words crafted to meet the expectations of a potential employer, later offered that he had "started a line of work that led company to establish its field analytical staff, and was given the opportunity of handling the Middle-West territory." His relatives recalled the situation in a less flattering light: Charles, one told an interviewer in 2001, "was fired from every job he ever had." The truth lies somewhere in the middle. If he in fact proved a poor fit for the journal (which in any event folded that August, after only five issues), Cushman evidently had not run entirely afoul of his employers at Standard: he remained in charge of the company's Chicago field office until July 1932.[29]

Cushman left New York with a bit more business and editorial experience, and with something more as well: a small black-and-white photograph of the streets under the Manhattan anchorage of the Brooklyn
Bridge (fig. 8). Common sense suggests that the street scene was only
one of a number of photographs he must have taken in his brief New
York sojourn, but this image is the only print to have survived his moves
of the subsequent decades; hence, it offers us our only clue of Cushman's first apparent turn to the serious practice of landscape and street
photography. Apparently taken with a traditional 8″ × 10″ view camera,
the image might be dismissed as being derivative of the sharp-focused
street photographs of Berenice Abbott—displayed in her successful 1934
exhibition at the Museum of the City of New York and subsequently made
more famous through publication of her federally sponsored "Changing
New York" project—were it not for the fact that Cushman's picture preceded by several years any widespread public awareness of Abbott's
now-iconic images.[30] Neither Abbott nor Cushman, naturally, was the only
New Yorker to carry a camera through the streets of lower Manhattan in
the 1920s and 1930s, but his interest in such an ordinary scene—and his
evident pride in the photograph, which motivated him to keep the print
for the rest of his life—speak both to his natural eye for the social and
economic dimension of everyday landscapes, and to his new facility
with visual media to express that dimension. The picture's contrasts—of
human and monumental scale, of light and shadow, of closely packed
buildings facing near-empty streets—offer a dynamic visual composition, but they serve at the same time to document a pregnant moment
in the life of the city. Not only do we see a neighborhood momentarily
stripped of the movement and the noise that will animate it during the
coming working week, but we also feel, with Cushman, a deeper sense
of quiet—the hush of a neighborhood, and of a way of life, soon to be
abandoned to changing ways of conducting commerce. Here is the
closely mixed district of warehousing, wholesaling, manufacturing, and
living quarters that had been increasingly displaced by the more mono-
lithically arranged central business districts that, in turn, owed much of

their appearance to the rising economic and cultural power of the department stores that Joe Hamilton had helped to promote over the previous quarter-century. An eye naturally attuned to detail—an eye that Charles Cushman had threatened to turn toward "the floral life of the Amazon Valley" if the spirit so moved him—had found much closer at hand a subject worthy of its attention. The businessman and the social documentarian, both of whom had coexisted in Cushman from early in his career, had found a common medium through which to channel their interests.

Back in Chicago, Charles and Jean found little sign of the Depression around Joe and Gussie Hamilton's household. As Charles continued his research for Standard Statistics, Joe managed to expand his business affairs while taking on a more explicitly political profile. The opportunity to do so came to him courtesy of a 1931 national ad campaign for the eccentric publisher Bernarr Macfadden, whose company maintained its Midwest offices one floor beneath Hamilton's in the Lake Michigan Building. Hamilton's advertisements for Macfadden's *True Story* magazine, which appeared in selected newspapers across the country from 1929 to 1931, took the form of a series of editorial essays, shorn of visual information, and topped with Kaufman-esque headlines like "Essay on a Man Buttoning up His Vest." In their indirect style (more public relations than advertisement per se), they may reflect the influence not only of Hamilton's early Chicago partner but also of Edward Bernays, the prominent public relations pioneer who later recalled having spent a year "trying to untangle Macfadden's socially constructive ideas from his fads and cults" before giving up on his willful client in 1928.[31] Through these mock articles, Hamilton helped Macfadden to promote *True Story* not to the magazine's working-class female readership but to the men whose business would keep the publication afloat. Through aphorism and anecdote, they encouraged nervous capitalists to keep production levels and wages high in order to encourage leisure-oriented spending (on, among other things, newsstand magazines) among working men and their wives. The magazine would, then, serve as a conduit through which those same companies might market their products to the American families whose income they had helped to ensure.

Hamilton's April 1931 essay "Human or Dog Intelligence?" won for him that year's Chicago advertising guild prize for "best national campaign." Hamilton, speaking through Macfadden, used the piece to elevate advertisement and consumption into patriotic responsibilities in a time of national crisis. The American worker, he argued, "represent[ed] the entire balance of power in our production plants"; it was by furthering that worker's power as a consumer (rather than instinctively retrenching) that businessmen could demonstrate the "human intelligence" required to recover from the crisis. "We have two million of these wage-earning Americans," boasted Hamilton of *True Story*'s readership, "who represent the great central core of this social and economic change." Appealing to "the great advertisers of America," he offered *True Story* as a direct line into the homes, and pocketbooks, of the nation's consumers. The solution to the growing depression, he submitted, awaited the concerted effort and mutual goodwill of workers, manufacturers, and consumers.[32]

Hamilton did not lag in his own entrepreneurial efforts at the time; his efforts resulted, eventually, in allowing his son-in-law the financial freedom to travel and pursue his budding photography habit. Since at least the 1920s, the Hamilton agency had managed accounts for Puritan Malt Extract Company, one of a number of industries that brewed legal malt extract during Prohibition. Chief copywriter on the account was Theodore Rosenak, who advertised Puritan's products through simple, straightforward language ("Richest-Strongest. Why don't you try it?") that matched both the company's conservative image and the matter-of-fact tenor of much early twentieth-century print advertisement. As Prohibition appeared headed for its end, the Pabst Corporation of Milwaukee purchased Puritan; the Hamilton agency evidently ceased its representation of the product at around the same time.[33]

Hamilton's acquired expertise in the brewing industry did not, however, go to waste. On January 8, 1933, as Roosevelt's pending inauguration made repeal of the Volstead Act a virtual certainty, the Chicago

Tribune reported on the "mysterious activities of Drewrys, Ltd., of Win-
nipeg, which is understood to have secured options on considerable
land in Chicago for a proposed new low type brewery." The "activities"
hinted at in the *Tribune* in fact represented the culmination of a deal
to establish Drewrys, Ltd., USA, an American offshoot of the Canadian
brewery, in Chicago. By April, the new organization, "fully financed within
itself," announced its plans to deliver U.S.-made Drewrys ale to the consumer within sixty to ninety days. The president of this fast-starting, pri-
vately held business was the Hamilton agency's copywriter, Theodore
Rosenak; its treasurer, Charles W. Cushman. Their offices were located
in the Lake Michigan Building.[34]

In their dual roles as client and advertising manager, Hamilton and
his colleagues crafted an ad campaign for their Drewrys venture that
reflected both their experience as advertising men and their instincts as
corporate executives (fig. 17). Like the *True Story* advertisements, Hamilton's Drewrys campaign showed him to be still a man of words, a be-
liever in the power of verbal persuasion to sell products and build relationships. His new ads kept potential customers abreast of the brewery's
progress in preparing its first batches for retail shipment; they touted the
brand's long history; and they prepared drinkers for the slightly higher
alcoholic content that distinguished the brand from competing beers. As
he had in the days when he worked to entice Philadelphians to step into
Wanamaker's, he blended logic with a contrived intimacy that portrayed
the reader as a knowledgeable, independent thinker who could be
trusted to join the producer's world of privileged knowledge.[35]

Hamilton's insistence on the kind of reasoned, gentlemanly conversation represented in his Drewrys and *True Story* campaigns marked him
as an increasingly conspicuous holdout in the world of those who touted
ideas for a living. Around him, the "picture story," earlier suggested in the
appearance of publications like Tugwell's *American Economic Life*, was
evolving into a versatile medium of salesmanship, entertainment, and
political propaganda. His particular gift—and his legacy to Cushman—
was to bring together the commercial and social application of informa-

17. Drewrys Ale advertisement,
Chicago Daily Tribune, May 15, 1936

tion in a manner that wholly suited the avid partisans of neither goal. This middle way, with its effort to ennoble the economic networks and the cultural landscape of modern America, has lain buried beneath subsequent historical efforts to dramatize the Depression in terms either of the grimness of everyday life or of the consumerist fantasies by which people sought to escape it. Yet it offers the key to Cushman's thirty-year project, beginning with his first travels with color film in 1938.

Cushman had been weaned on words, as well, but he was clearly attracted to the newer opportunities afforded by photography and illustration. We know that he was shooting his own pictures from at least the early 1920s and experimenting with custom printing by 1930. We know that his Christmas present to Jean in 1930 was a book of cartoons by *New Yorker* contributor Peter Arno, the artist whose crisp line drawings and terse captions had helped to establish the cosmopolitan pretentions of that new publication. She (or at least he) must have liked it—a year later he gave Jean a second Arno volume. And we can guess—without knowing for sure—that Cushman was more aware than his father-in-law of a growing trend in American publishing and social science toward works that not only included illustrations—as his *Business Bulletin* had—but that made images, rather than text, their central content.

Continual improvements in printing and reproduction—a trend that Cushman, as a young traveling salesman and as an aspiring editor, had promoted firsthand—had motivated growth and change in the magazine industry for many years. As Albert Lasker's ruminations about the rise of pictorial advertising had suggested (see above, n. 35), the switch to illustration-based communication had been almost as unforeseen, to the first generation of professional admen, as it was inevitable. Commercial printing studios urged publishers to increase their visual content, with hopeful testimonials to the persuasive value of "pictures that scurry you off to king's palace or pirate's rendezvous . . . that quicken the pulse, tingle the blood, and chase imagination."[36] Yet, as Hamilton's and other agencies' products showed, some advertising continued to model itself on newspaper journalism into the 1930s. It is, perhaps, appropriate, then, that the profession received an extra push in the direction of the visual by the arrival of an innovative news venue that first appeared Thanksgiving week of 1936, and that announced its weekly appearance thereafter in four simple, white letters set on a rectangular red background. Unlike such text-heavy publications as *True Story* or the *New Yorker* (or *Your Money*, for that matter), Henry Luce's *Life* proceeded from its publisher's faith in the power of images to relate a story. Seeking to branch out from his earlier successes with *Time* and *Fortune*, Luce encouraged his newest publication's more diverse readership "to see and to take pleasure in seeing; to see and be amazed." The message was not lost on advertisers and their agents. "*Life* will prove there is a new editorial technique," enthused Young and Rubicam art director Vaughn Flannery, who dubbed the new medium "pictorial journalism—a process of telling a story with pictures or with a series of pictures and a minimum of text." That process would, Flannery correctly predicted, soon alter advertising conventions, as well. *Life*'s editors' decision to print (and, one suspects, possibly to solicit) Flannery's testimonial of course reflected their ongoing need to pursue the business of major advertising agencies—including those firms that, like Hamilton's or Lasker's, had yet to break from the news-bureau tradition pioneered by Wanamaker and innovated by the likes of Macfadden. The magazine's editorial content developed alongside its advertising, each competing with the other to master the task of "telling a story with pictures."[37]

By the time that *Life* (and its imitators, such as *Look*, which appeared the following year) began bringing pictorial journalism and image-heavy advertisement to American newsstands and mailboxes, the photographic news essay—a response, in part, to the new popularity of newsreel films—had already established a toehold in popular culture. Educated Americans newly accustomed to the "generalizing tendencies" of Tugwell, Mencken, the Lynds, and their counterparts among the social and cultural analysts of the 1920s had access, by the mid-1930s, to a growing number of pictorial variations on the same theme: books purporting to capture in images the singular qualities that brought Americans together. Charles Cross's *A Picture of America—As it Is—and As It Might Be: Told by the News Camera*, printed in 1932, captured in its title the straightforward aims of such works (fig. 18). Archibald MacLeish's *Land of the Free*, which set out to turn print conventions on their head by offering "a book of photographs illustrated by a poem," appeared in 1937, as did *You Have Seen their Faces*, a words-and-pictures collaboration of the husband-wife team of Margaret Bourke-White and Erskine Caldwell; their next effort, *Say, Is This the USA?*, followed in 1941. Dorothea Lange and her husband, Paul Taylor (like Stryker, a professor of economics), published their Depression documentary *American Exodus* in 1939, several months after the appearance of Walker Evans's uncaptioned *American Photographs*, the catalog of his recent exhibition at the Museum of Modern Art.[38]

Just as Luce's *Life* mixed serious reportage with entertainment and advertising savvy, the superficially similar pictorial publications derived

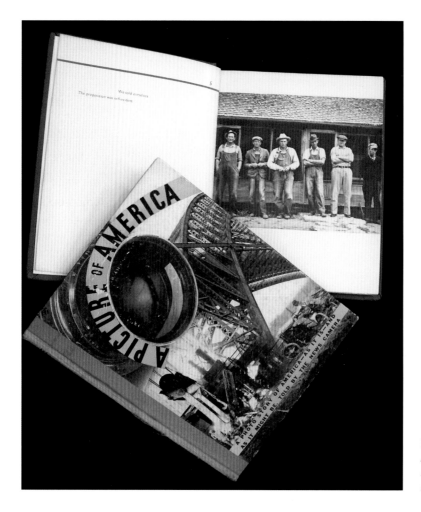

18. Documentary photography books of the 1930s: Charles Cross's *A Picture of America* (1932) and Archibald MacLeish's *Land of the Free* (1937)

their distinct flavors from differing mixes of commercial and documentary intent, and of artistic and political motivation. The desire to speak in pictures could serve a wide range of political leanings and personal ideals. Cross's book, sponsored by the League for Industrial Democracy, came replete with an introduction from socialist torch-bearer Norman Thomas. Bourke-White and Caldwell styled themselves, less politically, as roving observers in search of the colorful "cast of characters" who made the nation into "the scene of a mighty drama." Evans, claiming in personal correspondence to be "so *goddamn* mad over what people from the left tier think America is," protested that his own work carried no call for social change. Yet his "American Photographs," as curated and explained by Museum of Modern Art cofounder Lincoln Kirstein, did little to resist such a reading.[39] It bears notice, as well, that Kirstein had culti-vated his own leftist leanings amidst the comforts derived from his family's share of the Filene's Department Store fortune—and that one of Luce's rising reporters, Dwight Macdonald (who soon turned on both Luce and John Steinbeck for their roles in promoting the debasement of culture into what Macdonald coined its "masscult" and "midcult" strains), had himself trained for a retail career prior to taking up journalism and film criticism. In 1937 Kirstein's father's partner, Edward Filene, provided essential startup support (along with Edward Bernays) to the Institute for Propaganda Analysis, founded to track the effects of mass media upon American public opinion. The connection of such department store executives—and the application of their expertise in display and visual persuasion—to the rising tide of interest in pictorial and reportorial de-scription suggests another inevitable strand running through the mix of commerce, art, and social comment that typified the publishing and photographic worlds in the 1930s. It helps to position the eventual work of a businessman-photographer like Charles Cushman closer to the main-stream of the era's photographic traditions than historians of the docu-mentary tradition have suggested. And it provides some context for the invitation that arrived, in 1939, at the door of Wanamaker alumnus and Chicago advertising veteran Joseph R. Hamilton.

Hamilton found himself called to Washington, D.C., where he took up duties late that year as the newly appointed head of information for the Works Progress Administration (WPA). Joe and Gussie's removal to Washington followed on the heels of the sale of the Drewrys USA Cor-poration to the Muessel Brewery of South Bend, Indiana, in early 1937—a time at which many American breweries were closing or offering them-selves for sale in the wake of pressure to rationalize the newly revived industry.[40] Proceeds from the sale supported Joe's short-lived attempt at retirement, as they did the decision of son-in-law (and company trea-surer) Charles Cushman to take time off from his own work and travel west with Jean, in what proved to be the first leg of his decades-long avocation as a traveling photographic observer of the American scene.

Hamilton arrived at a WPA newly brought under the direction of Col. Francis C. Harrington, who had replaced Harry Hopkins as commissioner of the agency in December 1938. Harrington, an engineer, inherited the charge of bolstering the WPA against a rising tide of conservative criticism for its alleged leftist sympathies and wasteful spending. As the larger national economic emergency waned, Harrington and his successor, Howard Hunter (who would become a close friend to Steinbeck), set about trimming some of the WPA's more visible—and controversial— programs, including the Federal Theatre Project. In Hamilton, they found a spokesman for their new direction—one who represented at once experience in assessing and shaping public opinion, and a faith (demonstrated well in the text of the *True Story* ads) in the ability of the business and managerial classes to restore the economy through cooperative, voluntary effort.[41]

Left to continue under the diminished New Deal was the Farm Security Administration's (FSA) Historical Section of the Division of Information, headed since 1935 by Roy Stryker, the Columbia economics professor who had in the 1920s helped Rexford Tugwell to select the images that would create a new kind of textbook for students of American economics. Stryker had assembled, since his arrival at the agency first known as the Resettlement Administration, a team of photographers to whom he assigned the task of documenting the need for—and beneficial impact of—the programs initiated under Roosevelt's New Deal. Echoing the sentiment of Archer Wall Douglas's treatise for traveling salesman, and advised by—among other social observers—*Middletown* coauthor Robert Lynd, the economist had insisted that his photographers, similarly, "should know something about economics, history, political science, philosophy and sociology."[42] The FSA photographic team, which included at various times Ben Shahn, Russell Lee, Carl Mydans, Arthur Rothstein, Gordon Parks, Marion Post Wolcott, and Jack Delano (who replaced Rothstein after the latter departed for commercial work at *Look*), in addition to Lange and Evans, found its work reproduced not only in government publications but also in the news media and in the new picture books, such as MacLeish's, appearing at the same time. The FSA photographers' efforts rendered particularly strongly the tension between social criticism, economic reportage, and pictorial patriotism that characterized the documentary photography of the 1930s. For Delano and others of like sympathies, the assignment invited a chance to apply artistic skills to a reform agenda: "Here was art," he later recalled, "seriously concerned with the plight of the dispossessed, the needy, and the landless." Yet the entire operation, viewed in another light, represented an effort to enhance through personal appeal the support given a federal project—disaster relief—that offered specific and temporary assistance to those most affected by the Depression without upsetting the economic status quo.[43] The task of securing populist political support for the larger endeavor (funding for which had exceeded $9 billion in the period from the WPA's inception in 1935 to the end of 1939, when Harrington called for a general review of the agency's costs and benefits) having been largely accomplished, Hamilton came in to "tackle the problem of trying to break down a mutual antagonism existing between the business world and the WPA."[44] In a manner that would have come easily to the director of *True Story*'s pro-business ad campaigns, Hamilton had come to Washington to sell New Deal relief as a good business proposition. Stryker's team's pictures, marketed through *Life* and other media venues, would—regardless of the social or artistic ideals of the artists themselves—help him to make his case.

Cushman and his cousin, John Steinbeck, exemplified the divergent directions in which common experiences—a passion for documentary depiction, an interest in encompassing the national experience through travel—could direct themselves in 1930s America. The two men represented, in this sense, not only the divergence of Joe Hamilton's artistic and business temperaments in the lives of his two aptest pupils, but also the dual audiences to which the WPA's documentary programs had to appeal. Steinbeck, for his part, had visited the residents of FSA-sponsored work camps in California's Central Valley since 1936, as he prepared the newspaper series first serialized in the San Francisco *News*

under the title, "The Harvest Gypsies" (1936), and later published col-
lectively in a brochure known as "Their Blood is Strong" (1938). In the
summer of 1937, he had traveled east to Washington, D.C., where he
enjoyed access to the FSA/RA photographic archives and received a
promise of federal assistance in his ongoing research on the migrant
situation. Returning west via Chicago, he visited with the Hamiltons before proceeding home to California via U.S. Route 66. These experiences
contributed to the literary portraits of the Joad family as they appeared
in the novel that gestated through this period, *The Grapes of Wrath*, which
enjoyed immediate acclaim on its publication in the spring of 1939. With
the book out from under him, Steinbeck faced sudden and, he claimed,
unwelcome celebrity status. In response, he spent some weeks in the
early fall of that year "just driving and stopping and sleeping" across the
West with his wife, Carol, then turning east and once again staying with
the Hamiltons in Chicago, where he took some time to work with director
Pare Lorentz in *The Fight for Life*, a documentary film about childbirth
and health care. In June of 1940, after a stint in Mexico, Steinbeck saw
the Hamiltons yet again, this time at their rented home on Hillyer Street
near Dupont Circle in Washington, where the now-well-known author
met with his now-well-placed uncle, as well as with President Roosevelt
himself, in an effort to garner government support for his proposal to
produce anti-Nazi propaganda films for Latin American audiences.[45]

Steinbeck's cousins Jean and Charles likewise spent much of the
late 1930s on the road together, but they left behind a different sort of
record. From spring 1937 through early 1941, the Cushmans traveled
nearly continuously: through the West from the Mexican border to Vancouver; back to the Midwest; south to Miami; briefly back home, then
west again to California and the desert Southwest; east to Jean's parents' Washington house (where they overlapped with Steinbeck on another of his visits with FDR, in September 1940); home to Chicago. Along
the way, Cushman indulged the photographic interests he had developed in his New York sojourn, if not earlier. His images from the first year
of his travels were black-and-white scenic views, the best of which

19. "Clouds after Sunset, Farm near Eureka [California]," 1938

he had custom printed by commercial photo studios (fig. 19). California, and particularly San Francisco—where Cushman's mother Mabel had lived with her husband Adolphe Roome since at least 1930, and where Jean's Moskowitz relatives lived still—constituted the center of their spiraling itineraries. Despite their frequent presence in northern California, no evidence suggests that the couple visited with Steinbeck at his Los Gatos home, where for much of 1937–39 the writer sat immersed, alternatively, in the tasks of drafting *The Grapes of Wrath* and of entertaining a steady stream of Hollywood visitors. Nor do Charles's extant images reveal anything of the same concerns—for migrant labor, for the trials of work in the fields or life in the camps—that Cushman would have read about in Steinbeck's book or seen in the photographs, published in *Life* in Spring 1939, that staff photographer Horace Bristol had taken on his travels with Steinbeck to the Visalia area in 1937–38. If anything, the contrasting records kept by the two men of their crisscrossing itineraries— one in literature, the other in image—suggest the contingency of our eventual visual memory of the Depression, and the degree to which it

depends upon the published record of writers and artists seeking to promote specific agendas. This suggestion evidences itself, as I will explain,
not only in the choice of subject matter, but also in the means through
which those subjects are rendered.[46]

Cushman's 1937–41 photographic collection is weighted heavily
with the standard tourist repertory of wilderness scenery. He and Jean
made a point of visiting Glacier and Yellowstone National Parks on their
1938 travels out of San Francisco; the Smoky Mountains as they headed
north from a Miami vacation in the early months of 1939; and, one year
later, Bryce, Zion, and the Grand Canyon as part of a season spent in the
Southwest (figs. 20–22). The possibilities of color particularly fascinated
Cushman in the Southwest, where morning and evening shadows across
great expanses like the Grand Canyon afforded him the opportunity to
capture the full range of hues for which such sites were known.

Yet he began to show a knack for doing something more, as well. At
Yavapai Point, on the canyon's south rim, he positioned his tripod one
autumn morning in 1939, setting the timer and stepping into the picture

20. "Abiathar and The Thunderer in
late evening." Yellowstone Park, 1938

21. (Opposite, top) Charles and Jean
Cushman, Hotel Wofford, Miami
Beach, 1939

22. (Opposite, bottom) Grand Canyon
from the South Rim, 1940

frame in time for the exposure (fig. 23). The artist stands at the left side of the picture, gazing east from beneath the shadows of a broad-brimmed fedora, as though having just pulled back the curtain on the scene spread before him. One of the iconic views of American nature (a status due, in part, to the rise of American business—specifically, the promotional work of the Santa Fe Railroad earlier in the century) is here subsumed in the self-portrait of this cosmopolitan man, surveying his land. In his sport coat, pleated wool slacks, rep tie, and hat, Cushman looks well suited for lunch at Chasen's, cocktails at 21, or—as may have been the case on that November morning—breakfast at the El Tovar Hotel. Like his well-polished cars, which figure prominently in many of the photographs of the early travels, Cushman's attire signals a sense of distance from even his closest surroundings, a measure of pride in the style and the knowl-edge and the wealth that have brought him to this place far from his small-town roots or his big-city jobs, and that will allow him once again to leave it. As in his views of other western sites, his lens trains itself on the culturally framed, "natural" view itself—not on the infrastructure that

23. Charles Cushman, Yavapai Point, Grand Canyon, 1939

The personal nature of Cushman's photography distinguished even those images that resembled the work of professional documentarians at the same time.

24. Grand Canyon of the Colorado River, Grand Canyon, Arizona. Russell Lee, 1940.

helped him to arrive there, on the people (four separate CCC teams in the Grand Canyon alone) whose labor makes the site accessible, or on the commercial world that inevitably arises in the wake of tourist traffic.[47] Unlike Russell Lee, visiting the same site on assignment for the FSA a year later, Cushman's vantage point takes us down from the canyon rim, placing both him and his viewer further into the dramatic scene (fig. 24). A documentary impulse motivates both men's photographs—but in the case of Cushman, working for no one but himself, that impulse turns itself explicitly to the task of self-documentation.

"I am in it and I don't pretend not to be." Those are the words with which Steinbeck, writing a decade after his cousin's Grand Canyon portrait, reflected on the manuscript soon to become *East of Eden*.[48] Every work reveals its writer, the novelist explained to editor Pascal Covici; owning up to that fact, Steinbeck believed, he could discover—and reveal—himself in the Hamilton family saga without ever appearing as a character. It was through something akin to the same process that Charles Cushman learned to reveal himself in his art without showing his face. As

25. Boulder Dam, 1939

the post-Drewrys travels continued, Cushman developed a style and a focus that eventually became as self-revelatory as the portrait beside the Grand Canyon. The man himself rarely appeared before his own lens, but as he and Jean pointed their car across the countryside, through the small towns, and into the cities, his collected views began to take on the recognizable dimensions of a life's project.

What were the distinctive terms of Cushman's vision? From his 1938 trip through the ends of his travels in the mid-1960s, he showed the world as it appeared before him—a fact that explains the mundanity, and the relative lack of political import, of many of his views in comparison with those of the professional documentarians of mid-century America (figs. 25–27). While we are accustomed to believing, with one historian of the New Deal landscape, that the WPA and related projects "definitively shaped the nation's topography," few sites along Cushman's prewar itinerary would have suggested as much. He did stop to see the Grand Coulee and Boulder Dams, and he did travel through some of the nation's most impoverished rural and urban areas, but even

26. (Opposite) Elephant Towers and Tower of the Sun, Golden Gate International Exposition, San Francisco, 1940

so, he likely found, along with his professional counterparts in the FSA, that the Depression and the New Deal did not push themselves into vision at every turn.[49] Without a specific brief akin to the famous "shooting scripts" handed by Stryker to his photographers—a mandate to seek out breadlines or migrant camps or other such obvious emblems of Depression—Cushman chanced upon either the era's symptoms, or its federally subsidized cures, only as he did many other sorts of scenes. Of equal interest, to him, were the sorts of amusements that entertained millions of others at the time—San Francisco's 1939 Golden Gate International Exposition, for instance, circus scenes, and historic-railroad fairs. The blandishments of the American landscape were attraction enough, in good times or bad. And finally, much of the life of urban, rural, and small-town America presented a pedestrian and relatively unchanging aspect through both the Depression and the period of prosperity that followed it.

Hard times retained, for the Cushmans as for other Americans who had managed to avoid them, a "picturesque" quality that seems to have

27. Main St., Poseyville, Indiana, 1945

28. Johnstown, Pennsylvania, 1940

done more to attract his eye than did any identifiable political motivation. It also comprised a common theme, uniting otherwise disparate views of farm field and city street (figs. 28–30). In the mill towns of Pennsylvania and the farm fields and cities of the South, the Southwest, and the Mexican border, Cushman framed scenes of hardship and perseverance. Yet these scenes comprise, in his own work, less the building blocks of a systematic case (either against the cruelties of capitalism or in favor of the beneficence of the New Deal) than they are little keepsakes—human-interest stories of life on the margins that could have been found in equal abundance ten years earlier or—as Cushman continued to find them throughout his travels—twenty years hence. While there is nothing random in his fondness for scenes of poverty and decay, their setting within a broader range of scenes—both rural and urban—of abundance, amusement, beauty, or simple everyday-ness reminds us of the limitations of professionally made visual images as documents of the Depression and wartime crisis as it played out in the minds and eyes of many Americans.

29. (Over) Nogales, Mexico, 1952

30. Eutaw, Alabama, 1941

A few of Cushman's black-and-white images, in particular (the last of which date from the 1938–39 trips) do resemble the sort of straightforward descriptive quality of the work taking place in Stryker's Historical Section (figs. 31, 32). The best of these images—a street view of the Savannah Cotton Exchange, a straight-on view of two Charleston women cleaning out their possessions in front of a house—would not look out of place among the work of the better-known professionals of the period. But the far more numerous color images, which commenced in 1938 and continued for thirty more years, touch on what would become a familiar, and increasingly personal, set of motifs: people (usually women, children, or elderly men) passing the photographer on the streets of old urban neighborhoods; the buildings of those neighborhoods, often in some state of desertion or decay; images of the road itself, sometimes showing the family car set against a backdrop of farms, ranches, or wilderness; and establishing shots of towns and cities, taken from the vantage of a nearby hill or other viewpoint on the way into or out of town.

31. House Cleaning, Calhoun St.,
Charleston, South Carolina, 1939

More generally, Cushman's carefully archived slide boxes and their accompanying notes, all of which remain, illuminate the geographic and temporal continuities of his photographic experience, giving us a sense of the movement that connected single images into a larger passage through time and space (fig. 33). Knowing, as we do, Cushman's complete routes—as opposed to the reconstructed, redacted itineraries of Margaret Bourke-White or other road photographers whose work appeared in condensed form—offers some perspective on the rhythm of the modern landscape in which he had been raised and on which he trained his eye as an adult.

32. (Opposite) Savannah Cotton
Exchange, 1939

Cushman recorded the location,
shutter speed, and aperture of every
photograph that he took. Having
his complete notebooks, we can
reconstruct in entirety his itineraries
across three decades of travel.

33. Charles Cushman notebook,
Jan. 9, 1952

PORTFOLIO: FROM THE COUNTRYSIDE TO THE CENTRAL CITY

Cushman's photographs, sequentially arranged, reveal a world characterized by the continual passage of goods and people from the central city, to
the urban periphery, to small towns and rural landscapes, and back again.
The fluidity with which Charles and Jean moved from one such setting to
the other in their travels mirrors, in a way, the ease with which he and other
twentieth-century Americans like him moved, in the course of their lives,
from the farm and small-town environments in which they were born into
the metropolitan sphere. Charting a route along two-lane highways, he
traversed a landscape that encompassed the arc of his own career from
small-town boy to urbanite—a landscape that still reflected, in its basic
contour, the hierarchy of agricultural regions, market towns, and urban
trade and manufacture centers that had been set in place by people like
his grandparents in Posey County or Samuel Hamilton's clan in the Salinas
River valley. In the countryside, Cushman finds relatively small farms,
tilled either by motorized tractors (by 1945 a presence on half or more of
American farms, at least outside of the South) or by animal-drawn vehicles;
they give onto small towns like Poseyville, Indiana, and striving cities such
as Sioux Falls, South Dakota, as the state or county highway transforms
itself into a central Main Street crowded with the buildings in which
residents of the region meet their banking and retail needs.[50] Scattered
across the countryside, too, Cushman came upon evidence of the great
agricultural and extractive industries—coal in the Midwest, oil or ores in
the Southwest—that supplied the materials for the industrial processing
plants that he photographed along the edges of metropolises like Chicago.
In smaller cities like Johnstown, Pennsylvania, or Birmingham, Alabama,
these edges also provided the photographer with a vantage from which to
view the city as he entered it—vantages that confirmed the persistence
of the essential structure of the industrial city well into the postwar era.
Continuing past the industrial edges, into the neighborhoods, he documented the range of housing—from laborers' flats, to the office workers'
apartment houses, to the mill owners' mansions—that had been established by the end of the previous century. Further in still, he depicted the
central business districts—domain of the stores that Joe Hamilton had

34. View from near Sawtooth
Mountain, Highway 166, Texas, 1951

worked to publicize and of the offices of men like him and Cushman—
where the riches of the countryside and the labor of the worker were
mingled and abstracted into capital, real estate, and cultural spectacle.
From the city center it was back out into the countryside, once again.
Taken together, the sequences of images resembled a would-be FSA
assignment less than they did a photographic version of the old *Business
Bulletin* maps, with Cushman highlighting the interconnected landscape of
American business and industry and linking it, in the process, to his own
path from childhood to adulthood.

Cushman logged most of his half-million miles on rural highways, many of which had existed in one form or another since before the advent of motorized traffic. These two-lane roads appear to sink into, rather than dominate, the landscapes of Cushman's photographs.

35. U.S. Highway 89A near Sedona, Arizona, 1952

36. (Opposite, top) California Highway 150 from Santa Barbara to San Marcos Pass, 1952

37. (Opposite, bottom) Marrs Township, Posey County, Indiana, 1941

38. (Opposite, top) Cotton Pickers along U.S. 67 near Cumby, Texas, 1953

39. (Opposite, bottom) Farm, west of Harrisburg, Pennsylvania, 1941

40. Workers' Housing, Billeaud Sugar Factory, Broussard, Louisiana, 1951

Cushman, himself raised "pretty close to the soil," documented the range of midcentury agriculture: company mills and homesteads; migrant workers and family laborers; motorized tractors and animal-drawn wagons.

Cushman's eye for sites associated with the extraction and processing of minerals reflects the businessman's perspective that distinguished his photographs from those of more casual travelers. Once arrived at the edge of town, Cushman often pulled the car over to record the prospect of stores, banks, and hotels along Main Street.

41. (Previous spread) Coal Tailings, Highway 63, Perrysville, Indiana, 1946

42. Richardson Carbon Black factory, Odessa, Texas, 1959

43. Pyrite Mine, Etowah, Georgia, 1951

44. Main Street, Shawneetown, Illinois, 1949

45. Bisbee, Arizona, 1959

46. (Over) Phillips Avenue, Sioux
Falls, South Dakota, 1959

47. (Opposite, top) View North from
Radio Station WBRC, Birmingham,
Alabama, 1951

48. (Opposite, bottom) Johnstown,
Pennsylvania, 1940

49. Carnegie-Illinois Steel
Corporation South Works,
South Chicago, Illinois, 1958

Approaching larger cities, Cushman sought out an overlook along steep hillsides that had
provided local manufacturers with a source of water power or mineral ores. At the urban
edge, he also found the great processing plants that had been forced out from more
valuable land in the city center.

50. (Oposite, top) S. Santa Fe Street, El Paso, Texas, 1952

51. (Opposite, bottom) Cameron Hill, Chattanooga, Tennessee, 1951

52. Annapolis, Maryland, 1940

Moving toward the city center, Cushman passed through the older residential areas that still clustered closely around downtown. Here, in the days before streetcar or automobile travel opened up distant property for development, the mansions of the mill owner had stood not far from the tenements of his workers.

In a few cities, such as New Orleans or New York, conservation laws or a sheer continued demand for land would arrest the turnover and decay of inner-city neighborhoods, leaving blocks that looked much the same in Cushman's time as they do today.

53. St. Phillip Street, New Orleans, Louisiana, 1951

54. (Opposite) Jackson Square, New Orleans, 1959

55. (Over) Broome Street and Baruch Place, New York, New York, 1941

At the heart of the American city, the early twentieth-century central business district was a place of consumption, display, and sometimes discard. Downtown accommodated large-scale retailers and their customers, highrise office tenants, entertainment audiences, government workers, and—along its fringes—a population of single or transient workers.

56. "Three bums from South Ferry flophouses," New York, New York, 1941

57. (Opposite) Garrick Theatre, St. Louis, Missouri, 1949

58. Transit Tower, San Antonio, Texas, 1951

59. (Opposite, top) Main Street, Los Angeles, California, 1952

60. (Opposite, bottom) Rodeo Parade, Tucson, Arizona, 1940

In 1951, Cushman stopped near the foot of Atlanta's Peachtree Street to photograph Coca Cola's Neon Spectacular—erected by the home-town company three years earlier. A later stay in New York placed him above Herald Square, home to the retail giants that had recently put Wanamaker's New York branch—opened when Joseph Hamilton was with the company—out of business.

61. Peachtree Street, Atlanta, Georgia, 1951

62. (Opposite) Chrysler and Empire State Buildings, seen from the Gov. Clinton Hotel, New York, New York, 1960

Idiosyncratic as were his subjects and his itineraries, Cushman's equipment itself distinguished his approach from that of the men and women who made their living producing images of American society at the time. He carried on his journeys a new Contax IIA 35 mm "minicamera"— one of the instruments of choice of a small number of professional and serious amateur photographers of the day (fig. 63). Like its chief rival, the Leica, the Contax (introduced in 1931) featured small, "fast" lenses (capable of responding to a wide range of light conditions and of maintaining focus across a deeper picture plane) and a light weight, enabling its user to carry it easily and to set quickly his focus and exposure. The minicameras were one more innovation of the information age that had been pioneered by manufacturers like Addressograph and heralded by journals like *Your Money* and the *Business Bulletin*. Contax's manufacturer, Germany's Zeiss Ikon, was the same company that had earlier pioneered optical machinery for automated statistical analysis, an innovation of which Cushman had likely been aware during his work for Standard Statistics. For a device with seemingly recreational applications, the new

63. Charles Cushman's Contax II A viewfinder camera

minicameras—optical recording devices as sophisticated, in their way, as the early Zeiss calculators—were, as *Fortune* editors put it, "a costly hobby" in the mid-1930s. Of an estimated 20 million cameras in use in the United States, minicameras numbered only 100,000; at an average retail price of $245, they seemed unlikely to capture a larger market share any time soon.[51] Inevitably, professionals comprised a certain percentage of what the press termed the "minicamers," although the new equipment was likely to appeal particularly to those among them not already steeped in traditional photographic careers. Russell Lee, for example, bought his first Contax in 1935, just as he was turning to photography from his earlier careers as a chemical engineer and artist. Ben Shahn, a commercial engraver before he turned first to painting and finally to photography, later recalled convincing his brother to buy him a Leica after receiving the most cursory of lessons ("'Look, Ben, there's nothing to it'") from his studio-mate Walker Evans.[52] For Lee, Shahn, and other photographic innovators, the new, smaller cameras helped to facilitate a shift away from formal composition and posed portraiture, and toward spontaneous street photography. But the photographic and popular press treated the new machinery more as a democratizing influence than as a professional prerogative. "It is our opinion, and it is not unique to us," wrote the editors of the new magazine *Photo Technique* in 1939, "that the hope of the professional lies in the amateur."[53] Small but sophisticated cameras would take documentary work out of the exclusive domain of the professional, and in the process, put greater technical capability in the hands of dedicated amateur observers—men who, like Charles Cushman, might decide to turn their attention to "the floral life of the Amazon valley," if moved to do so.

Cushman further differentiated himself from the ranks of professional documentarians by his choice of film. The drive across the Golden Gate Bridge on that September day in 1938 marked the start of his thirty-year experiment with the technical and artistic capabilities of Kodachrome color transparencies. The ability of the new product's "living color" to render more real the images captured upon its surface made

Kodachrome a natural choice for someone seeking to show the world as he believed it to be. To some in the photographic establishment, however, it signaled a diversion from the formal essence that constituted their ultimate quest. To take color photographs in the 1930s and 1940s was to make not only a visual but also a sociological statement.

The search for a means to photograph the world in its color, rather than in shades of gray, had occupied photographers since the craft's mid-nineteenth-century beginnings. Steinbeck himself, likely drawing from his Uncle Joe's recollections, would describe in *East of Eden* one such experimenter, a man identified only as "Anderson," who had married Joe's oldest sister, Euna Hamilton, in the 1890s. The new family member appears briefly, in the novelist's rendering, as "an intense dark man—a man whose fingers were stained with chemicals, mostly silver nitrate. He was one of those men who lived in poverty so that their lives of questioning may continue. His question was about photography. He believed that the exterior world could be transferred to paper—not in the ghost shadings of black and white but in the colors the human eye perceives . . . in the end, it is said, he found what he wanted—color film . . . he took her away to the north, and it was black and lost where he went— somewhere on the borders of Oregon."[54]

Steinbeck's suggestion of a sorcerer, plying his black art in the distant forest, strikes an intriguing and troubling note in his larger saga of ranch-country family life. Its mood and mystery stem in some part, perhaps, from a simple lack of information about Euna's married life, and in larger part from the fact that Euna had died, possibly by her own hand, a short time after her marriage—an episode that functions in the book as a trigger for the decline of the aging family patriarch, Samuel Hamilton. But the passage also carries an echo of the suspicion directed from a variety of quarters toward those who would seek too greedily to comprehend in their art the full reality of the physical world—the "thing," to borrow again from Wallace Stevens, rather than "the version of the thing." For these critics of the new color-film technology, the representation of color on film was an inevitably artificial process that, in hiding its artifice behind the allure of realism, could only lessen the photographer's unique contribution to a new and original art form.

The task of succeeding where Steinbeck's obsessive uncle had left off was finally accomplished, not incidentally, under the direction of two amateurs. Leopold Mannes and Leo Godowsky, both professional musicians, had worked independently on the challenge since the late 1910s. In 1930, the two received an invitation to join Eastman Kodak's Rochester, New York, laboratory. Building on efforts by Kodak and other companies to expose chemically treated surfaces separately to each of the three color components of the light spectrum, Mannes and Godowsky managed the task of binding onto a single piece of film three color-receptive layers, each of which filtered out, or "subtracted," a specific color so that, together, they could reveal an image in the full spectrum.[55] Kodak first applied the new subtractive technique to its 16 mm movie film, which the company released in 1935. Kodachrome 35 mm still-camera film, offered commercially the following year, promised a wider potential market but still came with some impediments to mass-market success. The first version of the film came back to consumers in the form of transparent strips of images, each of which had to be cut manually and mounted within frames by the photographer for viewing in a slide projector. In 1938, the company removed a portion of this impediment by returning the developed exposures premounted in individual cardboard sleeves.

Professional photographers responded to Kodak's innovation with less than the enthusiasm that one might have expected in response to a breakthrough so long in the making. German film director Ernst Lubitsch, anticipating the arrival of color motion picture film, acknowledged that while color might prove appropriate for "fantasy" movies, only black-and-white photography would suit "'those films which attempt to place their emphasis on naturalism.'" Evans, known for his stark tonal contrasts and formal compositions, later complained that "color photographers confuse color with noise"; his younger counterpart Robert Frank later stated baldly that "black and white are the colors of photography."[56]

Museum of Modern Art curator Beaumont Newhall, author in 1938 of the first comprehensive critical history of photography, sounded a less judgmental, but still cautionary tone in regards to the new innovation. Writing of the "candid" picture best suited to the new minicamera, Newhall stressed that it "differs radically in its whole point of view from 'straight' photography"—the latter being the term he had coined for the sharp-focused, carefully composed black-and-white images produced by the likes of Evans, Edward Weston, and Berenice Abbott. Such straight works had, to Newhall's eye, already acquired a "classic" quality that promised to stand the test of time. Of color work, he could only say in contrast, "[i]t is too early to form any esthetic opinions." Newhall's survey, expanded, revised, and republished in his lifetime, eventually devoted still more attention to the straight tradition. As late as his 1964 edition, however, the author could still call color work the pursuit of amateurs, remarking that "[s]urprisingly few photographers . . . have chosen color as a means of personal expression." As if to emphasize the onus on color photographers to "express" something more than the visual reality of the scene before them, he warned that "[t]he esthetic problem is to define that which is essentially *photographic* in color photography." By lessening the distance between the pictured object and our knowledge of its true appearance, Newhall and others suggested, color film threatened the photographer's distinctive role as a creative mediator between the world and the image, as an artist capable of drawing a scene's formal or emotional essence out from behind its surface distractions and adornments.[57]

Newhall, Evans, and Frank's wariness of color as an appropriately sophisticated medium with which to document the landscape resonated with other trends in the artistic establishment of the 1930s. It bears notice, for instance, that their attitude dovetailed closely with the efforts of those architectural proponents of the movement known in Germany as the *Neue Sachlichkeit* and publicized in the United States, by Newhall's Museum of Modern Art colleague Philip Johnson, simply as the Modern Movement. For Walter Gropius, Ludwig Mies van der Rohe, Le Corbusier, and their American champions, white and black expressed an architecture stripped of its surface showiness, reduced to its elemental functions of shaping space. Le Corbusier had shown no compunction about doctoring the photographs in his 1923 manifesto, *Vers une architecture* (translated in the United States, in 1927, as *Towards a New Architecture*), yet he pointedly likened the integrity of his own work to that of a mythic time "when the cathedrals were white, above the nations in search of identity."[58]

Yet just as the multihued Art Deco–styled spires of the Golden Gate International Exposition—an event that Cushman visited and photographed, in color, on his 1940 stay in San Francisco (see fig. 26)—partook of a popular, "modernistic" contrast to the formal architectural world of Le Corbusier and Johnson, so did color photography itself offer an alternative to the monochrome starkness that, having once been imposed by technical limitations and prohibitive printing costs, would later be constructed as an artistic end in itself. "No spectator," wrote critic and filmmaker Lewis Jacobs, "whose emotions have been stirred by color, will ever be satisfied again by its pale echo, black and white." Speaking from the standpoint of the working photographer, *Photo Technique* pronounced that "[c]olor is the new medium for photographers. It is more difficult, more technical, more exciting than black and white." Most perceptively, photography educator and writer Herbert C. McKay offered a different take on Newhall's implicit judgment about expression and reality. Asking why, given Kodachrome's new availability, "our photographs are still largely the dull, drab black and white caricatures we have always known," McKay offered that "[p]erhaps the reason may be related to the fact that photography is an artistic convention . . . [With color, n]o longer do we have a conventional symbol; we have faithful reproduction." To assist them in the task of surpassing convention with fidelity, photographic publishing houses obliged sophisticated hobbyists with a steady offering of how-to books. In addition to their requisite instructions about exposure speeds, depths of field, and composition, these guides typically flattered the serious recreational photographers who constituted their ideal readership. "Thank your lucky stars," as German color-enthusiast Walther Benser put it, "that you are an amateur." (For their own part, amateurs organized local camera clubs in cities across the United States, sponsoring contests and exhibitions of their new color photographs and creating through social networks a measure of the respect and recognition that black-and-white-bound professionals seemed unlikely to extend their way.)[59]

Kodachrome being an expensive medium (at roughly $3.50 per roll, six times costlier than black-and-white 35 mm film), and color print film being as yet unavailable, color slides remained for amateur or professional alike a rarefied medium, one better suited to private exhibition (whether on a living room wall or a meeting room screen) than to public display. Farm Security Administration photographers took some color photographs (roughly 1400, less than 1 percent of their total negative count), but the cost associated with printing such images in the popular media ensured that most of these images remained unseen and ultimately forgotten. The editors of *Life*, the pace-setter among popular pictorial publications, delved only cautiously into the world of color, reserving its use in their earliest issues for features on art, the social scene, or entertainment. A full-color series of images of a chick developing in its egg, published in October 1937, extended the rhetoric of color to scientific features as well. News reportage continued to bespeak its own seriousness through the medium of black and white.[60]

To work with color film in the 1930s and 1940s, then, was to reveal something about one's background and one's ambitions. The ability to afford the medium—without expectation of profit from the sale or publication of one's photographs—indicated a measure of financial success. But using color in place of black and white also implied, to observers of the photographic scene, one's status as an amateur. For the middle-aged businessman Charles Cushman, aware of the growing aesthetic and political credence given black-and-white documentary photography, aware too that he would never join the ranks of the sorts of professionals who associated with his cousin and father-in-law, color slides conveyed an almost defiant expression of artistic will. They served one man's passion for depicting the world around him, at the same time that they side-stepped any perceived ambition to compete with the professionals who did the same. Cushman's photographic career paralleled his decision to write about—not play—college sports, as it did his later predilection for documenting—not taking part in—big business. Like the college journalist of the 1910s who had protested the futility of naming "the REAL" All Star team, only to set about doing just that, the amateur photographer of the 1930s demurred from the task of capturing the "real" America, even as his persistence suggested a strong desire to do so, and to do so more thoroughly and convincingly than those better-known artists whose works appeared in the pages of books and magazines or on the walls of museums.

AFTERNOON
Death at Midlife, 1941–1951

Cushman had ceased taking black-and-white pictures altogether by 1941, when Joe and Gussie returned from their Washington residence. Joe later wrote of having been "kicked off" the WPA staff, and Steinbeck's personal correspondence suggests that the advertising man's brief tenure as government bureaucrat had not been a happy one.[1] Hamilton supplemented his post-Washington income with a "quite lucrative" engagement for his old client (and subsequent New Deal foe) Bernarr Macfadden, this time drafting a weekly unsigned editorial, headed "We, The People," which kicked off each issue of the publisher's *Liberty* Magazine for the better part of 1942. In his *Liberty* essays, Hamilton added a flavoring of wartime urgency to his customary paeans (evident since the Wanamaker's days) to the virtues of American consumerism, labor/management cooperation, and self-reliance.[2]

At about the same time Charles, possibly facing the end of his profits from the Drewrys sale, found work in the Liquidation Division of the Custodian of Alien Property, a federal office that employed as many as 1,200 men and women in its Chicago headquarters between its establishment in March 1942 and its removal to New York two years later. Cushman was well compensated for his financial skills, earning some $316 weekly (roughly three times the average salary of a professional WPA employee of the time) for attending to the sale of everything "from postage stamps to railroad trains" seized from Axis-based companies or individual investors. Bigger than stamps or railroad trains alike were the American assets of the Zeiss Ikon Corporation, which the custodian's office vested in August 1942. We can only guess at Cushman's response to the prospect of appropriating for the U.S. government the profits obtained from sales to him and his fellow American photographers of his favored cameras and lenses.[3]

In June 1941, the Hamiltons bought a house at 56th Street and Kenwood Avenue, a leafy block of professors' homes beside the University of Chicago campus (fig. 65). That fall, Charles and Jean gave up their apartment on nearby South Shore Boulevard. Possibly inspiring his father-in-law's subsequent caution to a ration-constrained American

64. Maxwell Street near Morgan Street, Chicago, 1949. Following their travels in the late 1930s, Charles and Jean settled back in Chicago. In the decade that followed he crafted a melancholy portrait of the aging corners of his adoptive city.

public ("Certainly we shall travel . . . But fifty miles, seventy-five miles, is as good as five hundred"), Cushman took Jean out of town once again, this time for several months of what he later described as "some extensive traveling"—east to New England, New York, and Pennsylvania, through the South to New Orleans, then back home again to the Hamiltons' house in Hyde Park, where the couple established their new residence.[4]

Since returning to Chicago from his prewar travels, Cushman had begun to explore the city itself with the same restless gaze (and the same Zeiss Ikon camera and lenses) that he had previously reserved for farther-flung sites. His eye for local attractions settled first, in the spring and summer of 1941 before he undertook his work for the Alien Property Custodian, on a new subject that would remain a fascination for the rest of his life (figs. 66–71). Apparently leaving Jean at home, he ventured out along the South Shore beaches on warm afternoons, convincing good-looking young women in their bathing suits to pose for his camera, then

recording their names in the same small, brown-covered spiral notebooks in which he had written all of his meticulous camera notes (including details of the date, site, aperture, and shutter speed of every photograph). Soon the names or descriptions of Cushman's beach rendezvous filled pages: "Anni Sokal-discovered on Promontory P.-55th St."; "Light and Dark Meat-Promontory Visitors."[5] Now in his mid-40s, caring for aging in-laws and temporarily adrift in his professional life, Cushman had found in his camera a means for establishing contact—from behind the protective screen of his rangefinder—not only with the sites of his fascination with the American system in which he had grown up, but with the women whose inviting smiles, supple bodies, and bright clothes also connected him in some way to the youth that the events of early 1943 would force him at last to leave behind.

On January 3, Joseph Hamilton suffered a fatal heart attack. Steinbeck, living in Los Angeles as he worked fitfully on government writing commissions and prepared for the filming of the screen adaptation of his war-themed play *The Moon is Down*, received the news in a cable

65. Hamilton-Cushman House, 5557 Kenwood Avenue, Chicago, 1946

66. "American Airlines stewardess, Doris Irwin, takes sun," 1941

Some of the young women who posed for Cushman along the South Shore lakefront appeared on repeated occasions, sharing their names and perhaps a bit of their life stories; others, identified only by a first name or a brief (and occasionally offensive) caption, appeared once and vanished.

from his older sister, Esther. He quickly telegraphed his condolence to Gussie and then, the next day, tried to tell his aunt more of his feelings. "[H]undreds of little pictures and gestures and tones and laughter" ran through his head, he wrote, and yet no words seemed enough. To Esther, he opened up a bit further. "He was the last of his generation wasn't he," Steinbeck reflected in a letter, adding that "I wish he had never gone to Washington. That made him unhappy. He wanted something he couldn't get." Hamilton's obituaries proved less revealing. They duly noted his long and prominent career in advertising and government service, mentioned his famous nephew, but said nothing of his impact as a creative muse, father figure, and financial benefactor to his son-in-law, the unknown, itinerant photographer.[6] Nor could they predict the effect of Hamilton's death upon his only child, Jean. For evidence of the last fact, we have only her own words, as reported by Chicago newspapers two months later.

On the night of March 19, Charles sat working in his study on the third floor of the Hamilton house on Kenwood. Jean called to him from

67. "Anni Sokal—from Dusseldorf—
tans her legs at promontory," 1941

68. "Pictures of Annette, girl in yellow
bathing suit," 1942

69. "Eunice in mid-August sun," 1942

below. Walking to the head of the stairs, he recalled, he heard her say "something about going away." As he turned back toward his desk she followed him. "The next thing I heard two revolver shots," Cushman later said. Both bullets hit him in the head. As he collapsed, Jean turned the gun on herself, firing a shot into her own mouth. Cushman managed to stagger to the home of his next-door neighbor, Dr. Daniel McMillan, as Jean somehow called the police from a telephone on the second floor. By the time officers arrived on the scene, McMillan was administering first aid and family friend and lawyer Angus Roy Shannon was already present to handle their questions.[7]

"I am of an unhappy disposition," Jean told officers that night at Hyde Park's Illinois Central Hospital, where both she and her husband lay recuperating from their wounds, "and thought it would be nice to die. I didn't want to leave without him and I tried to kill him and my-self." Cushman added that Jean's father's death two months earlier had placed her under even greater emotional strain than normal. "[A]ll she had in mind was to kill me and herself," he confirmed.[8]

70. "Light and dark meat. Promontory visitors, 1941."

It could not have been a complete surprise. Moskowitz family lore holds that Gussie's mother, Amelia, had died a suicide while staying in Chicago with her daughter and son-in-law, Gussie and Joe; a search through San Francisco newspaper records reveals that Amelia's brother, Herman, had taken his own life in 1904.[9] The self-inflicted death of Joe's brother Tom, in Salinas, would later appear as a key feature of Steinbeck's *East of Eden*. At some time—maybe many times—in Jean's past, her own "unhappy disposition" must have revealed itself to those close to her. Perhaps it had done so in the form of chronic moodiness, perhaps through other violent outbursts, less spectacular in their results but not altogether different in their intensity from the events of March 19. Cushman's personal files, so meticulous in recording the particulars of each of his fourteen thousand photographs, each oil and tire changes given his automobiles, each purchase of a new lens or light meter and each ticket to a college football game, yield not a clue as to his wife's problems.

The silence tells its own story, of course, even if we cannot be certain of that story's plot line. Knowing the eruption of sadness and vio-

lence that would surface in the nineteenth year of their marriage, we can wonder anew about the reasons for the couple's quick retreat from New York—where Jean had lived, for the first time in her life, away from her parents. We can speculate that the months-long trips together, in the years that followed, represented Charles's attempt either to take Jean's mind off her troubles or, quite differently, to give himself a break from the tensions of daily life together (albeit one that required him to keep her close by, just in case). We can ask whether the growth in Charles of a near-obsessive preoccupation with the details of unfamiliar sites does not itself suggest a pattern of avoiding the world much nearer at hand. We can note that, in contrast to the ample images of women taking in the sun by the lake, Jean appears in no more than a dozen of the photographs Cushman took in the years and months before the shooting—and then either alongside Charles (in dual portraits likely taken, and possibly even suggested, by a friend or onlooker), or at a distance, as though present only to provide human scale for a viewer seeking to determine the size of a nearby building or height of an adjacent cactus. We can even question whether Jean's decision that evening was really the product of the perverse devotion ("I didn't want to leave without him") that she described, or was in fact a deliberate act motivated by some terrible resentment, some hatred for what he had done in the past. Could her actions suggest as much about his personality and his deeds as they do hers? Each speculative path, regardless of its final destination, leads at some point to the common realization that Jean's depression, invisible to the latter-day researcher but for a single day's sensational newspaper clippings, colored Cushman's view of the world around him as surely as did his own rural roots, or his business and journalism training. Like the tinted layers of his film that, bound together, produced a single, full-color image, the obvious artistic and documentary purposes of Cushman's pictures joined themselves to a third function, unseen: for a fractional second, each image opened onto an escape route—away from pain, from worry. Cushman disappeared momentarily into the newly framed scene, free from fear or guilt of leaving behind the people who depended upon him.

71. "Maria Grygier," 1949

He could do "something about going away," and he could soon come back. When the shutter closed again, the world around him returned.

In terms of the outward character of Cushman's life and the appearance of his photographs, however, Jean's actions and moods left little obvious trace. Rather than proving an irreparable rupture, the events that nearly ended their lives in March 1943 marked instead the beginning of a long second act of their marriage. As Jean's wounds healed, Charles brought her to Rogers Sanitarium in nearby Oconomowoc, Wisconsin (a town that four years earlier had hosted the world premiere of the film adaptation of former department-store window-dresser L. Frank Baum's novel, *The Wizard of Oz*). On Saturdays, Charles—finally noticing his wife?—snapped her picture among the trees and flowers on the hospital grounds or in the Morton Arboretum, outside Chicago. In contrast to the sylvan surroundings, her portraits from the period reflect the emotional toll taken by the events, and they suggest the physical damage, as well: the right side of her face appears stiff, perhaps the result of a paralyzed

Photographs taken before and after the 1943 shooting suggest its emotional and physical toll on Jean.

73. Jean Cushman, Morton Arboretum, Chicago, 1950

facial nerve. Her right eye, which wanders from the apparent direction of her gaze, may be artificial (fig. 73).

Cushman considered, and may have obtained, work at the War Department's Chicago Ordnance District after the 1944 removal of the Alien Property office to New York.[10] If he did acquire the job for which an application remains among his files, he may have left it by late that year or early the next, as his photographic records indicate that he took a number of pictures on weekdays.

PORTFOLIO: CHICAGO

Cushman's main collection of Chicago pictures, taken from 1943 to 1949—a period during which he appears to have left home only for the purpose of taking a few trips back to Posey County—favor several subjects: women, as I have mentioned; flowers, which I will not focus on other than to note his interest in the challenge that they present to the color photographer; and, most interestingly in retrospect, the city in a state of transformation. In a continuation of the pattern set in his already-extensive photographic travels, Cushman found his view drawn to the losing end of that transformation—to the disappearing, rather than emergent, landscape, to the structure of the city as it had evolved during the time in which his parents came of age and as it had remained when he himself arrived, a young man, in Chicago. Faced with the full diversity of the nation's Second City, his wandering eye came to rest on particular sites where the past lingered or seemed most imperiled: the aging Maxwell Street market area on the West Side, and, on the south, the streets of the old Black Belt, near his familiar South Shore and Hyde Park haunts. In 1949–50, in particular, as reports in each day's paper tracked the pending clearance of great tracts of South Side land for public housing, for publicly assisted private developments such as New York Life's Lake Meadows project, and for the new campus of the Illinois Institute of Technology, Cushman took to the streets, exploring along Drexel, Michigan, Dearborn, Wabash, South Park, State, and their side streets from the Loop south to Hyde Park. These were blocks where he had lived and worked as a younger man, blocks that he knew now would soon change or, in some cases, disappear altogether, as the South Side's original gridded landscape gave way to a super-block pastiche of plazas, walkways, and parking lots. On the West Side, where Jane Addams had established her legendary settlement house in the former Charles Hull mansion, similar plans brought expressways, new housing, and university buildings to a neighborhood once dominated by the busy pedestrian life of the Maxwell Street market.[11]

74. Mather Tower and Carbide Building from Rush Street, Chicago, 1941

Cushman captured the dynamic skyline of Chicago's late-1920s office building boom, when tapered skyscrapers stretched north from the Chicago River; a few blocks north and west he sought out remnants of nineteenth-century workers' housing.

75. 20 N. Wacker Drive (Civic Opera Building), Chicago, 1948

76. (Opposite) 505 N. Clark Street, Chicago, 1948

77. 400 block, Sullivan Street,
Chicago, 1946

78. (Opposite) 316 W. Erie Street,
Chicago, 1951

On the far South Side, steel mills and railyards dominated Cushman's views of the lakefront. Further inland the photographer encountered the rush-hour crash of a southbound streetcar and a gasoline truck.

79. "Day after street car crash and fire—33 dead, 6240 S. State Street," Chicago, 1950

80. (Opposite, top) Steel mills, Calumet River, Chicago, 1939

81. (Opposite, bottom) Carnegie South Works, 91st Street, Chicago, 1941

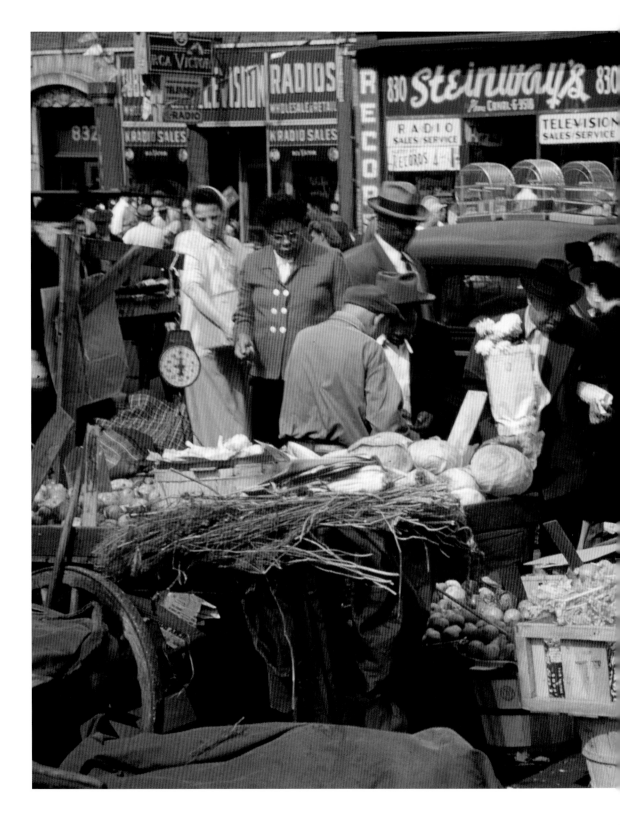

In 1889, Jane Addams had established Hull House "amidst the large foreign colonies" of the near west side. As early as 1943, city officials—envisioning an altogether different scale of neighborhood improvement—slated the area for demolition.

82. (Previous page) Newberry and Maxwell Streets, Chicago, 1950

83. Hull House, Chicago, 1950

84. (Opposite, top) Maxwell and Halsted Streets, Chicago, 1950

85. (Opposite, bottom) Maxwell Street near Miller Street, Chicago, 1944

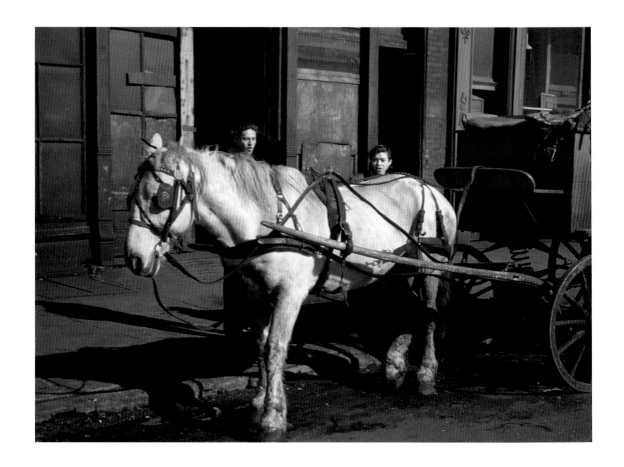

86. Horse and Wagon, W. 14th Street near Sangamon, Chicago, 1949

87. (Opposite, top) S. Throop Street near Adams Street, Chicago, 1949

88. (Opposite, bottom) 710 W. 14th Street, Chicago, 1949

89. (Over) Confectionary cart, Lexington and DeKalb Streets, Chicago, 1949

Cushman frequented blocks that
he knew were soon to give way to
publicly sanctioned demolition. As
newspapers projected images of a
modern city yet to come, he searched
for fragments of the old city soon to
perish.

90. Soda shack, 520 W. 13th Street,
Chicago, 1949

91. 3200 block, Rhodes Avenue,
Chicago, 1941

92. Otis House, 1709 Prairie Avenue,
Chicago, 1941

93. (Opposite) "Old Capone GHQ,"
2220 S. Dearborn Avenue, Chicago,
1944

As he set about the task of photographing the streets of Chicago, Cushman—by his own and others' accounts a charming and outgoing man—proved himself no ethnographer, nor even a particularly devoted portraitist. Aside from his ongoing preoccupation with the lakeshore bathing beauties, people—and not just Jean—appear seldom in his work, and then in a manner that suggests that their acquaintance with the photographer lasted for only a few seconds before and after the moment at which he opened his shutter. In contrast to a professional documentarian like Wayne Miller, whom the Guggenheim Foundation supported in his efforts to photograph "The Way of Life of the Northern Negro" in the postwar Bronzeville neighborhood, Cushman seems from his work along the same streets an interloper, a voyeur with little lasting interest in the lives of the people whose homes and businesses appear in his rangefinder. While he occasionally approaches children for direct portraits, he remains at a respectful distance from most of his human subjects, and all but a handful remain unidentified in his notes. The expansion of Bronzeville and the transition of the surrounding South Side from a White to an almost entirely African American neighborhood goes unremarked—except in the implicit awareness that Cushman carries with him as he walks long-familiar blocks. He was not oblivious to social and political issues—and the Hamilton's family friend, Angus Shannon, who had in 1940 represented the opponents to real estate agent Carl Hansberry in the latter man's efforts to integrate the Woodlawn neighborhood, represented an unusually close personal connection to one of the landmark moments of the northern Civil Rights struggle—but people, of any color, serve as ephemeral presences amidst a built environment whose slow decay remains his ultimate subject. Given the absence of a public audience for his work, social statements would have fallen on deaf ears, in any event. In their place, the personal memories and emotions associated with seeing changes in familiar streets would have spoken loudly enough for the artist—and his audience of one or two—to hear clearly.[12]

At the same time, however, Cushman's Chicago images show that he was no systematizer of the urban landscape. In contrast to another

94. 2944 S. Michigan Ave., Chicago, 1949

95. Enolia and Leonard Brown, Jr., 230 W. 23rd Street, Chicago, 1949

96. "Still tenanted," 3117 S. Wabash
Avenue, Chicago, 1949

professional photographer walking the same streets, Mildred Mead—
who documented before-and-after conditions for the city's Metropolitan
Housing and Planning Council—his images added up to no comprehensive statement of the need for social betterment or physical redevelopment. Each building, each storefront performs in Cushman's work as
a unique character, a collection of particular details that, in conjunction
with the abbreviated, often ironic captions that he scrawled in his brown
notebook, make up the dramatis personae of a script that remained
within his own head. The particular comparison of his images of the
"still-tenanted" rowhouse at 3117 S. Wabash (fig. 96) with Mead's photograph of the same site (fig. 97) makes the contrast clear: Mead posi-

tioned her camera at such an angle as to show the building as the final holdout in an otherwise-cleared landscape that awaits the development of the IIT campus; Cushman's photographs of the building focus on the home itself, capturing the detail of the makeshift store that projects from its ground floor and, in one case, of a woman—likely the same one who appears in Mead's image—returning through the door of the place that evidently still serves as home. We do not know her name, or how she earned her living on that day—but neither do we see her home as a blighted parcel whose existence retards the otherwise inevitable march of progress. There is, indeed, a great deal of "noise," to borrow Walker Evans's phrase, in the color and detail of images like those that Cushman took in front of 3117 S. Wabash. It is the noise of the city, a noise that echoes—for a few lingering weeks—off the walls of this urban remnant.

97. Mildred Mead. Illinois Institute of Technology, with 3117 Wabash Avenue in foreground.

TWILIGHT   California, 1952–1972

Jean was in and out of Oconomowoc in the years that followed the shooting. Neighborhood children knew her only as the dour, slightly palsied lady living in the home on the corner with her husband and aged mother. Pressed for any remaining memories more than fifty years later, one acknowledges sensing "something odd and a little scary" about the house, but nevertheless remembers Mrs. Cushman gratefully as the person who came to her aid after she hurt herself skipping rope on the street; her brother, a child of five in 1951, was the occasional beneficiary of offerings of milk and cookies in the Cushman kitchen.[1]

Cushman brought Gussie up to Oconomowoc to spend his fifty-fifth birthday with Jean. It was, apparently, her final stay there. Later that year, he decided to resume their travels together. Their fall 1951 itinerary took them south to New Orleans, west through Texas and then along the Mexican border to California, where they turned north for San Francisco. Week after week, the woman who had wanted to die and the man whom she had hoped to take with her sat, a camera's width apart, in the front seat of Cushman's Mercury Zephyr. The following spring they turned back east, this time through the Sierra to Nevada and northern Arizona, home again via U.S. Highway 66. After a few months in Chicago, they cleaned out the Hamilton house, preparing to leave the scene of their mutual tragedy for good. To Ted Laves, the five-year-old neighbor who had enjoyed Jean's cookies, Charles offered the little wire-backed chair from which he had once imagined the world beyond Poseyville, Indiana.[2] Packing a few of their belongings into the Mercury Zephyr, he and Jean turned south and then west once again, winding through Arkansas, Oklahoma, and Colorado before heading to their new home in San Francisco. Gussie went west too, eventually making a new home for herself in nearby Santa Clara County.

In the years that followed their arrival in the Bay Area, Jean and Charles rented several modest apartments, one in the city's Western Addition and the other in nearby Pacific Heights, before settling into what would become their last home: a bay-windowed corner apartment near the northern terminus of Broderick Street, in the flat blocks of landfill

98. Sunset over the Palace of Fine Arts, San Francisco, 1959. Cushman spent his final years gazing on the Palace of Fine Arts, a building constructed for San Francisco's 1915 Panama Pacific International Exposition and left to fall apart gradually over ensuing decades.

known as the Marina District (figs. 99, 100). In this bayfront district the city had in 1915 erected its Panama Pacific International Exposition, a celebration of the new canal and its promise for California's continued growth. When the exposition closed, its flimsy pavilions were bulldozed and its grounds plowed under. The land was platted into city blocks and soon overtaken by middle-class apartment buildings and small homes. The exposition's sole remaining structure, the Palace of Fine Arts, crafted of steel, lumber, and stucco into a Baroque setpiece at the heart of the fairgrounds, stood, gently decaying as the new neighborhood grew around it.

The years on Broderick were, by later accounts, a peaceful time, at least for Charles. In the evenings, he enjoyed sipping a glass of his beloved Stitzel-Weller bourbon and listening to his opera records as the sun set over the nearby Palace of Fine Arts. Daytime wanderings through the streets of his new home town afforded him a wholly different sort of view from those to which he had accustomed himself in Chicago. San

Francisco's ample natural light, reflecting off low-rising pale stucco and frame facades, accommodated the limitations of Cushman's slow color film better than did the deep shadows and dark masonry of the streets of his former home; its high vantages like Twin Peaks and Telegraph Hill offered plain-air views far above his accustomed myopic street-level perspective.[3]

99. 3465 Broderick Street, San Francisco, c. 2006

100. Marina District and Palace of Fine Arts, from Broadway and Broderick Street, San Francisco, 1960

Cushman traveled about the city and the surrounding state from 1953 until his death in 1972, always returning to his Marina district apartment.

PORTFOLIO: SAN FRANCISCO

Cushman's San Francisco is a recognizable place to anyone familiar with the city of sixty years hence. His walks through the city's Western Addition captured a bit of the pre-renewal streetscape of that now-altered neighborhood, but without anything like the cataloguing impulse that motivated his extensive walks through Chicago's South Side. Elsewhere, he recorded much the same streetscape that stands today. Absent the great turnover of population and of investment—and the growing dependency on federal redevelopment funds—typical of Chicago (or even of nearby Oakland), the city as it had developed after the earthquake and fire of 1906 remained largely intact for his exploration, as much of it does today. While he captured some vibrant moments along the streets of Chinatown, North Beach, Union Square, and the South of Market district, Cushman's San Francisco pictures suggest the growing detachment that accompanied him into his advancing age. His feel for the city's character seems less sure, less concise, than the sharp-focused, Depression-era San Francisco street photography of John Gutmann, and less romantic than Arnold Genthe's earlier, highly pictorialized Chinatown images. His true pleasure apparently lay less in the action of the sidewalk than in the more distanced attraction of the hillside views that await a San Franciscan willing to hazard even a few minutes' walk. Using a telephoto lens he purchased in 1957, he foreshortened the distance that separates those hills, accentuating and abstracting the already dense detail of the city's tightly knit architectural fabric.

Closer at hand, Cushman's nostalgic eye found an appropriate focus: the Palace of Fine Arts, standing peeled and faded in expectation of the wrecker's ball (figs. 119–20). He documented the original landmark's final days, composing moody, angled images of its deterioration that might have pleased architect Bernard Maybeck, who had hoped to see his masterpiece crumble picturesquely to dust.

101. View east from Twin Peaks, San Francisco, 1952

102. View south from Twin Peaks, San Francisco, 1953

103. (Opposite, top) View northeast from Sunset Heights, San Francisco, 1955

104. (Opposite, bottom) Angel Island from Buena Vista Park, San Francisco, 1955

105. (above) San Francisco Bay and Oakland from 20th and Rhode Island Streets, San Francisco, 1953

106. (Over) Eureka Valley from Collingwood and 22nd Streets, San Francisco, 1955

Frequent hilltop views reflected both Cushman's aesthetic interest in San Francisco's famous topography and a growing detachment from the immediacy of the street.

107. Church and 21st Streets, San Francisco, 1952

108. (Oppostie) Grant Avenue and Jackson Street, San Francisco, 1952

109. (Over) Broadway west from Grant Avenue, San Francisco, 1957

110. (Opposite, top) Kearney Street north from Sacramento Street, San Francisco, 1954

111. (Opposite, bottom) Telegraph Hill, from the Embarcadero, San Francisco, 1952

112. Telegraph Hill, from Broadway, San Francisco, 1953

113. (Over) Telegraph Hill, from Russian Hill, San Francisco, 1953

Rising north and west from the original shore of Yerba Buena Cove (near today's Kearney Street), Cushman found the rooming houses of Chinatown and North Beach looking much as they had since the post-fire reconstruction of 1906, while nearby Telegraph Hill still included a few nineteenth-century homes among its more numerous post-fire flats.

114. (Opposite) View east on Market Street from Third Street, San Francisco, 1953

115. Powell Street cable car turnaround, 1954

The "slot"—the tracks that ran down the center of Market Street—continued to define a separation of land use and social class from the late 1800s up to the turn of our own century. A short time after Cushman's move to San Francisco, three of the city's defunct cable car lines were reopened and protected for future use.

Cushman returned often to the Golden Gate Bridge, the subject of his earliest color photographs. The Zephyr appears here in its final photograph; its replacement would be a distinctly less romantic Ford Fairlane.

116. (Previous spread) Fort Point, San Francisco, 1956

117. Jean in the 1940 Mercury Zephyr, Golden Gate Bridge, San Francisco, 1958

118. (Opposite) Golden Gate Bridge and Pacific Heights from Fort Baker, Marin County, California, 1960

A short walk west of his apartment, the Palace of Fine Arts' crumbling condition and eventual demolition presented an aging Cushman with picturesque evidence of the ravages of time. The structure was rebuilt in 1965.

119. Palace of Fine Arts, San Francisco, 1959

120. (Opposite) Palace of Fine Arts, demolition, San Francisco, 1964

The Fortmann House, seen here a short time after its cameo role in Alfred Hitchcock's *Vertigo*, stood awaiting the urban renewal bulldozer. Although similar nineteenth-century mansions further up Franklin and Gough Streets were spared its fate, the home at the corner of Jackson Street would soon fall victim to private development.

121. Fortmann House, corner Eddy and Gough Streets, San Francisco, 1959

122. (Opposite) Southwest corner Franklin and Jackson Streets, San Francisco, 1953

123. (Opposite) Western Addition
urban renewal: O'Farrell Street east
from Buchanan Street, San
Francisco, 1960

124. Playland, San Francisco, 1952

At the end of the streetcar tracks, Playland, and nearby commercial strips like the one seen
here, stretched along foggy Ocean Beach, south from such earlier attractions as Sutro
Heights, the Sutro Baths, and the Cliff House.

125. Tent behind the Hilton Hotel,
Republican National Convention, San
Francisco, 1964

126. (Opposite) "Haight and Masonic
Hippies," San Francisco, 1967

Cushman's rare foray into human-interest documentation resulted in memorable images but
also subjected him to some subtle ridicule.

PORTFOLIO: CALIFORNIA

Jean and Charles's road trips, from the mid-1950s forward, remained confined (save for two trips to Europe) to the West. They traveled along their familiar routes in the Sierra and in the Southwest, photographing along the way. They explored the canyons and hillsides surrounding the old Hamilton ranch, south of Salinas, and the coastline of Morro Bay, where the Moskowitz family had first lived before moving to San Francisco. Closer to home, they wandered the backroads of Marin and Alameda counties. It was beside one of those roads, in Niles Canyon—near the tracks that had carried the first transcontinental railroad to its western terminus in Oakland—that Charles stopped on a sunny day in February 1955 to take a picture of Jean (fig. 142). Her drab coat sets off the brightness of her pink dress and her accessories from the deep background greens and blues of a dewy East Bay winter morning. In a manner unlike her usual poses, Jean neither hides within the shadows of the car nor looks away from her husband; her gaze is as direct as ever it would be again. Gone are the traces of girlishness still evident on Miami Beach 17 years earlier; gone, too, it seems, is any remnant of the shame or shyness suggested by the photographs that followed the shooting and her hospitalization. "Take a good look," her pose says. "This is who I am. And you"—staring at the man behind the rangefinder—"remember, you're all I've got."

127. Highway 1 between San Luis Obispo and Morro Bay, California, 1952

128. Monterey Bay, California, 1957

129. (Over) Cushman's Mercury Zephyr, U.S. Highway 1 near Bixby Creek, 1957

Cushman's cousin John Steinbeck had drawn new attention to the rolling farm country of the upper Salinas River valley with his novel, *East of Eden*. The Hamilton family ranch may have looked much like the farm shown in this picture.

130. San Lorenzo Creek, near Bull Canyon, east of King City, California, 1956

131. Bridgeport, California, 1954

132. (Over) Sierra Nevada range from west of Bishop, California, 1955

The eastern face of the Sierra Nevada range rises precipitously to the west of US Highway 395, as the road hugs the valley floor from Bridgeport, past Mono Lake, to Bishop. Not much further south, Cushman passed often through Death Valley.

133. Death Valley, California, east of
Stovepipe Wells, 1955

134. (Opposite) Jean Cushman at
Bad Water in Death Valley, 1955

Cushman leapfrogged the suburbs surrounding San Francisco Bay in order to document the agricultural landscape that still clung to the inland hillsides and valleys of Sonoma, Marin, Contra Costa, San Mateo, and Alameda Counties.

135. Near Livermore, California, 1958

136. Beck Road, south of Mt. Diablo, Contra Costa County, California

137. Dairy Farm, Petaluma, California, 1957

138. C & H Sugar refinery, Carquinez
Straits, California, 1958

Industry and agriculture met at the strategic site where the combined waters of the
Sacramento and San Joaquin Rivers join the bay. Here, in 1906, the California and Hawaiian
sugar company had built a plant to refine sugar cane offloaded from oceangoing ships.

139. (Opposite, top) Sonora, California, 1956

140. (Opposite, bottom) Black Butte, from U.S. Highway 99, Siskiyou County, California, 1954

141. Cholame Hills, California, view north from U.S. Highway 466, 1955

Cushman's California drives took him from gold-rush boom towns, to Steinbeck's "black and lost" border country near Mt. Shasta, to the dry southern hills east of Cholame, where Cushman chanced to photograph the location at which the actor James Dean would soon meet his untimely end.

142. Jean Cushman, near Niles, California, 1955

Only slightly easier to avoid than California's beauty or Jean's needful gaze was the evidence of sweeping changes to the landscape that Cushman had known and photographed over the course of his lifetime. A trip back to Chicago in 1963 resulted in several photographs not *of* the new Prudential Building that dominated the Loop's skyline, but *from* it— looking out from the observation deck upon a mostly familiar city from the one spot that afforded a view of downtown free of its newest and tallest building. Still, it would have been hard for any American in 1960 to ignore fully a spatial order—fueled by postwar federal investments far surpassing the Depression-era construction and engineering programs— that revolved around rebuilt downtowns, expanded residential suburbs, increasingly dispersed retail and industrial sites, and the interstate highways that connected them across great distances.

If Joseph Hamilton and his department store and newspaper clients had personified the old logic of the downtown-dominated metropolitan landscape, Jean's cousin, Karl Moskowitz, tied the family to the newer spatial order of widely dispersed homes and workplaces. Moskowitz, a traffic engineer with the California department of transportation, spent his days calculating the optimal size and scale of the new express highways that were beginning to replace the two-lane roads along which Cushman had for so many years driven his beloved Fords.

"Not only do I live in an officially auto-oriented community," Moskowitz proclaimed to a group of his fellow transportation professionals in 1962, "but . . . I have come to the conclusion that I am auto-oriented myself." Moskowitz contrasted a Bay Area childhood, oriented around ferryboats, commuter trains, and streetcars, with his current—and apparently happy—life in suburban Sacramento: "[T]here are two cars in my family of two people. I have a 10-year-old car which I drive 4,000 miles a year to and from work, and my wife has a four-year-old car which she runs errands in and that we use when we go out of town." He criticized mass-transit advocates for equating the common good with limitations on the right to private transportation and on the attendant opportunities to live in spacious suburban neighborhoods like the one he described as his own.[4]

Moskowitz's relatively good-natured protest, which he developed into a magazine article a short time later, registers a degree of annoyance not only at mass-transit advocates in particular, but more generally at the wave of intellectual criticism that had, by the time of his speech, come crashing down upon the pleasures of the Affluent Society. In addition to Galbraith's book, which lent to that now-familiar phrase its initial un-complimentary overtones, American readers in the 1950s and 1960s demonstrated a steady appetite for the works of such critical observers of the national scene as Marshall MacLuhan (who, like Galbraith, observed American foibles through Canadian eyes), Dwight Macdonald, Vance Packard, C. Wright Mills, William H. Whyte, Jr. — all of whom took aim not at American poverty but at its abundance. More sharply than had their counterparts in the 1920s, the postwar critics of mass culture identified the "American grain" (Macdonald's term, paraphrasing William Carlos Williams's from the earlier generation) with a sense of failed opportunity: failure to organize a more just society, failure to foster creative genius, failure to encourage beauty or to nurture community.[5] Inevitably, a pictorial equivalent to such criticism emerged, just as it had in the 1930s. Architect Peter Blake's *God's Own Junkyard* (1962) offered a dour photographic reappraisal of the American built landscape that fit well with the mass-culture critique, even as it resisted any reader's potential effort to seek out some trace of the Dignity-of-the-Common-Man theme typical of the Depression-era pictorial essay books.[6]

Steinbeck, too, sought to take the measure of postwar America. Yet the author who had, in 1952, insisted on retitling his "Salinas Valley" manuscript with the biblically charged *East of Eden*—deciding that the big novel was an elemental human tragedy and "not primarily [a book] about the Salinas Valley nor local people"[7]—turned, in his *Travels with Charley*, toward precisely the sort of prosaic, local observation, precisely the acceptance of the "day in its color," that his businessman-cousin had practiced for years. Packing his books, clothes, and camping gear—and his pet poodle—into a small custom-fitted truck, Steinbeck set out in 1960 to capture the America of highways and country roads, small towns

143. Karl and Catherine Moskowitz, near Pardee Reservoir, Amador County, California, 1956

and farmlands—the everyday places from which years of growing wealth, fame, and isolation had separated him. The resulting book remains today, as *New York Times* reviewer Orville Prescott allowed in 1962, "likable and amusing," but it stands equally susceptible to Prescott's charge that it "contains nothing of much significance about the present state of the nation."[8] Steinbeck filled his travelogue with meditations on the changing American scene—and with criticism of the highways, suburbs, and homogenized customs that have replaced the landscape across which he traveled earlier in his life. His straightforward, avuncular prose reads almost as if it were meant to accompany the photographs of the cousin whose trips (along some of the same roads) had preceded his own by more than two decades. Unlike Cushman's picture collection, however, Steinbeck's monologue remains inarguably about *him*, the famous writer, a character who never disappears from the center of the scene. There is no equivalent here to the dramatic power of Cushman's color film to absorb the viewer in the tangible and seemingly unmediated presence of the landscape.[9]

PORTFOLIO: THINGS TO COME

Not surprisingly, Cushman's later pictures betray him as neither a detractor
nor a cheerleader of the emerging postwar metropolitan landscape. Aside
from a few glimpses of the residential developments rising alongside the
highways leading south along the San Francisco Peninsula or north to
Marin, we see little—in either good or ill light—of the new suburbia in
his work. Likewise, while he caught an occasional bit of the commercial
roadscape that had by this time accumulated along the nation's smaller
highways for the last thirty years or more, his images left no evidence of
the practice of national franchising and prefabricated commercial
construction that altered the American roadside by the 1960s. Cushman
remained as uninterested as he had been in previous decades in aligning
his vision with that of better-known photographers, travelers, and social
critics.

The Federal-Aid Highway Act, passed in 1956, built upon two decades of high-speed road
improvement. In Chicago, clearance for the Congress Expressway had begun in the 1940s.
The Bay Area's Eastshore Freeway extended a highway first built in the 1930s.

144. Carquinez Straits highway
construction, Alameda County,
California, 1957

145. Congress Expressway from
Marshfield Avenue, Chicago, 1958

At the edges of new developments like Linda Mar (soon to be incorporated into the town of Pacifica) and Terra Linda, Cushman offered an occasional passing glimpse of California's postwar suburban landscape.

146. Suburban construction northeast of San Rafael, California, 1961

147. (Opposite, top) Linda Mar, California, 1955

148. (Opposite, bottom) Motel Inn, San Luis Obispo, California, 1958

In the 1960s, federal mortgage guarantees and expanded powers of eminent domain spurred a rush of mixed-use downtown developments such as Chicago's Marina City and San Francisco's Golden Gateway.

149. Golden Gateway Center under construction, San Francisco, 1965

150. (Opposite) View west from Michigan Avenue Bridge, Chicago, 1963

151. (Over) Wigwam Village, Bessemer, Alabama, 1951

If he did not actively seek out the kinds of scenes that might have helped to shore up the cranky arguments of Peter Blake or John Steinbeck (or, on the other side, of Karl Moskowitz), Cushman may not have sought to avoid them, either. Imagining iconic images—the suburban ranch house, the highway cloverleaf, the public housing project—standing in for an entire landscape, we may forget, today, how scattered and gradual were the architectural and landscape changes of the postwar generation. Dwight Eisenhower signed the interstate highway bill into law in 1956, but years passed before significant interstate construction took place nationwide—particularly outside of the central cities, where funding formulas encouraged local governments to move forward more quickly with their clearance plans for the new roadways.[10] The housing and urban renewal acts of 1949 and 1954 promised quick changes to aging urban centers (and resulted in some conspicuous experiments in inner-city, highrise living for both the poor and, to a lesser extent, the middle class), but the skylines of the 1920s continued to dominate central cities until well into the 1960s. For all his loyalty to living color, it was a dying world that captured Cushman's attention—and plenty of it remained to catch his eye. With little building taking place between the construction boom of the 1920s and the postwar recovery, the United States represented a vastly underinvested landscape into the 1960s.[11] Private automobiles, improved harbor and trucking facilities, enlarged and mechanized farms, telecommunications advances, increased foreign industrial productivity, all stood poised to render much of the industrial-era landscape obsolete, even as that earlier era's houses, offices, farm structures, and factories—underinvested, obstinately solid as built things are—continued to remind Americans of a bygone time. With America's economy preparing to move one step ahead of its stock repertory of cultural images (the family farm, Main Street, the billowing smokestacks, the tapered skyscrapers), the nation as it appeared in the 1940s and 1950s was coming to seem a picture of itself. A built environment dominated by sites for extracting and processing natural resources, by small family-owned farms, and by concentrated urban neighborhoods—in short, the landscape of Charles Cushman's life—had become a historical artifact. Viewed through pictures stripped of Newhall's "classic" scrim of black and white, the persistence of that older environment seemed less the evidence of crisis, as many documentarians had portrayed it, than it did a reminder of the continued, tangible immediacy of the aging world that our business leaders, architects, and policy makers told us we'd left behind.

Charles took his last picture of Jean in the fall of 1968 (fig. 152). Fittingly, her figure is half-obscured from view by the couple's 1958 Fairlane, which they are preparing to trade in at a Corte Madera car lot. By the time of the photograph, they both knew that she was dying of stomach cancer. As her condition worsened, he put down the camera altogether. When she died on June 12, 1969, Cushman filed away his slides and

152. Jean Cushman and the 1958 Ford Fairlane, Corte Madera, California, 1968

his notebooks. Some months later, on one of his neighborhood walks, he stopped to help two women loading their suitcases into a car. Fifty-three-year-old Elizabeth Gergely Penniman and her younger sister, Elsie, were, like Cushman, natives of Indiana. The two had grown up in a cultured and relatively privileged household in Gary. Elizabeth, the oldest, had left Indiana for Washington, D.C., and it was after a number of years there that she met the man who would become her first husband: William Frederick Penniman, the retired director of the Home Owners' Loan Corporation. After his death in 1959, she had moved to San Francisco, where she found work with the Social Security Administration.[12]

Elizabeth and Elsie were impressed with the "proper gentleman" who helped them with their bags. A few weeks later, Elizabeth and Charles bumped into one another on the street once more; this time they talked at greater length, discovering their common interests in opera and theatre. Soon, the two began seeing one another. Not long after their affair began Charles became seriously ill. As he lay in his bed at Mount Zion Hospital, recovering from a repair to his carotid artery, Elizabeth confronted him: "Charles," she later recalled saying, "we have to get married." They did so on Thanksgiving weekend, 1970, in a service officiated by Jean's cousin (and Karl's brother) John Moskowitz, a Santa Rosa judge. Charles and Elizabeth remained together until his heart finally gave out, June 8, 1972.[13]

After Charles's death, Elizabeth packed up most of his slides and camera equipment, along with his prized collection of RCA Red Seal opera recordings. In accordance with plans he had made several years before, she sent them to the Indiana University Archives in Bloomington. Not exactly unknown, the slides remained unexplored—an eccentric bequest of seemingly dubious value. In 1989 Elizabeth sent an additional 1,500 slides, along with more of his equipment. Rather than arriving at the archives, however, this latter shipment went to the Indiana University Foundation, the university's fundraising arm, to which Cushman had also left a financial contribution in his will. From the foundation, the second collection made its way to the office of a professor in the university's

School of Journalism. Six years later, photographer and historian Rich Remsberg rescued the slides from among the materials left behind by his colleague, now clearing out his office in preparation for retirement. Struck by the hitherto-unnoticed images, Remsberg tracked down Elizabeth, who gave him permission to include them in a book he hoped to write. In 1999, Remsberg and university archivist Brad Cook rediscovered the connection between the two pieces of the collection and brought them together for cataloguing. In 2000, the university's digital library program won a federal grant from the Institute for Museum and Library Services to restore and digitize each image, placing them and the accompanying notebooks in an online database that brought this private collection at last before a public audience.[14]

The online collection of Cushman's images, endlessly searchable to researchers and daydreamers, is so full in its coverage, so bright in its appearance, so distracting in its presentation, that one easily forgets the hole that yet remains in its center. How do we fill that hole? Charles and Jean, only children both, left no offspring of their own. His only close relatives, two elderly cousins in Posey County, both died in 1978. His paper records—an employment history form, a couple of letters, some miscellaneous paperwork—fit into a couple of slim folders in the university archives. Family friends and relatives—as well as the relatively small number of photographic subjects whose names Cushman recorded in the notebooks—are, not surprisingly, few in number and vague in their recollections. Adolphe R. E. Roome IV, whose grandfather had married Charles's mother Mabel in the 1920s (only to return to his first wife some years later), fondly recalls the woman the family knew for a time as "Mumsie," but does not remember meeting her grown-up son, Charles. Jack Moskowitz, whose Uncle Karl and Aunt Catherine traveled with Jean and Charles in the Sierra foothills, vaguely remembers a dapper man flirting with Catherine at a family holiday dinner, but cannot be sure of his name. One of Charles's photographic subjects, pictured with his first wife in a World War II–era portrait, still lives—but his second wife protects him from a curious researcher and insists that, in any event, he would have no recollection of the photographer. Another subject from the same period—a toddler when she appeared through Cushman's rangefinder—wishes that she could remember the man whom her mother allowed to photograph her on a long-ago Chicago summer morning, while her father fought in Europe. As for Elizabeth Gergely Cushman, she offered valuable impressions of Charles's life—including details of Jean and her family—to Rich Remsberg in 2001. Somehow, she neglected to mention the fact that her husband's first wife had placed two bullets in his head in 1943.[15] Elizabeth passed away in 2003. Her younger sister, Elsie, may be the last living person who, as of the date of this writing, remembers Charles well.

What, then, remains of the lives of these two people who, instead of dying together, grew old together? And what of the nation through which they moved? Like an untold number of other Americans whose visual records lie as yet unappropriated by historians, Cushman saw the nation neither as an "average" snapshooter nor as a member of the ranks of self-described artists, academics, or social reformers. His sensibilities and experiences combined conservative and reformist instincts, complacency and dissatisfaction. Without rejecting his privilege, he accepted its limits. Cushman would, as I mentioned earlier, perhaps have been a familiar sort of man to the insurance executive and poet Wallace Stevens—an observer and a daydreamer, perhaps, but a man of business to the end, unwilling to exercise the "complete ruthlessness" that John Steinbeck had proclaimed the necessary condition of his own life as an artist. Cushman seems not to have fretted over his inability to see beyond what Stevens called "the day in its color."[16] He crafted an extraordinarily complete inner world from the fragments of life that he found around him, a world defined more in terms of his own experiences than in the service of a search for a hidden essence or an unknowable design. The medium of color film, ceded by the professionals of his day to amateurs and advertisers, offered such a man a new tool for capturing the brief glow and the long, slow fade of the country he once knew and of the woman who saw it with him.

NOTES

Introduction

1. Charles Cushman to Claude Rich, April 4, 1966, Indiana University Correspondence File, Charles W. Cushman Collection, Indiana University Archives, Indiana University, Bloomington (hereafter cited as Cushman Collection, IUA).

2. *Bound for Glory: America in Color, 1939–43*, introduction by Paul Hendrickson (New York: Harry Abrams in association with the Library of Congress, 2004); Els Rijper, ed., *Kodachrome: The American Invention of Our World, 1939–1959* (New York: Delano Greenridge, 2002); Andy Grundberg, "FSA Color Photography: A Forgotten Experiment," *Portfolio* (July–August 1983): 53–57; Sally Stein, "FSA Color," *Modern Photography* 43 (January 1979).

3. Wallace Stevens, "The Pure Good of Theory," in *Transport to Summer* (New York: Alfred A. Knopf, 1947).

Chapter 1

1. Charles W. Cushman to A.B. Keller, International Harvester Company, June 29, 1944, Genealogy File, Cushman Collection, IUA.

2. University of Virginia, *Geospatial and Statistical Data Center: Historical Census Browser* http://fisher.lib.virginia.edu/collections/stats/histcensus/php/newlong3.php; U.S. Census, *Population of Counties by Decennial Censuses, 1900–1990: Indiana* http://www.census.gov/population/cencounts/in190090.txt.

3. *City of Mount Vernon, Indiana* http://www.mountvernon.in.gov/.

4. Ralph Waldo Emerson, "Farming," in *The Collected Works of Ralph Waldo Emerson,* vol. 7, *Society and Solitude*, ed. Ronald A. Bosco and Douglas Emory Wilson (Cambridge, Mass: Harvard University Press, 2007), 73. On the "neomercantilistic" quality of an early American network of sites of commerce, manufacture, and agriculture, see Lawrence A. Peskin, *Manufacturing Revolution: The Intellectual Origins of Early American Industry* (Baltimore: Johns Hopkins University Press, 2003), 5–6.

5. Charles W. Cushman to Thomas Grant Hartung, Dec. 2, 1968, Genealogy Files, Cushman Collection, IUA. U.S. Census Enumeration Manuscript, Poseyville, Indiana, 1910.

6. Charles W. Cushman to Indiana University Registrar, December 5, 1913, Genealogy Files, Cushman Collection, IUA.

7. Charles W. Cushman college scrapbook, Cushman Collection, IUA.

8. University of Virginia, *Geospatial and Statistical Data Center: Historical Census Browser* http://fisher.lib.virginia.edu/collections/stats/histcensus/php/newlong2.php.

9. Indiana University *Bulletin* 11:5 (June 1, 1913); Charles W. Cushman academic
   records, Cushman Collection, IUA.

10. *Indiana Daily Student*, December 2, 1915, Cushman Scrapbook, Cushman
    Collection, IUA.

11. Ibid., n.d., Cushman Scrapbook, Cushman Collection, IUA.

12. Charles W. Cushman, "Application for Federal Employment," March 1, 1944.
    Genealogy File, Cushman Collection, IUA.

13. Charles W. Cushman to Horace A. Hoffman, November 14, 1917; "Information for
    the War Service Register of Alumni and Former Students," n.d. Genealogy File,
    Cushman Collection, IUA.

14. "Information for the War Service Register," Genealogy File, Cushman Collection,
    IUA.

Chapter 2

1. U.S. Census Enumeration Manuscripts, Chicago, Illinois, and Terre Haute, Indiana,
   1920. On changing standards of salesmanship in early twentieth-century
   America, see Walter A. Friedman, *Birth of a Salesman: The Transformation
   of Selling in America* (Cambridge, Mass.: Harvard University Press, 2004).

2. Charles W. Cushman, "Application for Federal Employment," March 1, 1944;
   Charles W. Cushman to A.B. Keller, International Harvester Company, June 29,
   1944, Genealogy File, Cushman Collection, IUA. Archer Wall Douglas, *Traveling
   Salesmanship* (New York: Macmillan, 1919), 2, 149, 141.

3. "Antique Mail Room Machines," http://www.officemuseum.com/mail_machines
   .htm; Walter Benjamin, "The Age of Mechanical Reproduction," in *Illuminations:
   Essays and Reflections* (New York: Schocken, 1969), 217–51.

4. Cushman, "Application for Federal Employment"; Adolphe R. E. Roome, IV,
   telephone conversation with author, January 5, 2005; Adolphe R. E. Roome
   listings in U.S. Census Enumeration Manuscript, 1900, 1910, 1920; Roome
   obituary, *Los Angeles Times*, January 6, 1951, A5; ibid. January 8, 1951, A24;
   Elizabeth Gergely Cushman telephone interview with Rich Remsberg, May 23
   [c. 2001], notes, Genealogy File, Cushman Collection, IUA.

5. Cushman, "Application for Federal Employment." On LaSalle Extension University,
   see *Los Angeles Times*, January 25, 1931, C1; *Chicago Tribune*, May 7, 1916,
   A6; February 19, 1926, 16; July 28, 1935, A12; July 3, 1937, 12.

6. *LaSalle Business Bulletin* 11:2 (February 1927): 1; Cushman, "Application for
   Federal Employment."

7. Douglas, *Traveling Salesmanship*, 146.

8. *LaSalle Business Bulletin* 9:11 (November 1925): 1; 9:3 (March 1925): 8; 10:8 (August 1926): 8; 9:9 (September 1925): 2, 4–5; 9:2 (February 1925): 7; 9:7 (July 1925): 8; 9:10 (October 1925): 4.

9. Ibid., 9:9 (September 1925): 2, 4–5; 10:8 (August 1926): 1. See also Daniel Horowitz, *The Anxieties of Affluence: Intellectuals and Consumer Culture in the U.S.* (Amherst: University of Massachusetts Press, 2004), for an account of the growth of the consumer economy and its impact upon writers and cultural commentators.

10. *LaSalle Business Bulletin* 8:2 (February 1925): 1; 10:1 (January 1926): 1.

11. Douglas's own earlier work seemed, to at least some academics, impressionistic and built from scanty quantitative data; cf. "Book Notes," *Political Science Quarterly* 37:1 (March 1922): 172. Rexford G. Tugwell, Thomas Munro, and Roy Stryker, *American Economic Development: And the Means of Its Improvement* (New York: Harcourt Brace, 1925), viii; among other classic cultural and social studies of the era, see Lewis Mumford, *The Brown Decades: A Study of the Arts in America, 1865–1895* (New York: Harcourt Brace, 1931), Constance Rourke, *American Humor: A Study of the National Character* (New York: Harcourt Brace, 1931), H. L. Mencken, *The American Language: An Inquiry into the Development of English in the United States* (New York: Alfred A. Knopf, 1921), and Robert Lynd and Helen Merrill Lynd, *Middletown: A Study in American Culture* (New York: Harcourt, Brace, 1929). The intellectual climate in which such studies flourished forms the focus of Christine Stansell, *American Moderns: Bohemian New York and the Creation of a New Century* (New York: Metropolitan Books, 2000), and Ann Douglas, *Terrible Honesty: Mongrel Manhattan in the 1920s* (New York: Farrar, Straus and Giroux, 1995).

12. See James Leiby, *Carroll Wright and Labor Reform: The Origin of Labor Statistics* (Cambridge, Mass.: Harvard University Press, 1960); Joseph P. Goldberg and William T. Moye, *The First Hundred Years of the Bureau of Labor Statistics* (Washington, D.C.: Government Printing Office, 1985).

13. Walter Benjamin, "On the Work of Art in the Age of Mechanical Reproduction," in *Illuminations*, 223. Michael K. Buckland, "Emanuel Goldberg, Electronic Document Retrieval, and Vannevar Bush's Memex," *Journal of the American Society for Information Science* 43, no. 4 (May 1992): 284–94.

14. John Steinbeck, *East of Eden* (New York: Penguin, 2002; first published, 1952), 41; see also Steinbeck's revealing account of the writing of the novel in his letters to editor Pascal Covici, later published as *Journal of a Novel: The East of Eden Letters* (New York: Penguin, 1990).

15. Steinbeck, *East of Eden*, 41.

16. Ibid., 275.

17. "'Joe' Hamilton to Spend Vacation in This City," San Francisco *Call*, September 12, 1908, 5. On department stores and urban geography, see James E. Vance, *The Continuing City: Urban Morphology in Western Civilization* (Baltimore: Johns Hopkins University Press, 1990), 393ff.

18. On changing corporate images in the industrial age, see Pamela Walker Laird, *Advertising Progress: American Business and the Rise of Consumer Marketing* (Baltimore: Johns Hopkins University Press, 2001).

19. William Leach, *Merchants of Desire: Merchants, Power, and the Rise of a New American Culture* (New York: Vintage, 1994), 56–61.

20. Joseph H. Appel, *The Business Biography of John Wanamaker: Founder and Builder* (New York: Macmillan, 1930), 390–91; idem., "Reminiscences in Retailing," *Bulletin of the Business Historical Society* 12:6 (December 1938): 81–89; *Washington Post*, October 2, 1895, 5; Herbert Adams Gibbon, *John Wanamaker* (New York: Harper and Brothers, 1926), 18–19; *New York Times*, October 2, 1895.

21. Albert Lasker, *The Lasker Story: As He Told It* (Chicago: Advertising Publications Inc. 1963), 19; *Advertising Age Advertising Century*, http://www.adage.com/century/people006.html; Alan Trachtenberg, *Shades of Hiawatha: Staging Indians, Making Americans, 1880–1930* (New York: Hill and Wang, 2004); "'Joe' Hamilton to Spend Vacation in This City."

22. "'Joe' Hamilton to Spend Vacation in This City," "How One Man Advertises," San Francisco *Call*, January 28, 1909, 6. Hamilton was, notably, among the group of influential businessmen (their numbers augmented, for the occasion, by the likes of Indian fighter General George Miles and artist Frederic Remington) that Wanamaker assembled at Louis Sherry's New York restaurant, in May 1909, to hear guest of honor Buffalo Bill Cody make the case for Wanamaker's proposed National American Indian Memorial. See "Plan Memorial to Red Man," *Philadelphia Record*, May 13, 1909, n.p., in Wanamaker Scrapbook, 1904–1909, Mathers Museum of World Cultures, Indiana University. For more on the unsuccessful Indian memorial, see Trachtenberg, *Shades of Hiawatha*.

23. San Francisco *Call*, February 6, 1910, 27; Jonas Howard, "Man of Ideas Earns $1,000 a Week in This Golden Age of Brain Worker," *Chicago Daily Tribune*, April 5, 1908, D2; Irwin Ellis, "Herbert Kaufman—Story of the Optimistic Accomplishments of a Worker," *Chicago Daily Tribune*, June 11, 1911, E1; *Chicago Daily Tribune*, June 28, 1914, E9; September 7, 1913, B8; October 13,

1912, E1. Kaufman was the son of Washington, D.C., department store pioneer Abraham Kaufman, and the brother of Pittsburgh retailer Harry Kaufman. See "Abraham Kaufman Dead," *Washington Post*, October 17, 1913, 14.

24. "Herbert Kaufman Buys McClure's," *New York Times*, December 26, 1919, 3; "Herbert Kaufman, Editor, 69, is Dead," *New York Times*, September 7, 1947, 63.

25. Rich Remsberg interview with Elizabeth Gergely Cushman. Dawes and Shannon are among the references listed by Cushman on his "Application for Federal Employment," March 1, 1944, a copy of which is held in the Genealogy File, Cushman Collection, IUA; for a review of their achievements see their obituaries: *Chicago Tribune*, September 30, 1952, C2 (Dawes), and *Chicago Tribune*, July 20, 1958, A12 (Shannon).

26. Jackson J. Benson, *The True Adventures of John Steinbeck, Writer* (New York: Viking, 1984), 91; Thomas Kernan, *The Intricate Music: A Biography of John Steinbeck* (Boston: Little Brown, 1979), 110. Less than one month later, Steinbeck wrote his parents that he had "been amputated from the American staff," but promised that freelance work would come his way. Steinbeck to "Folks," March 5, 1926, Wells Fargo Steinbeck Collection, Stanford University Libraries Special Collections, Box 1, Folder 83.

27. *Your Money*, 1:1 (December 1928): 2.

28. Ibid.

29. "Application for Federal Employment"; Remsberg interview with Elizabeth Gergely Cushman.

30. Bonnie Yochelson, *Berenice Abbott: Changing New York* (New York: New Press, 1997).

31. Edward L. Bernays, *Biography of an Idea: Memoirs of Public Relations Counsel Edward L. Bernays* (New York: Simon and Schuster, 1965), 361; "Essay on a Man Buttoning Up His Vest," *Chicago Daily Tribune*, February 17, 1931. The "Vest" essay eventually made its way into the testament of another business-leader-self-help-advisor of the time, Ralston Purina founder William H. Danforth, who retold the story in his *I Dare You*, 8th ed. (St. Louis, n.p., 1938), 52.

32. "Newspaper Advertising Awards Made," *Chicago Daily Tribune*, May 22, 1931, 9; "Human or Dog Intelligence?" *Chicago Daily Tribune*, April 28, 1931. On the Bernays connection, see Bernays, ibid., and Emile Gauvreau, *My Last Million Readers* (New York: E.P. Dutton, 1941), 130. On Macfadden, see Mark Adams, *Mr. America: How Muscular Millionaire Bernarr Macfadden Transformed the Nation through Sex, Salad, and the Ultimate Starvation Diet* (New York, It Books, 2009); Ann Fabian, "Making a Commodity of Truth: Speculations on the Career

of Bernarr Macfadden," *American Literary History* 5:1 (Spring 1993): 51–76; Robert Ernst, *Weakness is a Crime: The Life of Bernarr Macfadden* (Syracuse: Syracuse University Press, 1991); and Lizbeth Cohen, "Encountering Mass Culture at the Grassroots: The Experience of Chicago Workers in the 1920s," *American Quarterly* 41:1 (March 1989): 6–33.

33. Carl Spielvogel, "Advertising: Blatz Top Team Rises at Pabst," *New York Times*, August 29, 1958, 37; "Puritan Malt Merges with Pabst Corp.," *Chicago Daily Tribune*, March 29, 1930, 25; Puritan Malt advertisement, *Chicago Daily Tribune*, April 17, 1924, 30.

34. *Chicago Daily Tribune*, January 8, 1933, 18; April 6, 1933, 12. On post-prohibition brewing, see A. M. McGahan, "The Emergence of the National Brewing Oligopoly: Competition in the American Market, 1938–1958," *Business History Review* 65:2 (Summer 1991): 229–84, esp. 230–37.

35. Hamilton's better-known peer in the Chicago advertising world, Lord and Thomas agency founder Albert Lasker, had reminded a group of his colleagues in 1925 of his maxim that advertising was "salesmanship in print"; nonetheless, Lasker confessed, he had made a "mistake," through his career, in lacking "faith in art in copy." Lasker, *Lasker Story*, 21, 50. On the growing importance of pictorial imagery in American advertising, see Elspeth H. Brown, *The Corporate Eye: Photography and the Rationalization of American Commercial Culture, 1884–1929* (Baltimore: Johns Hopkins University Press, 2005), 165–68; Roland Marchand, *Advertising the American Dream: Making Way for Modernity, 1920–1940* (Berkeley and Los Angeles: University of California Press, 1985).

36. Grauman Studios advertisement, *Printers' Ink Monthly* 3:2 (July 1921): 100.

37. Luce quoted in Samantha Baskind, "The 'True' Story: *Life* Magazine, Horace Bristol, and John Steinbeck's *Grapes of Wrath*," *Steinbeck Studies* 15:2 (2004): 53. Flannery letter: *Life*, December 7, 1936, 7 (Young and Rubicam appears a week later in the magazine's list of its advertisers. See *Life*, December 14, 1936, 36–37.)

38. Charles Cross, *A Picture of America—As it Is—and As It Might Be: Told by the News Camera* (New York: Simon and Schuster, 1932); Erskine Caldwell and Margaret Bourke-White, *You Have Seen Their Faces* (New York: Modern Age Books, 1937); idem., *Say, Is This the USA?* (New York: Duell, Sloan, and Pearce, 1941); Archibald Macleish, *Land of the Free* (New York: Harcourt, Brace, 1938); Dorothea Lange, *An American Exodus: A Record of Human Erosion* (New York: Reynal and Hitchcock, 1939); Walker Evans, *American Photographs*, with an essay by Lincoln Kirstein (New York: Museum of Modern Art, 1938).

39. Caldwell and Bourke-White, *Say, Is This the USA*, 71, 3; Douglas R. Nickel, "'American Photographs' Revisited," *American Art* 6:2 (Spring 1992): 80; Alan Trachtenberg, "Walker Evans's 'Message from the Interior': A Reading," *October* 11 (Winter 1979): 10; John Tagg, "Melancholy Realism: Walker Evans's Resistance to Meaning," *Narrative* 11:1 (2003): 3–77.

40. McGahan, "Emergence of the National Brewing Oligopoly."

41. "Colonel Harrington Lauds Bill to Women's Press," *Washington Post*, February 1, 1939, 15. "Dismissed Theater Project Employees Refuse to Quit," *Los Angeles Times*, July 12, 1939, 2. Hunter, who took the national post upon Harrington's death in the fall of 1940, had come to Washington after several years as chief administrator of the WPA's Region IV, based in Chicago. It is likely that he knew Hamilton there, and it may have been through Hamilton that Hunter met Steinbeck.

42. Steven W. Plattner, *Roy Stryker, USA: The Standard Oil (New Jersey) Project* (Austin: University of Texas Press, 1983), 16, 22.

43. Jack Delano, *Photographic Memories* (Washington, D.C. and London: Smithsonian Institution Press, 1997), 31. Worthwhile critiques of the FSA project include Michele Landis, "Fate, Responsibility, and 'Natural' Disaster Relief: Narrating the American Welfare State," *Law and Society Review* 33:2 (1999): 257–318. For a summary of revisionist theories, see Stuart Kidd, *Farm Security Administration Photography, the Rural South, and the Dynamics of Image-Making, 1935–1943* (Lewiston, NY: Edwin Mellen Press, 2004), 21–22.

44. Felix Cotten, "Public Weighs Results of 9-Billion Expenditure" *Washington Post*, March 24, 1940, B3.

45. Michael Lesy, *Long Time Coming: A Photographic Portrait of America, 1935–1943* (New York: Norton, 2002), 318–20; Benson, *True Adventures of John Steinbeck*, 359–60, 415, 458; letter from Steinbeck to Hamilton, n.d. (1940), reprinted in Elaine Steinbeck and Robert Wallsten, eds., *Steinbeck: A Life in Letters* (New York: Viking, 1975), 207. The plan for Latin American films had developed earlier in the year, during Steinbeck's sojourn in Mexico to make the film *The Forgotten Village*. The plan comprises the subject of a long letter sent from journalist Richard R. Kilroy to Joseph R. Hamilton, July 6, 1940, Genealogy File, Cushman Collection, IUA. For Steinbeck's thoughts on this period of his work generally, see the diaries collected in Robert DeMott, ed., *Working Days: The Journals of The Grapes of Wrath, 1938–1941* (New York: Viking, 1989).

46. Mabel appears as Roome's wife in the 1930 Census enumeration manuscript for San Francisco. They subsequently divorced; Roome remarried his first wife.

Telephone interview with Adolphe R. E. Roome, IV. On Steinbeck's travels see Baskind, "The 'True' Story," and Steinbeck, *Working Days*. On Steinbeck's presence in Washington in September 1940 (during the same week in which Cushman photographed the city), see Benson, *True Adventures*, 465 (though the author mistakenly writes "1939" for the correct "1940"). Cushman's travels might be as fruitfully compared to those of another Ford-driving Hoosier of the same time, Ernie Pyle, who spent the late 1930s driving across the country with his wife, Jerry, and filing stories for the Scripps-Howard news syndicate.

47. Joni Kinsey, *The Majesty of the Grand Canyon: 150 Years in Art* (San Francisco: Pomegranate Press, 1998); David E. Nye, *Narratives and Spaces: Technology and the Construction of American Culture* (New York: Columbia University Press, 1997), 17ff.; Ethan Carr, *Wilderness by Design: Landscape Architecture and the National Park Service* (Lincoln: University of Nebraska Press, 1998), 117–35.

48. Steinbeck, *Journal of a Novel*, 24.

49. Phoebe Cutler, *The Public Landscape of the New Deal* (New Haven, Conn.: Yale University Press, 1985), 4; William Stott, *Documentary Expression and Thirties America* (New York: Oxford University Press, 1973), 67–68.

50. *United States Census of Agriculture*, vol. 2 (Washington, D.C: Government Printing Office, 1945), 326.

51. "The U.S. Minicam Boom," *Fortune* 14:4 (October 1936): 125, 160, 129.

52. F. Jack Hurley, *Russell Lee, Photographer* (Dobbs Ferry, N.Y.: Morgan and Morgan, 1978); "Interview with Ben Shahn, Conducted by Harlan Phillips At the Artist's home in Roosevelt, New Jersey, October 3, 1965," Smithsonian Archives of American Art, http://www.aaa.si.edu/collections/oralhistories/transcripts/shahn65.htm.

53. Keith Herney, "Black and White," *Photo Technique* 1:2 (July 1939): 3.

54. Steinbeck, *East of Eden*, 273. Anderson may or may not be a fictional character. If he is, like others described in the Hamilton clan, a real person, then his identity is of some interest. Thirty "Anderson" men appear in the 1900 U.S. Census enumeration manuscripts for the California counties bordering Oregon (Del Norte, Siskiyou, Modoc). The great majority are single laborers and lumber workers, many of them Scandinavian-born. The one who stands out by virtue of his markedly different professional and ethnic profile is Frank M. Anderson, a "mining expert" living in Yreka.

Frank Marion Anderson (1863–1945) was an Oregon-born geologist who divided his career between public service and private industry—oil companies

in particular. After a short career teaching school in Oregon, he earned his
bachelor's degree from Stanford in 1895 (several years earlier than Joe Hamilton
earned his degree, but still close enough in time that the two men would have
overlapped on the small campus), returned north for a year to teach high school
science in Yreka, then came back to the Bay Area to study for his M.S. at
Berkeley. In 1899 the California State Mining Bureau commissioned him to
examine copper deposits in the state's northern counties; he remained there for
several years. Anderson's obituaries show that he married twice: to Elinor Anglin
from 1900 until her death in 1916; and to Theresa Barry, who survived him.
Hamilton's sister, Euna, was born in 1861, taught at the Warm Spring School
near San Jose for at least some time in the 1890s, and died of an unknown
cause in the mining town of Northport, Washington, in March 1898. Her
obituaries in the Salinas papers confirm her married name of Anderson but
otherwise make no mention of her husband or of the reason behind the
"crushing suddenness" of her death (my search for a death certificate from
Stevens County, Washington, has been, thus far, fruitless). We can speculate
that she would have had opportunity to meet Frank M. Anderson during his
period as a student at Stanford or Berkeley, and to imagine that he would, as a
mineralogist (particularly one working in an area known for its ample deposits of
copper, a substance that has been shown to be partially suitable as a substitute
for silver in the composition of sulfide compounds used in film emulsion), have
been as prepared as anyone living in far northern California at the time to
experiment with photography. But no document yet found links the two of them,
nor documents Anderson as having lived or worked in Northport, Washington.
See "Death of Mrs. Euna Anderson," *Salinas Daily Index*, March 30, 1898, 3; C.
M. Wagner, "Frank Marion Anderson (1863–1945)," *Bulletin of the American
Association of Petroleum Engineers* 30:4 (April 1946): 636–39; "Frank Marion
Anderson (1863–1945)," California Academy of Sciences *Academy News
Letter* 71 (November 1945): 3–4; "Rich Minerals are the Study," *San Francisco
Call*, August 4, 1901, 19; "Copper District Vast in Extent," *San Francisco
Call*, October 9, 1901, 9; *Yreka Journal*, August 23, 1898 (1:5), October 13,
1899 (3:4), December 8, 1899 (3:5), December 22, 1899 (2:2); Carol Robles,
"California Connections," *Steinbeck Studies* 15:2 (2004): 171; email
correspondence between author and Julie Monroe, University of Idaho Special
Collections and Archives, August 28, 2009; email correspondence between
author and Danielle Castronovo, Archives and Digital Collections Librarian,
California Academy of Sciences, September 1, 2009.

55. Brian Coe, *Colour Photography: The First Hundred Years, 1840–1940* (London: Ash and Grant, 1978), 120–21.

56. Lubitsch quoted in *New York Times*, November 25, 1934, x5; Evans in Sally Eauclaire, *The New Color Photography* (New York: Abbeville, 1981), 9; Frank in Leslie Baier, "Visions of Fascination and Despair: The Relationship between Walker Evans and Robert Frank," *Art Journal* 41:1 (September 1981): 58.

57. Beaumont Newhall, *Photography: A Short Critical History* (New York: Museum of Modern Art, 1938), 71, 75; idem., *The History of Photography from 1839 to the Present Day*, rev. ed., (New York: Museum of Modern Art, 1964), 194. Anti–color photography sentiment echoed an earlier generation's suspicions of chromolithography as a means for reproducing original works of art. See Rob Kroes, *Photographic Memories: Private Pictures, Public Images, and American History* (Hanover: Dartmouth College Press, 2007), 59–60.

58. Le Corbusier, *When the Cathedrals Were White: A Journey to the Country of Timid People* (New York: Reynal and Hitchcock, 1947).

59. Lewis Jacobs, "Color and the Cinema," *New York Times*, March 17, 1935, x4; *Photo Technique* 1:3 (September 1939): 3; Herbert C. McKay, "Introduction," in Clifford A. Nelson, *Natural Color Film: What it Is and How to Use It* (New York: Galleon Press, 1937), 11–12; Walther Benser, *More Color Magic* (Neumunster: Dr. Diener KG, 1959), 11. See also Luis Marden, *Color Photography with the Miniature Camera*, *Theory and Practice of Miniature Camera Photography*, *Better Color Slides* (Canton, Ohio: Fomo Publishing Company, 1934).

60. *Bound for Glory: America in Color, 1939–43*, introduction by Paul Hendrickson (New York: Harry Abrams, in association with the Library of Congress, 2004). For examples of the range of topics that the early editors of *Life* deemed appropriate to experimentation with color, see November 23, 1936, 32 (a feature on Helen Hayes's appearance on Broadway); January 4, 1937, 33–36 (an article on WPA art); March 15, 1937, 37–42 (on England's crown jewels), and October 4, 1937, 45–46 (the embryonic chick).

Chapter 3

1. Joseph R. Hamilton to Esther [Rodgers], July 24, 1942, Stanford University Special Collections Library, Wells Fargo Steinbeck Collection, box 1, folder 68; John Steinbeck to Esther [Rodgers], Stanford Steinbeck Collection, n.d., box 2, folder 88.

2. Hamilton to Esther, July 24, 1942; "We, The People," *True Story*, cf. June 27, 1942, 6–7; July 11, 1942, 6; August 1, 1942, 7. Hamilton's last column appears to

have been published on September 26, 1942, after which a signed editorial by another *Liberty* writer takes its place. As with the early Wanamaker's ads and the *True Story* essays, there remains the possibility that the *Liberty* pieces originated either with the client himself, or with someone in Hamilton's employ. His claim of personal authorship, in his letter to Steinbeck's sister Esther, combined with the strikingly similar tone of all three assignments (across more than three decades) nevertheless leads me to conclude that he is likely their common author.

3. Office of Alien Property Custodian, *Annual Report for the Period March 11, 1942 to June 1943* (Washington, D.C: n.p., 1943); idem., *Annual Report, Office of Alien Property Custodian for the Fiscal Year Ending June 20, 1944* (Washington, D.C: Government Printing Office, 1944), 79–80, 153–7; *Chicago Daily Tribune*, March 13, 1942, 5; *Report on the Progress of the WPA Program* (Washington, D.C: n.p., June 30, 1941), 47.

4. *True Story*, June 20, 1942, 9; Charles W. Cushman to Thomas Grant Hartung, January 25, 1943, Genealogy File, Cushman Collection, IUA.

5. Cushman photographs P02336, P02344, P02360, , Charles W. Cushman Photograph Collection, IUA, http://webapp1.dlib.indiana.edu/cushman/index.jsp.

6. "Joseph R. Hamilton," *Chicago Sun*, January 4, 1943, 13; *Chicago Tribune*, January 5, 1943, 17; *New York Times*, January 4, 1943, 15. Steinbeck to Aunt Gussie [Hamilton], January 4, 1943, Stanford University Wells Fargo Steinbeck Collection, box 2, folder 89; Steinbeck to Esther [Rodgers], n.d., Steinbeck Collection, box 2, folder 93; telegram to Mrs. J. R. Hamilton, January 3, 1943, Steinbeck Collection, box 2, folder 87.

7. "Wife Turns Gun on Mate, Then Shoots Herself," *Chicago Tribune*, March 20, 1943, 5; *Chicago Sun*, March 21, 1943, 10.

8. "Wife Turns Gun on Mate."

9. Rosalie Hillier Washburn to Anne Moskowitz, August 31, 1979, courtesy John H. Moskowitz, Jr.; San Francisco *Call*, June 15, 1904, 7.

10. Charles W. Cushman, "Application for Federal Employment," March 1, 1944. Genealogy File, Cushman Collection, IUA.

11. For examples of the stories on urban renewal appearing in the *Chicago Daily Tribune* during the time of Cushman's South Side picture-taking, see March 3, 1949, 1; March 11, 1949, 8.

12. Wayne F. Miller, *Chicago's South Side, 1946–1948* (Berkeley and Los Angeles: University of California Press, 2000). Hansberry's experiences later formed the basis of his daughter Lorraine's play, *A Raisin in the Sun*. Cushman's Chicago

pictures bear more direct comparison to those of another and better-known photographer whose work appeared in a retrospective at the city's Art Institute from November 1947 to early January 1948: Walker Evans. Evans's show drew from images that had recently appeared in "Chicago: A Camera Exploration of the Huge, Energetic Sprawl of the Midlands," one of his numerous photo-essays for Henry Luce's *Fortune* (February 1947). The show included what Art Institute publicity termed his "psychological portraits of Chicago houses" (Chicago Art Institute press release, c. December 1947, Chicago Art Institute institutional archives). A museumgoer and a reader of financial news, Cushman was likely aware of both the article and the exhibition, and he photographed at least one of Evans's sites—the distinctive house at 1325 N. Dearborn Avenue—several years later (Charles W. Cushman Photograph Collection, IUA, http://webapp1.dlib.indiana.edu/cushman/index.jsp, P04469).

Chapter 4

1. Email correspondence: Edward Laves to author, July 19, 2008; Elizabeth Laves Marcuson to author, July 19, 2008.

2. Email correspondence, Edward Laves to author, July 19, 2008. Gussie, who died in Santa Clara County, California, in February 1957, may have preceded Charles and Jean in moving west. See *California Death Records, 1940–1997*, http://vitals.rootsweb.ancestry.com/ca/death/search.cgi.

3. Rich Remsberg–Elizabeth Gergely Cushman interview notes, Cushman Collection, IUA. Elsie Gergely Steg, telephone conversation with author, April 11, 2008, and correspondence to author, May 8, 2008.

4. Karl Moskowitz, "Living and Travel Patterns in Auto-Oriented Cities" (1962), *California Highways and Public Works*, July/August 1964, 1.

5. See, for example, Richard H. Pells, *The Liberal Mind in a Conservative Age: American Intellectuals in the 1940s and 1950s* (Middletown, Conn.: Wesleyan University Press, 1989), Howard Brick, *Daniel Bell and the Decline of Intellectual Radicalism: Social Theory and Political Reconciliation in the 1940s* (Madison: University of Wisconsin Press, 1986).

6. Peter Blake, *God's Own Junkyard: The Planned Deterioration of America's Landscape* (New York: Holt, Rhinehart and Winston, 1964).

7. John Steinbeck, *Journal of a Novel: The East of Eden Letters* (New York: Viking Press, 1969), 90.

8. "Books of *The Times*," July 27, 1962, 23.

9. Much closer to Cushman's methods and interests were the published works of a fellow Bay Area resident, the University of California English professor George R. Stewart, whose *U.S. 40: Cross-Section of the United States of America* (Boston: Houghton Mifflin, 1953) and *NA 1: The North-South Continental Highway* (Boston, 1957) paired black-and-white photographs with short historical and geographical descriptions of discrete portions of each of these national highways, along the route from one end to the other. While he spoke to a wide public audience and balanced his images with words, Stewart shared with Cushman a catholic interest in how the pieces of the American landscape fit together in a larger whole. "We must accept the slums of 'Truck Route,'" he wrote in a sentiment little shared by academics of his own time but widely echoed in the works of subsequent generations of students of the vernacular landscape, "as well as the skyscrapers of 'City Route,' and the fine churches and houses of 'Alternate Route'" (*U.S. 40*, 5.) We have no record of whether Cushman owned Stewart's books or may even have met the writer at some point in his California years. From 1957, Berkeley also offered a part-time home to another (and ultimately more influential) student of the American landscape, the geographer John Brinckerhoff Jackson.

10. *Statistical Abstracts of the United States* (Washington, D.C., U.S. Government Printing Office, 1938), p. 365; 1950, p. 481.

11. Richard Hurd, *Principles of City Land Values* (New York: The Record and Guide, 1903), 107; on low assessed values, see Jon C. Teaford, *Rough Road to Renaissance: Urban Revitalization in America, 1940–1985* (Baltimore: Johns Hopkins University Press, 1990), 80.

12. California Certificate of Death, Jean Hamilton Cushman, June 12, 1969, District 3801, certificate 4430; Elsie Gergely Steg, telephone conversation with author, April 11, 2008.

13. Elsie Gergely Steg, telephone conversation with author, April 11, 2008, Rich Remsberg-Elizabeth Gergely Cushman interview notes, Cushman Collection, IUA.

14. Cushman to Claude Rich, IU Alumni Secretary, April 4, 1966, IU Correspondence Files, Cushman Collection, IUA; Bradley D. Cook, email correspondence with author, February 18, 2005.

15. Adolphe R. E. Roome, IV, telephone conversation with author, January 5, 2005. Catherine Vanderpool, email correspondence with author, December 1, 2008. John H. Moskowitz, Jr., telephone conversation with author, May 10, 2006. Rich

Remsberg–Elizabeth Gergely Cushman interview notes, Cushman Collection, IUA; Cushman to Edward Von Trees, IU Foundation, January 30, 1967, IU Correspondence Files, Cushman Collection, IUA. Elizabeth died in 2003. Cushman's cousins Anne Fullinwider and Emma Fullinwider Barr died within a week of one another in their native Mt. Vernon, Indiana. http//home.hawaii .rr.com/fullenwider/web/genealogy/pafg21.htm#713.

16. Steinbeck, *Journal of a Novel*, 103; Wallace Stevens, "The Pure Good of Theory," *Transport to Summer* (New York: Alfred A. Knopf, 1947).

ILLUSTRATIONS

44. Main Street, Shawneetown, Illinois, 1949, CWCPC P04429

45. Bisbee, Arizona, 1959, CWCPC P10609

46. Phillips Avenue, Sioux Falls, South Dakota, 1959, CWCPC P10228

47. View North from Radio Station WBRC, Birmingham, Alabama, 1951, CWCPC
     P05152

48. Johnstown, Pennsylvania, 1940, CWCPC P01821

49. Carnegie-Illinois Steel Corporation South Works, South Chicago, Illinois, 1958,
     CWCPC P10344

50. S. Santa Fe Street, El Paso, Texas, 1952, CWCPC P05485

51. Cameron Hill, Chattanooga, Tennessee, 1951, CWCPC P05118

52. Annapolis, Maryland, 1940, CWCPC P02077

53. St. Phillip Street, New Orleans, Louisiana, 1951, CWCPC P05242

54. Jackson Square, New Orleans, 1959, CWC, P10428

55. Broome Street and Baruch Place, New York, New York, 1941, CWCPC P02522

56. "Three bums from South Ferry flophouses," 1941, CWC, P02302

57. Garrick Theatre, St. Louis, Missouri, 1949, CWCPC P04383

58. Transit Tower, San Antonio, Texas, 1951, CWCPC P05369

59. Main Street, Los Angeles, California, 1952, CWCPC P05736

60. Rodeo Parade, Tucson, Arizona, 1940, CWCPC P01769

61. Peachtree Street, Atlanta, Georgia, 1951, CWCPC P05130

62. Chrysler and Empire State Buildings, seen from the Gov. Clinton Hotel, New York,
     New York, 1960, CWCPC P11614

63. Charles Cushman's Contax II A viewfinder camera, Cushman Collection, IUA

Afternoon

64. Maxwell Street near Morgan Street, Chicago, 1949, CWCPC P04186

65. Hamilton-Cushman House, 5557 Kenwood Avenue, Chicago, 1946, CWCPC
     P03465

66. "American Airlines stewardess, Doris Irwin, takes sun," 1941, CWCPC P02343

67. "Anni Sokal—from Dusseldorf—tans her legs at promontory," 1941, CWCPC
     P02347

68. "Pictures of Annette, girl in yellow bathing suit," 1942, CWCPC P02639

69. "Eunice in mid-August sun," 1942, CWCPC P02652

70. "Light and dark meat. Promontory visitors," 1941, CWCPC P02360

71. "Maria Grygier," 1949, CWCPC P04542

72. Jean Cushman, Tucson, Arizona, 1940, CWCPC P01784

73. Jean Cushman, Morton Arboretum, Chicago, 1950, CWCPC P04786

74–96. Portfolio: Chicago

74. Mather Tower and Carbide Building from Rush Street, Chicago, 1941, CWCPC P02222

75. 20 N. Wacker Dr. (Civic Opera Building), Chicago, 1948, CWCPC P03998

76. 505 N. Clark Street, Chicago, 1948, CWCPC P04092

77. 400 block, Sullivan Street, Chicago, 1946, CWCPC P03116

78. 316 W. Erie Street, Chicago, 1951, CWCPC P05023

79. "Day after street car crash and fire—33 dead, 6240 S. State Street," Chicago, 1950, CWCPC P04757

80. Steel mills, Calumet River, Chicago, 1939, CWCPC P01661

81. Carnegie South Works, 91st Street, Chicago, 1941, CC IUA P02192

82. Newberry and Maxwell Streets, Chicago, 1950, CWCPC P04865

83. Hull House, Chicago, 1950, CWCPC P04857

84. Maxwell and Halsted Streets, Chicago, 1950, CWCPC P04883

85. Maxwell Street near Miller Street, Chicago, 1944, CWCPC P02857

86. Horse and Wagon, W. 14th Street near Sangamon, Chicago, 1949, CWCPC P04181

87. S. Throop Street near Adams Street, Chicago, 1949, CWCPC P04207

88. 710 W. 14th Street, Chicago, 1949, CWCPC P04210

89. Confectionary cart, Lexington and DeKalb Streets, Chicago, 1949, CWCPC P04280

90. Soda shack, 520 W. 13th Street, Chicago, 1949, CWCPC P04259

91. 3200 block, Rhodes Avenue, Chicago, 1941, CWCPC P02398

92. Otis House, 1709 Prairie Avenue, Chicago, 1941, CWCPC P02383

93. "Old Capone GHQ," 2220 S. Dearborn Avenue, Chicago, 1944, CWCPC P02853

94. 2944 S. Michigan Ave., Chicago, 1949, CWCPC P04252

95. Enolia and Leonard Brown, Jr., 230 W. 23rd Street, Chicago, 1949, CWCPC P04161

96. "Still tenanted," 3117 S. Wabash Avenue, Chicago, 1949, CWCPC P04265

97. Mildred Mead. Illinois Institute of Technology, with 3117 Wabash Avenue in foreground. Mildred Mead Collection, apf2-01576, Special Collections Research Center, University of Chicago Library.

Twilight

98. Sunset over the Palace of Fine Arts, San Francisco, 1959, CWCPC P10847

99. 3465 Broderick Street, San Francisco, c. 2006 (author)

INDEX